Smuggler's URCHINS

*A tale of hardship,
suffering, courage and,
most of all, love!*

PAT KELLY

Originally Published by The Manx Experience
10 Tromode Close, Douglas, Isle of Man
Printed by The Alden Press, Oxford

First published in Australia 2020
This edition published 2020
Copyright © Pat Kelly 2020
Cover design, typesetting: WorkingType (www.workingtype.com.au)

Kelly, Pat
Smuggler's Urchins
ISBN: 978-0-6487976-2-3
pp278

*Cover image of storm and shoreline: Iain Mackenzie
macfid (Instagram)*

*Back cover storm image: Susie Mackenzie-Fidlin.
Facebook: Susie Macfid Photographs*

About the author

The author was born in Scotland a year before World War II started, but swears she didn't cause it …

In January 1968 she arrived in Australia as a 'Ten Pound Tourist' with her, then, husband and four children.

After the breakup of her marriage after twenty-five years the author was contacted by a man named Mike Kelly, whom she had known in her teens and had had no contact with for nearly thirty years. Mike's marriage having broken up around the same time as the author's. On learning she was 'on the loose', he obtained her phone number by courtesy of his mother — International telephone enquiries — and the author's mother, so rang to see if she was okay.

One thing led to another, they were married in 1988 and returned to the Isle of Man to start a new life. On Mike's retirement, five years later, they followed the summers and spent half their lives in Australia and the other half in the Isle of Man.

In their months on the island each year, they ran a daffodil and plant nursery and were well known throughout the island for their roadside stall, where they sold their daffodils and plants.

As age caught up with them, they realised it was time to settle somewhere permanently. Being the warmer country, Australia won, and they moved there in 2014, to live in a retirement village in Lakes Entrance — one of the prettiest spots in Australia.

This, they both feel, will suit them until they climb in their boxes (but not for a long time yet) and move on to higher places.

By the same author

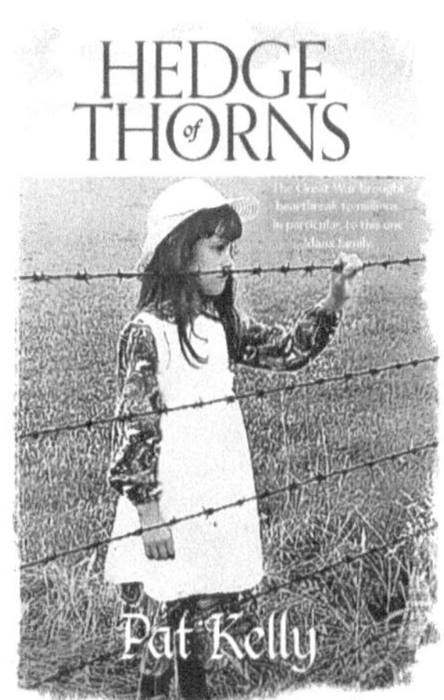

Shadow of the Wheel

The mighty water-wheel at Laxey mines in the Isle of Man has been set in motion. In its great shadow, Sarah and Patrick have fallen in love. It is a love that must be kept secret, for Patrick is Irish. Sarah's mother — Judith — has lost her mind and blames an Irishman for her husband being imprisoned 'across the water' in Liverpool, where she can never visit him.

The two young lovers desperately desire to wed and be together, but Judith's increasing madness, which began when she lost some of her childher to a savage disease and deepened on her husband's incarceration, proved too strong a pull.

Sarah's deep loyalty to her mother also stands between the lovers, indeed life itself thwarts their every effort to find a way toward their happiness.

Patrick's friend — Robert — is going to Australia to make his fortune mining for gold and has asked Patrick to accompany him. With no other option and seemingly with the cards stacked against them, Patrick and Sarah are both heartbroken.

Knowing that her mother will never recover from her illness and will always need her support, Sarah tells Patrick he must go with Robert to make a life for himself without her, and to forget her, and the love they share.

Hedge of Thorns

The author, who hails from Scotland, spent many hours listening to her mother-in-law recount, in vivid detail, memories of her child-hood days in the tiny village of Patrick, in the Isle of Man, during the First World War. As Lou talked, the author realised she was listening to history, a lot of which no one else could tell, and that if Lou were to die, all that history would be lost forever. So she wrote it all down and turned it into *Hedge of Thorns*.

In those days the village was dwarfed by the huge internment camp at Knockaloe, created for the accommodation of thousands of men classed as enemy aliens. Men whose only crimes were to have German, Austrian or Turkish origins.

Hedge of Thorns is a true account of the impact that the Great War and the monster of Knockaloe camp had on the lives of a Manx family which still followed the traditional crofting way of life. It is a most moving and memorable story of the stresses and strains which shattered the peaceful existence of a family whose loved ones were caught up in the emergencies of war.

Throughout Europe, during those dreadful war-torn years, millions of families were suffering similar deprivation, fear, loss and heartbreak.

Millions died in most dreadful ways and millions more eventually returned home crippled in either body or mind. Or both!

It was to be the war to end all wars, for no one could imagine such stupidity happening again but—!

This book is dedicated to my husband, Mike, for the many happy years he has given me, and for still being a big and important part of my life. My love forever.

Acknowledgements

I would like to acknowledge the Manx Museum in Douglas, for all the help they gave me when I was researching for this book. I'm sure there will be some things I will have got wrong, but any mistakes are entirely mine.

Many thanks to my Grandaughter Elissa for being my 'cover girl'. Elissa is my youngest grandchild and a very charming young lady.

A great big thank you also to her father, my son Andrew, who spent many hours scanning this book in and putting it into word for me so that I could edit and re-publish it. The best Christmas present he could have given me.

Thanks also to my other three children, Dawn, Alison and Kenneth for their support and encouragement.

I must also thank my friends at the Lakes Entrance Senior Citizens club for their great interest and encouragement.

Bless you all.

Introduction

MONA'S ISLE — our green and pleasant land — was not, in the mid-eighteenth century, an easy place in which to live. It was a period of abject poverty when most of the people seemed to have lost the ability or desire to earn an honest living. Fishermen had hung up their nets to make their livelihood by a more lucrative means — smuggling! Farmers had left the land to join them. Family life crumbled and the Islanders' most popular pastime became drunkenness.

Countless numbers of children became homeless and hungrily roamed the streets in search of food. There was no work. They could earn no money. So their only way to survive was to steal. It was common for these poor unfortunates to be imprisoned and whipped for thieving at the market or stealing bread from the baker.

People could not, with any degree of safety, air complaints about government officials, as we can today, for according to Manx statutes, this would render them likely to *forfeit ten pounds and have his ears cut off besides!*

In fact, Manx law seemed to have a thing about ears, for according to another entry in the statute books, The Marriage Act of 1757, *prohibits Nonconformist ministers in the Island from performing the ceremony of Marriage. The penalty for doing so is that the offender stand one hour in the pillory at Castletown, have his ears nailed to it and cut off; that afterwards he be imprisoned, fined and transported to the Americas for 14 years.*

For anyone misguided enough to steal a sheep — the penalty was death!

During the early eighteenth century, the free-traders of the Isle of Man entered into their own. English, Irish, Scots and true born Manx made the most of the Island's incongruous constitutional position.

On the north-west coast of England, at that time, revenue protection was made very difficult by the proximity of the Isle of Man, which was overrun by smugglers. The collector of excise at Whitehaven was particularly concerned about this. The Island sheltered bankrupts, thieves, rebels and murderers, outlawed from three kingdoms. Provided they committed no crime on the Island, the law would not touch them.

The whole Island lived entirely by smuggling. Brandy, tea, silks and other goods, with the exception of tobacco, were imported to the Island in foreign ships from France, Holland and Scandinavia. Rum came to the Island direct from the New World colonies, and sugar and spices from India.

A single smuggling ship from Man might take on as many as 12,000 gallons of brandy for shipping to Scotland and Ireland. Smaller craft ferried contraband over to the English mainland, loaded to the gunwales.

Other boats, called 'bumboats', were also used by the merchants of the Island. These would lie about a mile off the coast during daytime, loaded with brandy and rum, awaiting the return of the light colliers or other vessels from Ireland and elsewhere, bound for the Cumberland or Scottish coast. The bumboats sold their goods to these ships and then returned to the Island for fresh supplies. The practice was for the vessels which had received the contraband either to pass it off as stores or, if there was too much for this, to sink it in the sea and mark it.

The Isle of Man had become the centre of a vast trade network. As a result of this, the British government was being robbed of large sums of money that should have been paid as customs duties. The remedy which finally suggested itself was that the king of England would again become the sovereign of the Island, with the right to fix the Manx customs duties and to appoint officers to collect them. To effect this, it was necessary to buy the sovereign rights from the Lord of Man.

The Lord, however, refused to sell. Eventually, in 1765, his successor, the third Duke of Atholl, parted with his rights for the sum of £70,000. The bargain did not cover the Duke's rights as lord of the manor, but did include the customs duties of the Island, which were henceforth transferred to the English government.

It was the end of an epoch. And it was into this harsh world of smuggling and drunkenness that two homeless children, Daniel and Isabella were released, scantily clad, from Castle Rushen gaol in the winter of 1758 and sent forth to fend for themselves.

JANUARY 1758

Chapter I

Daniel reluctantly trailed his bare feet, trying to put off the evil moment for as long as possible.

Biting his lip, he fought to suppress a sob, as his mouth soured to the taste of vomit. Stopping, he gazed miserably around at the cold, bleak, grey stone walls of the castle. They towered above him, seeming to lean towards each other at the top, looking down on him, whispering darkly. His eyes were stark and dulled with fear. The boy shuddered, partly with awe at the Castle's threatening bulk, and also because of the cold of the January morning. But mostly it was a dark terror of his unknown future that made him tremble.

'Come on, Daniel.' The gaol's governor had stopped also, a little ahead of him and was turned now, looking back, waiting. 'You *have* to leave.'

Daniel nodded mutely, feeling a tear sting his eye. Walking slowly, he followed the gaoler across the windy forecourt and through the gatehouse. The guard on the gate straightened when he saw them approaching, watching the ill-assorted pair without any real interest. On the head gaoler's nod, the man drew back the huge bolt on the massive door, swinging it creakingly back on its hinges.

Daniel moved forward, stopping in the open doorway to look up at the governor, an unspoken plea in his eyes. Seeing no sign of the man weakening he drew a deep, ragged breath. 'Where should I go?' he enquired nervously.

The man looked down, not unkindly and shrugged. Rubbing the flat of his hand across his forehead in a tired gesture he asked, 'What age are you, Daniel?'

'Ten, sir. Almost eleven.'

'Go home then, Daniel. Surely that's where you belong? I had hoped that perhaps your father might have come to meet you.'

'I have no parents, Sir. Nor any home. I am, and always have been an orphan.' Again he felt the prick of a tear and was angry at his own weakness.

The gaoler drew a quick breath, wincing almost as though the boy's pain was his. Shaking his head in sorrow, he said quietly, 'I'm sorry, but then you must find your own way in the world. You're a good strong lad. Perhaps a farmer will give you work for a roof over your head and a bite to eat. Or a fisherman might, perhaps.'

Daniel still lingered in the doorway, gazing longingly back past the Governor, towards the grey courtyard.

Taking great gulps of breath to steady his unsteady heart, he pleaded, 'If I could only stay here I would happily work for my crusts. I'm strong and well used to hard toil. Please let me stay, Sir. I have nowhere else to go!' He stood looking up at the man, his hands clasped in an unconscious attitude of prayer.

The man looked down into the beseeching eyes, one a light brown, the other green. The eyes of a devil child they called them — those that were a different colour. But this poor boy was no demon — just a child of misfortune, parentless, homeless, shoeless, hatless and breadless. Without even a coat to his back. The governor was not a harsh man and would have liked to help. But there were so many of these poor urchins, both male and female, in similar poor circumstances on the Isle of Man, and he could not aid every such child who was sent to Castle Rushen by the Deemsters. He could only do what he was paid to do and keep them imprisoned for the term laid down by the courts. Then he must turn them loose — but to what he wondered. To freeze in winter; to starve; to steal food to stay alive and, ultimately, to end up back in Castle Rushen!

What could he do about that? He didn't know the answer. Did not want to know. It pained him to think of such young children homeless, cold and suffering, the man knew there was nothing he could do to ease their situation. Sighing unhappily and frustrated by his own inability to help, he told himself it was better to get this over with as quickly as possible. Placing his hand on the boy's shoulder, he pushed him gently beyond the doorway.

'I'm sorry, lad, but there is no work for you here. I wish I could help, but you must understand that you are only one of hundreds who are in the same situation. You must find some toil for yourself, but make it honest employment. If you come before the Deemster again, he will surely give you a far more severe sentence. It is likely you would suffer a birching and possibly transportation next time,'

Daniel clutched at the Governor's sleeve, but the man abruptly twitched his arm free, then stepping back quickly, before he had time to weaken, he nodded to the guard, who swung the heavy door closed behind him.

The solid clang it made was like the knell of doom to the boy. Daniel stood for many long moments gazing steadfastly at the door, willing it to re-open; hearing his heart thundering in his ears; feeling tears stinging his eyes.

Castle Rushen was the closest thing to a home he could remember. A sickening, scared sensation was churning away in his bowels. Absently running shaky fingers through his mat of dark hair, he kicked at a few loose stones on the flagged roadway. What now? The boy drew a deep, shuddering breath, letting it susurrate slowly out between his teeth.

All his life, as far back as his memory served him anyway, he'd had to fend for himself and he'd become quite adept at stealing a bun or a piece of fruit on which to survive. Then had come the day when he had picked up a piece of offal from the floor of the market. The butcher had seen him and made a grab for him, but years of experience stood him in good stead and he had easily ducked under the outspread arms and large, grasping hands.

'Stop, thief. Someone stop that boy! He's stolen my meat!' The butcher had shouted.

Daniel had run. Bobbing, weaving, ducking away from all his would be captors, until somebody stuck out a foot, when he was too close to jump over it. He had hit the ground hard, sliding along it winded and gasping painfully for breath. Feeling the skin grazing from his bare knees and arms.

Several pairs of hands had grabbed him and held on tightly. There was no escape.

Daniel had struggled to breathe as someone heavy sat on him, twisting his arm high up his back. In a confusing flurry of activity and shouting, the soldiers had been summoned, the butcher had explained Daniel's crime and with the blood from the offal still damp and sticky on his hands to prove his sins he was dragged, kicking and struggling to gaol.

For two days he was held, more scared than he had ever been in his life, at Douglas gaol, then taken to Castletown, the Island's capital, for trial and sentencing.

In the days and months that followed, he languished in the cell, more sheltered and better fed than he could ever remember. His food, though only bread and thin gruel for supper, with bread and water for other meals, came to him regularly. If it hadn't been for the lack of freedom and being locked in a dark cell, he would have enjoyed it there. But he was used to his freedom — to being able to wander where he wished, needing no one, his will to survive his only captor

When he stood, finally, in the dock at the Court of General Gaol Delivery at Castletown, the Deemster had sentenced him to three months imprisonment. Frowning, the man had glared at him across the courtroom and cautioned him, with severity, that if he were ever to appear in the dock again a far more terrible punishment would befall him.

Daniel had stumbled from the court between two guards, terrified of what unknown horrors might lie before him. Did it occur to His Honour, he wondered, or to any of the officials of Mona, that miserable little creatures such as he, would have little chance to avoid appearing at the Bar of Justice again and again and yet again as accused criminals. They would surely need something far more substantial than just a judicial caution to keep them out of trouble.

The months of imprisonment in Castle Rushen had been hard, but not as hard as the life he had been used to. All through the sentence he had looked forward to his release, but now the time had come he was not so sure. Being locked away behind the solid stone walls had given him some strange sense of security. It was the nearest thing to a home he had known for a very long time. The fellow prisoners were his family.

The boy looked once more at the door, now firmly bolted against him, then with a sigh of regret he started down the slope toward the harbour.

He had been alone, it seemed, all his life, but suddenly he felt an aching, terrible despairing loneliness. Sobs tore at his throat with a rasping noise that made him stuff his fists into his mouth to silence them. If he had been asked why, he could not have explained this rending reaction now to being alone.

Were it not for the January coldness, the day could not have been more perfect. There was a fresh, pale winter-washed sky and little, scudding puffball clouds, slightly pinked round the edges.

The harbour water danced in the crisp sunlight and the cries of the ever wheeling seagulls had an almost cheerful note as they crowded, greedy and hopeful, around the fishing boats.

Daniel stood silently, in doubt of which way to shape his course. What was he to do? The sentencing judge had been quick to tell him what *not* to do on his release from prison, but could he now tell him what he *should* do? Where could he go? He had heard that orphans such as he were supposed to be the responsibility of the Chancery Court, but he had never been offered any help or guidance from it — or from any other source. He had always been left to fight his own battle for survival.

Undecided, the boy settled in a nook by the Castle wall, hugging himself and tucking his bare feet under him to help stave off the bitter cold. The sick feeling in his stomach was getting worse, whether with hunger or fear he did not know, but he controlled it with a few deep breaths.

Daniel looked, through large, hungry eyes at the busy little harbour. He loved the sounds and atmosphere of the quayside, the bustle of activity and the squawking, squabbling herring-gulls, fighting over every little scrap of anything and often nothing.

The slapping of the water racing against the quay on the incoming tide excited ham. And the flapping of the sails and clinking of rigging against masts.

His nostrils flared to the scents of the harbour; the salt air; sea-weed; the smell of varnish, holystone and tar. The sight of the boats bobbing on the waves, the clean-scrubbed timber of their decks and the ropes neatly coiled. Sails furled and secured. Rigging slapping sharply. How he would love to be a part of it all. To belong somewhere. To have more to look forward to in his life than — what? Than nothing!

In an instant, he knew he was crying for the people he had loved and lost in the past. And for what seemed to him to be the death of his future. In the distance, he could hear the call of the elegant little oystercatchers as they picked amongst the rocks. He could picture them, strutting, proud, with their dapper black and white plumage and long, bright orange beaks. They sounded as melancholy as he felt. But with far less reason, he was sure.

A cloud passed across the sun, shutting out its paltry pretense at heat. Daniel glanced towards it, shivering. A gull flew over, attacked by another and momentarily loosened its grip on the scrap of fish it was carrying. The morsel dropped near the boy and instantly he was on his feet, snatching it from the dirt before the bird had time to recover it. Grasping it tightly, he moved back in against the wall.

The gull made several diving passes, screeching angrily, while Daniel flapped a fending arm at it. Disgruntled, and scolding still, it finally flew off in search of further spoils.

Daniel opened his hand, looking down eagerly to inspect his windfall. Not much more than the head and gills of a medium-sized bollan. Not a lot, but far better than nothing. Carefully he pushed it into the only pocket without a hole, to keep it safe for if nothing better came along.

*   *   *

Five people approached, three men and two women, all more fashionably dressed than any he had seen before. As they neared, he noticed they spoke with English accents and he remembered parts of conversations overheard in gaol. It appeared that the Isle of Man had become a sanctuary, in the last few years for criminals whose misdemeanours had been committed out of the Island. Many gentlemen who owed thousands of pounds in London, Paris, Amsterdam and many other places, now lived in the greatest tranquillity on the Island. Provided that they took care to do no harm against the law here, which is strictly put into execution, they were able to bide with no fear of arrest.

Daniel gazed hopefully at the Englishmen as they drew level, even daring to extend a thin, dirty, trembling hand in a silent plea. He was unaware of the cleaner channels where his tears had run through the dirt on his cheeks.

One of the men saw him and stopped, looking startled, into the different coloured eyes. His hand moved instinctively towards his pocket and Daniel felt his heart quicken in excited anticipation.

Suddenly one of the women noticed what was happening.

Seeing the boy's dirty, ragged state, she screwed up her face in distaste. Plucking at the man's sleeve, she edged him past.

'Don't go near the filthy creature, Charles. you don't know what infestations he might give you. He's probably covered in bugs!'

'He looks starved. I was just going to throw him a half-penny.'

The woman frowned crossly 'Don't encourage the miserable little urchin to beg. He'll follow you around and you'll never get rid of him.' She put a hand behind his shoulders, fingers spread, to propel him away.

The man looked around once more, almost apologetically then moved on. taking his hand away from his pocket.

Tears of disappointment stinging the backs of his eyes. Daniel slumped back against the wall. swallowing a great lump in his throat. He looked around helplessly. Where was there to go?

After a while he roused himself. Sitting there shivering would get him nowhere, he told himself crossly. First, he must find food. Perhaps somewhere around the harbour he would be lucky enough to find a fisherman who would give him some work for the price of a crust of bread and somewhere warmer than the street to spend the night. But where, he asked himself, his eyes silently searching the pale sky as if the answer might found there.

Standing up, he stretched his stiffening legs and shuffled towards the waters-edge. A herring gull swooped hopefully as Daniel passed, then wheeled away, with a squawk, to seek food elsewhere.

Seeing a boat preparing to sail, Daniel hastened his steps towards it. 'You want any help?' he called, looking hopefully down into the boat.

Four surprised faces looked up at him.

The man at the helm shook his head, giving a snorting laugh. 'Help? From a weak little bag o' bones the likes of you? I have doubts you could even lift the brush to scrub the decks wi'. Na, we ha' a full crew. Off wi' you, lad, an' don't be botherin' us.'

A crew member still on the quay dropped the last hawser into the boat, jumping down behind it, studying Daniel from stem to stern, laughing derisively

'I wouldn't want any pay. Just enough food to live on. Please take me on. I promise I'd work hard.' The boy moved right to the edge of the quay, balanced with his toes out over the water, boldly meeting the master's eye.

The man dismissively waved his hand and turned his back as the boat edged away from the dock.

Daniel turned abruptly away so that the men would not see the tears which sprang to his eyes again. He wanted to feel the wind on his face and run and run until his heart pounded in his ears. But to where? There was nowhere for him to run!

It was a tranquil afternoon, though the painful rumblings in Daniel's stomach spoiled its beauty for him. Gulls drifted lazily in the harbour, swirling and swooping around the high turrets of Castle Rushen. The sun shone brightly, casting clear cut shadows which lengthened with the approach of evening.

As the day wore on a chill wind sprang up, needling the boy's cheeks with sand blown from the shore. Scudding clouds raced across the grey winter sky, and from the docks came the sucking roar of the building waves against the harbour wall.

The January evening was clammy with the awful chill that always crept in with the bone-piercing, muscle-aching mist, which penetrated his thin rags and set his teeth chattering.

Somewhere across the harbour a flicker of light sprang and soon flames were leaping excitedly from a huge fire. Seeing it, Daniel felt his heart quicken with something akin to hope. Scrambling stiffly to his feet, he hurried toward it. A group of fishermen was gathered around, standing as close as they comfortably could to the flames, exchanging yarns. Daniel sidled to the far side of the fire, edging as close as he dared, breathing in the comforting homeliness of the wood smoke.

After a while the men drifted away, still laughing, toward the alehouse, leaving Daniel with the fire to himself. Looking around, he saw, with a sudden surge of joy, a tea-chest, battered and abandoned at the wharfside. Dragging it as near the dying fire as he safely could, he crawled inside, curling tightly, revelling in the warmth from the flames and their reflected heat from the tin lining of his box.

Tugging the morsel of bollan from his pocket, Daniel ate every crumb of it, bones, eyes and all. Then, feeling warmer than he had for months, he settled snugly in his makeshift home, before the weakening flames, and fell into an unsettled slumber.

Chapter 2

The governor of the gaol had a leaden feeling in his heart as he turned the tattered little dress in his hands, and the battered boots with more hole than sole on their underside. Sighing sadly, he bundled them up, carrying them to the dungeon where the girl was being held.

It pained him to make her remove her warm prison clothes and replace them with her own rags, which would hold out no cold at all. He had no choice. It was the law. The child must be released in her own clothing, but, like the boy he had sent away the previous day, this girl had been brought to the gaol in summer clothes. With some luck, he thought, there would be someone to meet the girl — somebody with warm clothing for her to wear.

Stepping into the murky cell, the Governor looked around the grimy faces — some wild-eyed, others defeated and empty — which turned in his direction. He shuddered and waited for his eyes to adjust to the almost total lack of light.

The child he sought was huddled miserably in the farthest distant corner, hiding in the gloom.

'Come, child. It is time for you to leave.'

The girl looked bleakly up at him. Her cornflower-blue eyes, glittering with unshed tears, appeared unnaturally large in her small, pinched, pale face. She pressed herself against the dank wall as if hoping she could dissolve into it.

A woman, Jane Quiggin, moved to the girl's side, putting an arm protectively about her. 'Must she leave, Sir? Can she not stay?'

The gaoler shook his head emphatically. 'She has served her sentence. Now it's time for her to leave.'

Jane tightened her embrace and the child clung to her, trembling as she buried her face against the scrawny bosom.

'There's nowhere for her to go. sir. If you send her away, she'll surely finish up back in here. Can you not find her work in the kitchens? She's such a tiny, helpless mite.'

The man gave an irritated, impotent shake of his head, tutting his tongue.

'There is no employment for her here. I can't be expected to provide work for every child who is sent here. Surely she has parents waiting for her? The child must return to her family. She can not be kept here just because you have formed a fondness for her. Now come child.' His voice was tight. Angry. His own helplessness making him so. He had no illusions about what the child would be up against after she stepped through the castle gate, but there were dozens — possibly hundreds — out there who were in the same sad position. He could not help them all, so he *had* to harden his heart.

'She has only a mother, sir. A harlot she would best be without. It is because of her mother she's here. The baggage tried to sell the girl's service's to a customer who desired someone younger than her.' Jane's voice, which had risen in pitch to a high treble, broke with a sob.

John Barton felt his stomach cringing. The child could be no more than eight or nine years of age and small into the bargain, probably because of a lack of food throughout her life. Looking at the emaciated little face, with its pointed chin, under the dirty mat of red hair, he thought of his own robust, well cared for, slightly spoiled daughter of the same tender years and felt pained by the knowledge he had to cast this fragile mite out into such a cruel world.

Angry with himself for what he had to do he moved forward, grasping the child's thin wrist. As his fingers met and overlapped easily round it, he gave an involuntary shudder. Gently he pulled her to her feet, easing her out of Jane's arms and edging with her towards the cell door. In the doorway he stopped, remembering the girl's clothes. Swallowing a lump in his throat he thrust the rags into her hands and turned away.

'Here. These are yours. I'll wait outside whilst you change into them.' He stepped from the cell, to lean against the stone wall pulling deep breaths to steady his turbulent emotions.

The child took the rags, her pale face crumpling into a mask of abject misery. Turning back into the cell, she looked beseechingly at the older woman, who could only shrug helplessly and bite hard on the insides of her sallow cheeks.

'I'll help you to change.' Jane's voice was trembling, barely controlled. Unbuttoning the warm, woolen prison dress, she drew it over the child's head, shuddering in dismay as she helped the girl into her own, poor, summer frock.

'Is this all you have Isabella?' A tear started to flow and she scrubbed it away with the back of her hand, not wanting the little one to see.

'Aye.' The small voice came on a sob, hardly more than a whisper.

Sinking to the cold stone floor, Isabella pulled on her battered boots, laboriously fastening the many tiny buttons. She did it slowly, making the task last as long as possible, hearing, all the time, the governor's foot tapping impatiently until finally, the last button was in place. Standing again, she looked up tearfully at Jane, her young shoulders shaking with suppressed sobs.

Jane drew her into her arms. giving her one last, tight hug. 'Well, you take care of yourself, love. Find your way back to your mother in

Douglas. Maybe she'll have changed if she thinks she's lost you. At least you'll have a roof over your head there, an' you must have that in this weather. Just don't let any of your mother's men do things to you or you'll finish up wi' as miserable a life as hers. An' you'll end up wi' childer just like yourself who have no food in their bellies an' know not who their fathers are.' Her voice wavered more with the delivery of each and every word.

Trembling, Isabella clung to Jane, her tears leaving a dark. moist patch on the grey wool of the older woman's prison dress. Then, tearing herself away, panic choking in her throat, she stepped out into the passage where the governor awaited.

'Come on, lass. Once you are out and away from here you'll soon realise how nice it is to be free. I'm sure your home will be so much better than you remember it.'

He put his hand on her shoulder, shuddering at the fragility of it and steered her gently, half a pace before him, along the dank, echoing passages. He could feel the child trembling — a tremor which increased with every faltering step she took.

Emerging from the darkness into the courtyard, Isabella's eyes were stung by the unaccustomed brilliance of the morning sun which slanted down between a tower and the high castle wall. Screwing her face up, she jerked, turning it away from the light, feeling the bite of the wind at her eyes and lips.

On the slope up to the gate, Isabella stopped to survey her surroundings. All around her hovered the different towers, their narrow, slits of windows, from whence archers had once sent their arrows speeding and, later, soldiers had fired their muskets.

Fat seagulls sat on the battlements, watching the harbour for any slight promise of food.

Isabella clearly remembered the day she had arrived at the Castle, the Deemster's doom-filled words of warning still ringing loudly in her ears. Even now she could feel her heart thudding and a sickness in her belly when she recalled the terror she had felt on that frightening day.

Castle Rushen had seemed so forbidding then — but that was before she had come to know other prisoners. They had seemed frightening at first, so rough and dirty, most of them, with harsh voices and rough language. Having to share her dungeon with men and boys increased her terror at first. Even Jane, with her wild eyes and the look of a witch, had scared her in the beginning. But then, after the first few miserable days, the women had started to fuss and to mother her. Quite suddenly, in those harsh surroundings, she had felt more secure and loved than ever before. Especially by Jane, who had appointed herself Isabella's protector.

Once she had settled, the days passed all too quickly and as the end of her sentence drew near, she found herself wishing for them to slow. Now the time had come and she was almost at the gate to the outside world. Her feet were leaden, her heart pounding as it hit her searingly, like the aftershock of some terrible injury, that she really was being sent away. There was an awful, sick emptiness squirming like worms inside her.

The Governor turned, eyeing her worriedly. 'Will your mother be here to meet you?'

Isabella shrugged helplessly. 'I don' think she'd come all the way from Douglas jus' for me, sir. 'Sides, she won' know.'

'I sent her word. Surely she'll come?' It was beyond him to understand that any mother might not care for her daughter.

Isabella shook her head. 'Mammy won't come.' A hot tear ran down her cheek, putting a salt taste in the corner of her mouth.

The man looked down on her for a moment, a nerve twitching his face. Sighing, he told her, 'Then you must find your way to her. Douglas is not such a very long way from here. If you don't make it by nightfall, perhaps some farmer will be kind enough to permit you to bed in his hay-shed.'

Taking her arm, the man led her forward to the gate, nodding briefly to the guard to open it.

Forcing the giant bolt back, the guard lifted the latch, throwing his weight against the huge door until it swung wide. At the threat of the harsh world, Isabella gasped and took an involuntary step backward, feeling vomit burn the back of her throat.

All at once the thought of home was terrifying. The child had sudden frightening visions of the last time she had been there. The day she had been forced to run, naked, into the street, with her clothes clutched to her breast. She could still see the man; the ugly, leering man; coming at her with his rotten green teeth bared in something between a snarl and a smile, his arms outstretched, trousers unbuttoned, trying to grab her.

There had always been men, of course. All her life. As long as she could remember there had been a succession of lecherous men coming and going in the tiny damp hovel she shared with her mother. Some of them had stayed for a few months and become the nearest thing she had known to a father, but mostly they were strangers her mother would bring home from the alehouse. They would stay for an hour or two, or sometimes all night, threshing with her mother on the grubby mattress. Later, with their lust satisfied, they would don their clothes, throw a few coins to her mother and leave.

Isabella would lie in her loft; the type common in Manx cottages, in that it extended over only half of the single-roomed building; listening to the giggling, grunting and the men's lewd laughter. Sometimes more than one man would come and they would all roll together. The child had seen more pale, sweaty rumps and aroused male organs than she cared to remember.

In the beginning, she had wondered about it, but as she grew older, peeping down over the edge of her loft, innocence deserted her and she had become fully aware of what was going on. At times, young though she was, she had felt a strange excitement and curiosity, strangely mingled with revulsion. Several times she had challenged her mother, begged her not to fetch any more men home, but her pleas been met with scorn.

'Where in all hell do you believe the money comes to put food in your belly and clothes on your back? 'Tis the men I bring home who pay for all that. They do you no harm. Do they? Not one has ever touched you, has any? Of course not. You know they haven't. So why do you complain now? 'Tis my men friends who have kept you alive all these years So keep your bloody nose out o' my business, child, and allow me to live my life how I want to.'

Several times after, when her mother had seemed more sober and affectionate, Isabella had tried to talk to her, but she was not to be reasoned with.

'I need love,' Esther had said in a less angry moment

'I love you, Mammy,' her daughter cried feelingly, pressing against her mother, desperate for a cuddle.

'But I need more than that. I need the love of a man.' Esther gripped the girl's arms, putting her firmly away from her.

Stung, Isabella asked, 'Do these men love you then, Mammy? Even strangers you fetch home from the alehouse?' Isabella's blue eyes were wide. Puzzled. Struggling to understand.

Esther shrugged dejectedly. 'They think they do, at least while they're lyin' with me. They desire me. They love my body, so I suppose that's the best I can hope for. It's what I have to settle for.'

Feeling worthless, Isabella had shrunk away from her mother then and that was the last time she had said anything about the men until the night she had left home.

Remembering it, Isabella started, gasping and clasped a shaking hand to her mouth. Disturbed from her reverie, she realised the Governor was waiting, watching her intently, the Castle gate wide open behind him. Wordlessly, he extended his hand towards her.

The girl reluctantly stepped forward, passed him and moved beyond the gate. The man turned to follow a pace behind, walking with her down to the outer edges of the castle walls.

An icy gust of wind blew in their faces, chilling Isabella to the very marrow in her bones. It combined with her fear, causing a violent shiver that shook her very soul.

The governor looked down sadly on the frail little figure. 'I'm sure it can't be as bad as you imagine at home. Now go there and don't get yourself into any more trouble. Remember the Deemster's words. If you are convicted of any other crime you will surely be birched and transported to the New World.'

Isabella nodded mutely, looking up at the man through waterlogged eyes. 'I'm scared to go home for fear that man is still there.'

'What man?' The Governor frowned

'Mammy brought a man home from the alehouse. They were both laughin' an' shoutin' an' drunk. First they drank some more jough that they had brought home wi' them, then they went on the mattress an' did…'

Isabella stopped, flustered. Fumbling for words she finished lamely,

'Well — they did the things Mammy does wi' men!'

The man blanched. 'She does these things in your presence?'

'Aye.' Isabella agreed, surprised at his mortification. 'Our house has only one room, and the half loft where I sleep.'

He shook his head in shocked disbelief. 'And what happened after they had — em — finished their activities?' When Isabella did not reply, he took a hold of her arm. 'Did he leave then?' he prompted.

He gazed fixedly at the ground, as he waited for her reply. Shuffling his feet uncomfortably, he felt the heat of colour rise in his neck and face. He was appalled to be having this conversation with a female — especially one of such tender years.

'They fell asleep for a while an' so did I. Then a long time later I heard them movin' about an' talkin'. He was sayin' he must get off home to his wife. I peeped over the edge o' the loft to watch him leave an' he must ha' heard me 'cos he looked up. 'Is that a girl you got up there?' he asked. My Mammy nodded an' he asked how much it would cost for him to ha' me.'

The Governor's face was black with fury. 'To have you? You mean for fornication? Your mother surely would not agree to that?'

A gathering wind swirled around the harbour basin, whisking up sand, pieces of straw and paper, snatching and whirling them high above the water.

1 heard her tell him that I was not yet nine years old an' was still a maiden. Then he said he would pay tuppence to serve me. Mammy told him that was not enough. He stood, for a moment, lookin' up at me then he pulled open the top two buttons o' his trousers an' said something else, too quiet for me to hear. Mammy nodded, then called me to come down from the loft. I went down slowly, 'cos. I was feared, an' he put his hand up my shift an' started touchin' me. Then he caught my arm roughly before I reached the bottom an' pulled me off the ladder.'

Isabella, stopped suddenly, trembling as the memories of that awful night assailed her mind. Her breath spurted out in sobbing gasps and she saw the Governor's fists tightly clenched, his breathing sounding ragged and laboured.

'Go on,' he managed to rasp.

'Well, he started to feel me all over with one hand, like they do wi' the animals at the market, an' all the while his other hand was working on his trouser buttons. When they were all undone, he pulled off my frock an' petticoat an' pushed me down onto Mammy's mattress. Then he knelt beside me, leaning over an' I could see the stubble on his face, 'cos he needed to shave, an' a vein was throbbin' in his temple an' his eyes was ugly an' bulging'.'

'Surely your mother didn't just permit this to happen? She stopped him, didn't she?' The Governor's voice was dry and harsh and murderous. His face was grey — green almost.

Isabella was silent for a moment, startled, wondering whether she should continue her tale. Her listener looked as though his temper would erupt at any moment and she did not want to be at the receiving end of his fury.

'Continue,' he prompted finally when he had managed to get his feelings back in hand.

'His thing was big an' swollen an' suddenly I was frightened sick an' I knew I couldn' do the things my Mammy did wi' him because it looked as if it would hurt me.'

'I should think not!' The Governor agreed vehemently 'Is there no decency left in the world? Is that when you ran away?'

'Well — sort of. I tried to roll away an' get off the mattress, but he caught my hands in one of his an' held them above my head. Then he bent my legs up high an' tried to push his thing into me. I felt as if I would tear in two an' I screamed and jerked my bottom away from him. I managed to kick his thing. Then when he let go of my hands I scratched at his face. He crumpled on the bed an' I jumped from the mattress an' snatched my clothes up an ran out the door. I thought I might ha' kilt him.'

The Governor recoiled, his face a mask of horror. 'They're the ones who should have been in prison. Do you know the man's name?'

Isabella shook her head, trembling with the memory, instinctively pressing her knees tightly together. 'Na. He was just a man Mammy met in the alehouse. He sounded English an' was quite poshly dressed. But I remember his teeth was green. Probably one o' the merchants the smugglers deal wi'.'

'Then he has almost certainly gone by now and should be no further trouble to you.' Regretfully he added, 'So it would be best if you went home.'

Isabella nodded resignedly. Looking up, she noticed the governor was gazing past her, frowning irritably. Then he turned abruptly, walking briskly back towards the gate, his back stiff and angry looking.

'Take care of yourself, Isabella,' he called over his shoulder, then he was gone, the gate clanging shut behind him with soul-destroying finality.

Isabella stood motionless for a while, gazing longingly at the gates, the misery of her aloneness sweeping over her in great black waves of undiminishing pain and self-pity. Her eyes were bleak as she turned away to gaze, sightlessly out over the harbour. Now what? Where? What was to be her future? Did she even have one?

A noisy clutch of herring-gulls pestered a fishing-boat which was newly arrived in the harbour with a full catch. A black cloud came across the sun, ominously darkening the day.

Isabella shuddered and shrank back into the shadow of the castle wall, trembling now with fear as much as cold. She wanted to be safe at home, but a better home than she remembered. She wanted anything but this shivering, frightening loneliness. Suddenly she desperately wanted her mother.

Slowly she moved towards the edge of the water. Standing on a rock, she looked longingly north towards Douglas. Perhaps the Governor was right. Maybe it would not be so bad at home now. Her Mammy would be there. An' she did love her Mammy. No matter what had happened, she did still love her.

Feeling more alone than she ever had in her life before, Isabella looked sightlessly towards the harbour. She listened sadly to the cry of the gulls and the sighing of the wind in the rigging of the many boats at anchor. A gusty wind blew cold, salt spray in her face.

Clouds were piling up in the west, darkening the cowering sun, turning it from its usual cheerful orange to a glowering crimson. Only half-seen; misshapen; veiled by the oncoming weather. *There's going to be a storm,* Isabella thought, shuddering. Her skinny, starved body was racked with tearless sobs.

Chapter 3

Daniel opened bleary eyes to the angry squabbling of seagulls and the low mutterings of some early risen fishermen. Shivering and cramped, he struggled painfully out of the tea-chest to take a look at the day.

Stretching and flexing his cold, stiffened limbs, he gazed around. The dark looming bulk of the castle across the harbour caught his attention, drawing him. He knew it was hopeless, that he would never be allowed back in, that he must move on and somehow find a way to live. But it was hard to tear himself away.

The castle had been his home, his security, for what seemed like so long. But he knew he could not survive too many nights out of doors before the spring. Finding the fire and tea-chest last night was a bit of luck that would not be repeated often — if ever.

In the east, the sky was lighter, like a translucent scarf laid across the blackness of the night. A bridge of light; the dawning of a new and, Daniel hoped, better day. He heard small sounds and after a moment, a yellow flame flickered as someone in one of the boats lit a lamp.

Like a moth, Daniel found himself drawn toward the light, feeling the whip of the chill, early morning wind racing in from the water. In a smelly, battered boat an old man, stooped and starved looking, bent over a dirty table pecking hungrily at a piece of dry bread.

Daniel watched, licking his lips, listening to the quietude of the gentle sea lapping at the wharf stanchions, and the creaking of the dark, brooding boats at anchor. He heard the plaintive cry of a sea bird far out on the water and his stomach grumbled painfully about its emptiness

'Please, have you any food to spare? I'll gladly work for you. Do anything you ask, if you will only give me a crust!'

Startled, the old man jerked his head to peer up into the dusky dawn. The old tired eyes stared up at Daniel without expression, appearing not to comprehend.

'Food?' he asked absently.

'Aye. I've had none since yesterday morning. I'm terrible hungry. I can work hard.'

'I have no work for you, boy — nor food. I have barely enough to keep myself alive.' The old man's face darkened, his eyes suddenly dulled with pain. 'Time was when I had it all. Riches. A wife. A beautiful daughter. Sons to carry on my business. Now I have nothing!'

'What happened?' It was difficult to believe that this bent skeleton of a man had ever been any other way.

The old man looked up at the boy, not really seeing him, his mouth working grotesquely to form the words he struggled to utter.

'There came a fever, which carried off my wife,' he said slowly, the elderly voice tasting every word. 'My daughter died at childbed — and the baby wi' her. Then a merchant persuaded us into smugglin' an' a Customs cutter fired on my boat. Ten more minutes an' we would ha' bin inside the three miles.' A faint tremor began at the corner of the old man's mouth, the shrunken, yellowing eyes dulling with pain.

It seemed to Daniel he was about to crumble with the weight of his misery and anguish.

'Were your sons captured, then?' Daniel wanted to leave; to walk around and warm up. But he felt pity for the old man and realised the poor soul needed to talk of his heartbreaks. The cold of the morning breeze cut into Daniel's legs and needles of pain shot through them like splinters of broken glass.

'Not captured!' The old man's face folded like a worn concertina. 'We all went down wi' the wherry. At first two of my son's were wi' me, clinging to some flotsam, but the cold took 'em an' when they could hang on no longer they drifted away. I tried to hold 'em, but my hands were numb. The third son, John an' my son-in-law, I never set eyes on after the boat was holed.'

The lamp sputtered and went out. The old man sank to his knees on the floor, his head buried in his skinny arms and his shoulders heaved as he wept in huge, convulsive sobs.

Daniel felt his eyes stinging as he stepped back from the wharf's edge. Perhaps, he realised, there were folks worse off than himself. At least he, who had never had anything, had lost nothing. Life could be terribly cruel, he sighed.

Over to his left the sky was pearled lavender now, the slowly ascending sun merely a ghost through the morning's heavy mist.

The boy listened carefully to the familiar sounds of morning, wishing desperately that he belonged to it all.

Booted feet tramped heavily on the tarred, stained decks of the fishing boats. Hoarse shouts and curses filled the briny air as fishermen readied their vessels for the day ahead.

He wandered around the quay, stamping his feet from time to time to keep the blood flowing. Aimlessly he watched the men coiling ropes checking rigging, nets and sails, hurrying from one task to another.

Not many found time even to spare an incurious glance at the ragamuffin who looked on.

Very quickly, before the sun had properly lit the morning sky, the fishing fleet sailed, the growing wind flapping the sails and clicking the rigging against the masts.

Daniel watched longingly until all the vessels were out of sight, and for a long time afterward. He heard, in the distance, the whispering sea breathing gently against a headland. Mournful seagulls mewed somewhere overhead, well out to sea, he thought, probably following the shoals of fish.

The magnitude of the dark castle across the harbour beckoned to him, the whistle of the wind in its crevices like a siren call, hypnotising, pulling him towards it. Without knowing why, he made his way around, to stand, looking up. Feeling, too distinctly, the vulnerability of a chill void at his back, Daniel backed against the nook in the wall and squatted down to wait, though for what he did not know. The emptiness within him was in his soul as well as his belly.

For a while the boy toyed with the idea of committing some crime. That would soon put him back inside the gaol. The thought was tempting. But then the Governor had made it all too clear what the consequence would be. He fancied neither a flogging, nor transportation. He knew not where this place called The Americas was but had heard it took several weeks to reach.

He had been told by one of the other prisoners that convicts were carried in far worse conditions than the animals — for they were of less value — and very great numbers of them died on the passage. Even if he did survive the journey he felt certain that The Americas would almost certainly yield a harsher life than the Isle of Man. Better the devil you know, someone had once told him.

With a sigh, Daniel huddled in against the wall, embracing himself, hugging his knees tightly to his chest in a futile attempt at warmth.

After a while, above the other sounds of the harbourside morning, the boy heard the castle door creak mournfully. Standing, he edged towards it. Voices drifted to him, though for several moments he could see no one. Then a small girl appeared, disheveled and tearstained — only a little less ragged than himself. He remembered seeing her before — when they had been exercising. She had always clung around the women as if the men frightened her.

The Governor appeared close behind, and involuntarily Daniel moved back against the wall, wishing there was a shadow he could hide in.

The man and the girl stopped close by and it was impossible for the boy to avoid hearing what was said. When he tried to steal away, the movement caught the man's eye and Daniel could not fail to notice his look of anger before he turned and stalked back into the castle.

Daniel warily watched the girl, wondering if he should speak to her. From what he had overheard, it was obvious she had always had a home and was not used to caring for herself, as he was. His heart lurched as he studied her fragility. Her plight, somehow, seemed so much worse than his. Was it not to Douglas the governor had told her to go? A long walk for such a tiny girl alone. To Daniel's eyes, she did not look strong enough to survive such a journey.

For a while she stood, motionless, undecided, gazing morosely out over the harbour. Her shoulders were slumped as though she bore an awesome burden.

Clouds came across the sky, dulling the sun to a ghostly halo against the lowering sky. When the girl started to move away he quietly followed, drawn to her by her loneliness. In her, he sensed a fellow spirit. Another innocent whom life had brutalized, with nowhere to go and no one to turn to for help.

The girl glanced briefly in his direction but seemed not to see him as she strolled aimlessly towards the water, her eyes fixed always towards the north. Stopping on a rock close to the edge, she leaned forward. For a heart-stopping moment, Daniel thought she was going to let herself fall into the freezing water and with a gasp he broke into a run. Then she straightened and, hearing his footsteps, turned.

Daniel had his hand outstretched towards her when she saw him coming and in sudden fear she took a backward step, her foot slipping on the slimy rock.

The boy leapt forward, grasping her arm, dragging her away and together they fell, breathless, to the ground.

'No! Don't Jump!' he gasped. 'Nothin's so bad it's worth dying for.'

'I wasn't goin' to. You gave me a fright an' I nearly fell. That's all.' Isabella glared reprovingly as she scrambled to her feet, straightening her clothes and rubbing at a trickle of blood where the fall had grazed her leg.

'Sorry. When I saw you so near the edge I thought you were goin' to jump.' Daniel shuffled his feet awkwardly, feeling the blood burn in his face and neck.

'I was only lookin' at the fish in the water an' wishin' I knew how to catch some.'

Daniel looked down into the dirty harbour water sloughing and sucking against the rocks, and the seaweed below swaying and eddying on the outgoing tide. Schools of fish swam lazily there, but with no way of catching them, it was self-torture to watch.

'Where do you live?' Isabella looked up at Daniel through innocent blue eyes. Eyes that, to him, looked to be filled with nothing but painful memories,

'Anywhere and nowhere.' The boy shrugged, sighing tremulously. 'I've never had a proper home. Not for a long time, anyway! I sleep wherever I can find shelter and eat, whatever food I can find to take.'

'Take? Do you mean you steal it?' The blue eyes widened in horror.

'Most often that's the only way to get any. It's either steal or starve. So I steal.' He expressed it with childlike simplicity.

'You must be clever not to be caught. I had to run away from home and when I knew I must either steal, or die of hunger, I pinched a bun from the baker. I wasn't very good at it though, because I was so busy watching the baker-man I didn't see a lady come into the shop behind me. When I tried to run out, she grabbed me an' I was arrested. I have been in gaol in the castle for four months.'

'So have I,' it pained Daniel to have to admit he had been careless enough to be captured. 'I must never be caught again, though, or next time I'll be birched and sent to The Americas.'

'The where?'

'It's some place a long way away across the sea. I heard you tell the Governor why you had to run away. You aren't goin' to go back there are you? To your Mammy, I mean.'

'I think I must. I've nowhere else to go. An' I love my Mammy. She's not really bad, you know. Jus' can't think o' no other way to get money. I must make sure she's all right.'

'You still love her? After what she did to you?' Daniel asked incredulously.

Isabella shrugged wearily. 'She couldn't help it. I suppose she needed the money. I must go home.' Her head nodded as she spoke, as though trying to convince herself.

Daniel nodded. Home! What a lovely sound the word had. 'Can I come wi' you? As far as Douglas, anyway? My name's Daniel.'

'I'm Isabella. Is that where you're goin'? To Douglas?' Isabella brightened, her heart soaring with relief She had been dreading the journey alone. Especially with the days so short and dark.

Daniel shrugged. ''Tis as good a place as any. I might have more luck at finding a living there.'

Side by side the two children turned their faces towards the north, their footsteps hesitant, reluctant to leave Castletown. At the bridge, they stopped for one last, lingering look at Castle Rushen.

'Goodbye Jane,' Isabella whispered, biting her lip as a single silent tear burnt a path down each cheek.

'Who's Jane? Was she a friend?' Daniel asked quietly.

Isabella nodded distractedly. ''The best friend I've ever had. An' soon she's to be transported. I don' think I would have survived wi'out her in gaol at first. I'll never forget her as long as I live.'

Sensing her melancholia, Daniel took her arm, gently pulling her forward. 'Come. We'd best be on our way. There looks to be a storm comin'.'

Isabella nodded, following him slowly, shuffling sideways, swallowing a sob as she paused just once more to glance sadly over her shoulder at the darkening castle.

A strong wind picked up before they had gone far. A wild, whipping wind that ceaselessly swirled, gathering layers of powdery snow from the hills and driving it in stinging sheets around their ill-protected bodies. The icy blast tugged and reeled them about as if they had no will of their own.

Daniel walked in front, trying to afford the girl the best possible protection from the storm. On occasion, as they stumbled around the bay, he took her hand to help her over the hard, frosted sand and tussocks of coarse grass.

All of a sudden his life had a purpose and he felt very grown-up. He would be this tiny waif's protector! He was worthwhile! He was important! Pride lifted his head a little.

A thick mist came off the sea, closing tightly around them, clinging damply and chilling them right through into their bones.

'Hold on to me so we don't lose each other.' Daniel reached back, plucking at Isabella's fingers, nodding with satisfaction when he felt her tiny hand grasp his tightly.

'I'm so cold,' she whimpered, complaining for the first time. 'I don't know how you can bear it with no shoes.'

Daniel looked down, only fully aware, for the first time, of the nakedness of his feet. Suddenly he was aware they felt no cold. They felt nothing. Blessed numbness had taken away the pain.

'I've never had shoes.'

'What — never ever?' Isabella's eyes widened in disbelief.

'Na. Never. Never had no one to buy them for me. Never needed them.' In fact, it was something he had never missed, nor even thought much about before. None of the street urchins wore shoes. Unless they managed to steal a pair somewhere, of course. From what he had seen of Isabella's, hers were no great improvement on bare feet. Certainly, they would not keep out much cold.

The wind increased yet more, bringing with it a violent mixture of sleet and hail. Shivering uncontrollably, Daniel looked around for a place to take refuge, but could not see any distance. Gritting his teeth, he took a firmer grip on Isabella's hand, keeping her moving as quickly as he could.

The ground was starting to rise quite steeply and they stumbled upwards, their heads bent low, faces turned sideways from the weather. They winced and gasped as the full fury of the storm smote them, hail battering their faces and bare limbs with bruising, frozen pellets of hail.

'We must find somewhere to shelter!' Daniel shouted, but the wind whipped his words away before they reached Isabella.

Trustingly, blinded by the weather, she stumbled in his wake without a whimper. The lip she had clenched between her teeth bled — but was too numb to cause her pain.

A large, dark shape loomed just off the right and, heart bounding with joy, Daniel realised it was a building of some sort. Stopping, he pulled Isabella to him, pointing.

Following his gaze, the girl saw the dim outline, her face lighting with relief. 'Is it a house?' she asked tremulously.

'Dunno!'

They struggled towards it, leaning sideways against the tearing gale, seeing as they drew near, that it was, in fact, a stack of hay.

'Oh! Is that all?' Isabella asked, her heart plumbing a new depth, her blue eyes swimming with tears of disappointment.

'All? That's good!' Daniel contradicted. 'If we dig ourselves right into the inside it will be quite warm. Much better than being out here in the storm.'

Isabella nodded mutely, clinging trustingly to his hand. Anything had to be better than staying out in the storm, though a cottage with a nice, roaring fire would have been so wonderful.

Battling their way to the leeward side of the stack, the children frantically pulled out handfuls of hay, until there was a large enough hole for them to wriggle into its depths. Daniel pushed Isabella in first, crawling in behind her and pulling hay loosely down to protect his back.

Cuddling up tightly, they curled around each other, listening to the storm growing and raging outside. Warmth and feeling gradually returned to their bodies and limbs, bringing pain at first. Excruciating pain that had Isabella once again punishing her gnawed lips in her determination not to cry

At times the gusts outside were so fierce the haystack shuddered under the onslaught as though the storm grasped it and shook it.

Hay dust invaded the children's' lungs and noses and at first they were convulsed with violent fits of coughing and sneezing, but after a while they grew used to it and breathed more easily.

'The storm seems to be getting worse. Do you think it'll ever stop? Isabella asked fearfully.

Daniel shrugged. 'I s'pose so.'

'I'm so hungry.'

'Me too. When the wind dies down a bit I'll go out an' see if I can find anythin' to eat.'

For hour after endless hour, they huddled in the hay, while the storm strengthened and raged outside. Insulated, even their damp clothes now warm, they dozed, awakening startled, on occasions, when a particularly strong gust battered their nest.

Daniel stirred and was suddenly wide awake. By straining his ears he could just make out strange sounds of movement — very quiet, but there, just the same. He tensed, alert, pushing up onto one elbow, holding his breath, listening intently. It came again — and closer now. A rustling and the sound of strong, small teeth gnawing. Relieved, he sank back into the hay, expelling the breath in a long, slow sigh.

A mouse — or a rat — that was all. Nothing to fear. Hiding from the weather, just as he was doing.

Suddenly he realised there was a silence. The storm had finally quietened. The wind had dropped and the world seemed at peace once more.

It would be wise, he thought, to look outside, try to get his bearings. By the time they had found the haystack, he had not been sure which direction they were facing. They might well have been walking round in circles in the swirling sleet and hail.

With infinite care and slowness, to avoid wakening Isabella, Daniel lifted himself from the hay, extricating himself gently from the girl's entwining arms and slid backwards from the stack. The ground where his feet landed was slippery with quickly freezing sleet and snow. Looking around, he found he could see almost nothing, the day having turned black with early winter night. A wispy mist hung over the hill and the moon was almost completely obscured by heavy, banking clouds.

'Daniel! Where are you Daniel?' The girl's voice was cracked and dry, with a note of rising panic.

'I'm here,' he called back. 'Jus' takin' a look aroun'.' The cold was so profound that his legs were already numb. Turning, he crept back into the nest, pulling hay down behind him and cuddling up to Isabella. 'Has the storm stopped?'

'Aye, but 'tis dark now. There's no sense to try to go any further before mornin'. We'd best stay here for the night or we could easy get lost, or fall an' be hurt.'

'I'm so hungry though.'

'We'll find some food in the mornin'.'

Isabella nodded, sighed and fell promptly into the deep slumber of exhaustion.

Chapter 4

A group of quarrelsome rooks, perched, squabbling atop the haystack, wakened Daniel and Isabella.

'Is it morning?' Isabella asked. Rubbing her eyes, she tried in vain to stretch her cramped, stiffened legs. 'Dunno'. Probably.' Daniel backed out, flinching as his feet landed in the frozen snow.

Isabella followed him, her teeth chattering and goosebumps rising when the chill breeze blew through her damp, threadbare clothing.

'Where are we?'

Daniel lifted one shoulder in a half-hearted shrug. 'I lost direction a bit in the storm.'

A patchy ground mist hung around, giving the world a surrealistic air. Daniel stumbled around the stack, trying to get his bearings. There was a brighter patch in the lowering clouds, so that must be east. Straining his eyes, he peered downwards and thought he could just see a faint glimmer of the sea through the mist.

Returning to Isabella, he waved an arm in a vague, sweeping gesture. 'I think north must be that way.'

Isabella nodded, ready to believe anything he told her, and follow wherever he cared to lead her. It was clear he was more able to take care of her than she was herself.

'I'm awful hungry. Can we find anythin' to eat?' she asked plaintively.

Daniel looked around at the few bare trees on the hillside, stunted and grotesquely misshapen, constantly battered by the prevailing wind. Above, a flock of seagulls wheeled and dipped, wailing and screeching.

The ground, hard and white with frozen snow, offered no chance of food. Daniel shook his head, then noticed a movement in the corner of his vision. A sheep! Crouching, he started to move towards it.

Watching, Isabella suddenly drew a sharp breath realising his intention. 'No! You musn't.' She clutched at his arm.

Daniel jerked himself free. 'We have to eat.'

'Not a sheep. You can't kill it. Anyway, how would we eat it?'

'I'll make a fire an' we'll cook it.' He shrugged at the simplicity of it.

Surely even a girl should be able to see that.

'But we haven't anything to start a fire with! Have we?'

Daniel stopped. No! He hadn't. What then? He sighed resignedly.

'I bet you wouldn't have had the heart to kill it!' Isabella looked up at him, smiling. 'Anyway,' she added defiantly, 'They hang you for stealing sheep!'

'They'd have to catch me first,' he replied, remembering past sheep he had encountered — and tasted! He heaved a hearty sigh. 'But you're right about the fire.'

When they were ready to be on their way the sun had broken through to lend a pale watery glow to the scene. Below them, to the right, they could see its light reflected, glinting from the rippling wave crests in a million shimmering lights.

'North is that way.' Daniel pointed across the slope of the hill. Already his feet were numb and turning blue. He was keen to get moving, in the hope it would put life into them. One step at a time, he told himself. It was a long way to Douglas, but if they could just set their eyes on something on the skyline and keep going, then eventually it would be the town they were seeing and taking their steps towards.

Motioning with his head, he led Isabella toward the smudgy outline of a stand of trees.

Everywhere around were draperies of snow. Ice spread treacherously on the steeply sloping ground or hung from rocks or trees. Only an occasional column of slate or Manx spa stood barren, rising like some ancient tombstone.

Several times, Isabella fell, lying winded, and would have been happy to stay where she landed had not Daniel pulled her to her feet and bullied her, sobbing, into going on.

'You can't stay here.' If you stop to rest in this cold you will never get up again. You will lie here and die.'

'I can't go any further. Please let me rest. Just for a few minutes. I'm so tired and hungry.' The cornflower blue eyes, water filled, pleaded, but Daniel would not give in.

'Only a few miles left to go.'

'You keep saying that. It is always just a few miles. It never gets any nearer!'

That was true in a way, Daniel thought, because it was not really far from Castletown to Douglas, so there had only been a few miles to face when their journey started. Because he had been the one to continually urge them onward, he had ignored the signs of utter exhaustion on Isabella's face.

A hawk flew overhead, banking and gliding against the washed blue sky. His black eyes glittered as they scanned the awful sameness of the black and white landscape for a movement that would give away the whereabouts of some poor, unsuspecting creature.

If only I could glide in the heavens like him, to find food, Daniel thought, sighing heavily.

'What's wrong?' Isabella gazed trustingly up at him.

Daniel smiled wanly. 'Nothing. I was just wishing our lives could be as easy as his.' He nodded towards the hawk.

The hawk dived with frightening speed, then soared away, some poor, terrified, struggling creature gripped firmly in its talons. Daniel looked around. Apart from the swishing and whipping of tree branches, nothing moved in that harsh, unforgiving landscape.

The wind whipped loose snow about their legs as they walked. Isabella stumbled behind Daniel, clinging grimly to the back of his shirt, uncomplaining, though choking down silent sobs. Never, never, never in her life had she felt so cold. And she had shoes. She worried about Daniel with his feet bare, looking so dark and unrealistically large. She had heard of people losing feet with frostbite and feared this might happen to him.

'It'll be good to get home. It seems such a long time since I saw my Mammy. I hope that man isn't there still. Do you think he will be?'

Daniel shrugged. 'I dunno'. Was he really so bad?'

Isabella nodded, trembling. 'Yes. He was awful.' She shook her head jerkily, as though the action would somehow cleanse her.

'Listen!' Daniel held a hand up to silence her chatter. His head was turned sideways, listening intently.

'What is it?' Isabella could hear nothing, save the squabbling of some birds, far off.

'Can't you hear them?'

'All I can hear is seagulls.'

'No. Not them. Hens. I can hear hens.' Isabella frowned in bewilderment.

'Come on. Let's find them. Over this way somewhere.' Daniel started off quickly up the hill.

At the top of the rise they found themselves in a thicket of trees. The wind whistled amongst them, playing with their tips, tossing handfuls of hard snow down on the children passing below.

Isabella caught the smell of peat and wood burning. 'There must be a cottage near here. I can smell a fire. Should we ask for food?'

Daniel looked thoughtful. 'I dunno', We'll take a look at them first. A lot o' folks don't like strangers being aroun'. They might think we've come to cause trouble.'

In a few minutes, they saw the dim glow of lamplight through the trees and soon found the cottage. The warm, inviting smell of the fire was closer here. Moving to the edge of the clearing, Daniel caught Isabella's wrist as she was about to hurry past him.

'You stay here until I check it's safe.'

'No!' She clung to his hand. 'I don't want to be left. Let me come wi' you.'

Daniel hesitated, eyeing her thoughtfully. 'Well, all right,' he sighed.

'But be careful — an' quiet. An' be ready to run quickly if we ha' to.'

Isabella nodded and, crouched over, scuttling across the clearing. Daniel reached the cottage first, turning quickly to put his back against it, placing his finger to the girl's lips, when she reached him. For what felt like hours, they stood there motionless, watching and listening. They heard no sound from inside the cottage, but from round the side they could hear the contented chuckling of the hens. The smell of the burning peat was magnetic.

Carefully Daniel edged along until he could peep through the small square of window. The turf hut was tiny, but no less than he would have expected. In the far corner was a rough mattress filled, it looked like, with dried bracken from the hills. A few grubby, threadbare blankets were strewn untidily atop it. A battered old chair leaned drunkenly against the wall, and a rough shelf on the wall held a few odd pieces of chipped crockery. In the centre of the single small room blazed the fire whose smell had attracted them with, hanging on a chain above it, a large, steaming black pot.

Daniel's first thought was the warmth as he watched the fire leaping, the logs crackling and the sweet-smelling peat smouldering, with its cheery orange glow.

Pressing his face close to the window, he tried to see into the very farthest reaches of the room.

'What can you see? Who's there?'

'It looks like the home of someone very poor. But there don't seem to be nobody home. I can't see anyone.'

'What shall we do?'

Daniel looked around thoughtfully. The glow of the fire tempted him, dulling his wits. 'First, we'll knock on the door. If the person who answers looks nice, then we'll ask for food.'

Isabella huddled behind Daniel as they approached the door. Pulling himself up as tall as he could, the boy took a deep breath, raised his hand and, after only a momentary hesitation, rapped loudly on the gnarled door. When there was no reply he knocked again and the door swung open just a crack. Pushing it a few inches farther, Daniel called, 'Is anyone home?'

There was still no answer, so after listening carefully for a few moments, he pushed the door wide, poked his head inside, and looked around carefully.

The heat of the fire glowed on his face and made him want to move closer, but for a moment caution prevailed and he could not budge. Isabella's hand was on his back, pushing gently.

'Is there anyone there?' Her whisper was close to his ear.

Daniel shook his head. 'Don't seem to be.'

'Should we go in?'

'I don't know. Suppose they come back?'

'Surely they can't be angry about us just gettin' warm?'

'I don't know.' Daniel was apprehensive. A lifetime of battling to survive had taught him to be overcautious. But he had never before been responsible for anyone else's safety.

'Come on. Please let's go in near the fire.'

Daniel stepped through the doorway first, carefully checking, once again, that the room was empty. 'All right. Come on in.' He stepped aside to allow her passage. Following her in, he pushed the door to behind him.

Isabella rushed straight to the fire, huddling as close to it as she comfortably could. More cautious, Daniel edged around the other side, from where he could easily watch the door. Looking around carefully, he studied the room, finding, to his chagrin, that there was only the one door and window. Both were on the same wall, and the window too small to escape through anyway. Sighing deeply, he crossed his fingers and settled to enjoy the warmth.

Isabella's cheeks glowed pink as she felt the fire's warmth seeping through her body. Quite quickly she felt her frock drying against her.

Daniel stood, alert and ready to run, holding first one foot, then the other, towards the fire. There was a spell of sheer agony at first when the blood began to circulate again. Then gradually it changed to a comfortable tingle.

'I think we'd better leave soon,' he said reluctantly after a while.

Isabella's gaze was moist, her lip quivering. 'Must we? Can't we stay just a little while longer?' She dreaded facing the soul-destroying cold again.

Daniel frowned, sorely tempted, then shook his head. 'We must go. See if we can reach Douglas tonight. You know how early the light is gone an' we don' want to be travellin' in the dark.'

Isabella stood, nodding sadly and glanced into the black cauldron. ''Tis soup!'

Daniel's eyes lit. 'Should we ha' some?' He ran his tongue hungrily along his top lip.

Isabella nodded. Looking around, she saw a grubby, chipped mug on the shelf. 'This should do.' Crossing. she picked it up.

Suddenly the door flew open with a loud crash and the children found themselves confronted by a wild-eyed old lady.

With a squeal of terror, Isabella darted behind Daniel.

'Who are you? What do you want? Why are you in my house?' Suddenly the woman appeared to see the cup in the girl's hand. 'You've come to steal from me!' she screeched. Her grey hair, dirty and unkempt, stood out from her head in wild disarray. What had once been her teeth were now no more than black stumps.

'No! No! We haven't. We were cold an' saw your fire an' came in to get warm,' Daniel said desperately.

'She's a witch!' Isabella bleated from behind Daniel's back.

If he'd been alone he could have ducked past the old lady and escaped easily. He looked around wildly, but could see no means of escape.

The old lady's eyes were fixed on the mug. 'you came to rob me!' she cried again, lunging at Isabella.

Screaming, the girl released her hold on the mug, darting away and watching it fall, as though time stood still for a moment, to the earthen floor and shatter.

'That was my only cup!' The old lady screamed, agonised

The spell broken, Daniel grabbed Isabella's wrist, swinging her towards the door. 'Run!'

With the sudden surge of inner strength which is often lent by fear, he ducked under the outstretched, scrawny hands, pushing Isabella before him, gasping as the cold air hit him. Without faltering they ran out well beyond the copse of trees, to huddle together a hedge.

'She was a witch!' Isabella repeated, shivering more from fright than cold. Let's get away from here quick lest she puts a spell on us.'

'Soon.' Daniel popped his head above the fence, peering back towards the cottage. 'I want to go back an' see if I can get a hen.

Isabella gasped. 'No! She'll turn you into a frog, or a lump of stone or somethin'.'

'I won't let her see me. But we must ha' something 'to eat Stay here.' In an instant he was over the hedge and moving stealthily back the way they had come.

Isabella watched until she could see him no longer, then she hunched down behind the hedge. After a few moments there was the most awful squawking, then the old lady's screeching voice, followed by the sound of running feet. Daniel suddenly came scrambling down beside her.

'Run Isabella,' he yelled, hardly missing a stride.

It was a full ten minutes before they stopped their terrified flight, gasping for breath, hearts pounding painfully. Sitting, Daniel held out a hand, offering Isabella an egg. 'Here. Eat this.'

Frowning, she turned it over. 'Raw?' She asked, startled.

Daniel nodded. 'Like this.' Producing a second egg, he tipped his head back, dug his fingers in to crack the shell and let it empty into his mouth.

Isabella shuddered, but was hungry enough to copy him.

'Sorry that was all I could bring. I couldn't catch the hens an' they was makin' too much noise.'

Isabella started to giggle. 'I thought you would be changed into somethin' horrid.'

Recovering their breath, the children continued on their journey. When they finally topped the rise above Douglas and saw, thankfully, the town nestled in the basin below, it was becoming quite late. Though the clouds had long since obscured the winter sun, it was not yet quite dark. As their eyes grew used to the trailing mist which clung wispily to the harbour water, they saw that the quay was cheerful with lamplight from boats and warehouses and taverns. A ship was unloading and an occasional burst of rowdy laughter cheered the grey January day.

Isabella brightened the moment Douglas came into her view and her steps quickened. Daniel sensed her excitement and found himself almost running to keep pace with her down the hill. They hurried over the bridge to the other side of the river, then round the harbour side.

Isabella felt her heart quicken excitedly. Home! Nearly home! An' Mammy would be waiting. She hadn't realised, until now, how much she had missed the little house and her mother. Isabella could see her now. Knew she would be thrilled to see her daughter home. Reaching the corner, she broke into a run racing down the filthy, smelly lane to knock happily on her mother's door.

That awful man, the Englishman with the green teeth, would be gone now. Isabella was sure her mother wouldn't have let him stay after what he had tried to do.

No one opened the door and the girl knocked more loudly.

Daniel had run with her and stood behind her now, looking at the outside of the scruffy little hovel. Besides the battered door, there was only one very small window in the chipped stone front of the building. It was very tightly shut, with a wooden slat nailed across it.

Isabella knocked harder. 'Open the door, Mammy. 'Tis me, Isabella. I'm home, Mammy.' She stepped back looking up at the house, frowning in bewilderment and her lips trembling.

'Maybe she's out,' Daniel offered, a little worm of fear starting to gnaw in his stomach.

Isabella sensed something badly wrong. The cottage had a bad feel about it. 'Why is the window boarded? It didn't used to be.'

Danny gazed at it and shrugged. How would he know?

Heads appeared out of the surrounding doorways, wondering about the commotion.

'Who are you? What do you want here?' A dirty looking woman barked the question.

'I'm lookin' for my Mammy — Esther Cain.'

The woman peered at her through ale-bleared eyes. 'Is that you, Isabella?'

'Aye.'

'I thought you was in gaol. Your Mammy said you was.'

'I was, but I got out yesterday. Do you know where my Mammy is?'

'Na. Can't say I do, lass. She went away. Left soon after you got took.'

'Went? Went where?' Daniel could see panic building in the girl and moved closer to her.

'Dunno'. Jus' went. Maybe she thought the police would come for her too. I heard she went "across" wi' some Englishman she picked up wi' in the ale house.'

'No! Mammy! Mammy!' Isabella screamed. Running to the door, she started pounding on it with both hands, rattling it on its hinges. 'No! Mammy wouldn't go wi'out me!' When there was still no answer she sank. sobbing, to the cold street, burying her face into the corner of the doorway.

Daniel knelt behind her, placing his hand on her back in a lost, helpless gesture. He wanted to help, but knew not what to say. Turning, she put her arms tight around him, pressing her cheek against his neck.

'What am I to do? What will become o' me?' she sobbed.

Daniel's voice, when he found it, was charged with emotion. 'I'll take care o' you!' he promised. Then his arms were about her, holding her so tightly her ribs felt to be cracking. His tears were on her cheeks along with hers.

'I swear I'll allus take care o' you!' he promised!'

Chapter 5

Daniel and Isabella huddled in the doorway until long after the night had turned black. 'We'd better leave an' see if we can find somewhere warmer to spend the night,' Daniel suggested through chattering teeth.

'No!' Isabella shook her head emphatically. 'Mammy would know I'd be out o' gaol soon. She'll come back for me. I must stay here where she can find me.'

Daniel sighed. 'Well we can't survive another night in the open. We must find some shelter.'

The girl nodded mutely, but did not move.

Daniel stood up, looking around. Wind gusted up the alley, screaming in his ears, rushing unheeded, sucking in amongst the cracks and crevices of the old buildings. Loose snow picked up to whip stingingly round his legs.

'Come wi' me.' He plucked at Isabella's sleeve. 'Let's look aroun' the town. Maybe we can find shelter somewhere.'

Pulling her arm free, she looked up at him, her eyes like black holes in the darkness of night. 'You go. I must stay.'

Daniel lingered, undecided. 'If I go, will you promise you won't stir from here?'

'Aye.'

Reluctantly he edged away from her, walking backwards at first, afraid to take his eyes off her lest she should vanish. When he reached the end of the street, she was still huddled there, exactly as he had left her.

Wending his way towards the harbour, he stopped for a few brief moments, to scan the sea to the east. The moon was riding free, its intermittent cloud cover racing westward, and its light pale and glittering against the smooth surface of the water. Daniel stared for a moment, but then the moon disappeared behind the rushing clouds and he could discern a new mist rolling in off the sea. With a final glance, he moved on around the harbour.

The market place had been long closed by the time Daniel found his way there. He walked all around it, as far as he could, but could find no way in. Beyond it stood the Market Hotel, a dim gaslight shining through its doorway, but he knew there would be little chance of finding refuge there. Someone had told him once, he remembered, that the hotel was a popular den for smugglers, having secret passages which passed under the street to emerge in the harbour wall itself. There was little chance, he felt, of smugglers finding any pity on two abandoned children. Sighing, he moved on.

The dark bulk of St. Matthew's church blackened out the stars, bringing Daniel's attention to it. Crossing, he went quickly up the few steps, trying the handle, his heart leaping with excitement when it turned. Slowly, he pushed the huge door open and slipped inside.

All was in total blackness. Daniel stood for a few minutes, quietly listening while his eyes adjusted. Faint glimmers of moonlight peeped in through the small windows from time to time as the clouds momentarily flitted clear of the moon.

No sound came. The church was cold and draughty but, Daniel thought, warmer than outside. Satisfied, he moved back, sliding the door shut behind him. He stood for a moment, breathing deeply in the chill air, then he made his way back along the harbour, past the line of fishing boats, their hawsers firmly secured on the bollards.

Across from the Market Hotel he made out, when the moon cleared its cloud mantel, shadowy forms, low down the side of the quay, moving stealthily. Stopping in the shadows, he watched boxes and barrels being brought out from a tunnel in the harbour wall and hefted onto a fishing boat. Voices whispered urgently and the contraband was quickly whisked below decks.

Suddenly Daniel's shoulder was grasped by an iron fingered hand.

'What you doin' here, boy?' a voice boomed in his ear.

Startled, he tried to whirl round, but found he could not move.

'I asked you a question, boy!'

'Jus' — jus' watchin'' Daniel stammered.

'You spyin' for Customs are you?' The fingers dug in even harder, making the boy wince.

'Customs?'

'Aye. Custom's an' Excise. Government officials.'

'Oh! No! I wouldn't ha' nuthin' to do wi' the like o' them!' Daniel shook his head vigorously.

The fingers slackened and the boy felt himself being turned around.

At first, he found himself looking low on the man's chest and had to tip his head well back to see his face.

Daniel gasped. Never before had he seen a man so tall. And large in every way, with wide shoulders topped by a round, not unpleasant, face with a full, but close-cut beard. The head was supported by a bull-like neck.

The man glared down at him, then suddenly he looked startled and his penetrating, almost black eyes widened. 'Alexander?' he whispered. Shaking his head, as though to clear away an impossible thought, he muttered, 'Can't be Alexander!' After staring bemusedly at Daniel for a long moment he asked, 'What're you doin' out here so late?'

'I was jus' lookin' for a place to sleep for the night.'

'Don' you have a home?'

'Na. Never have. Been an orphan as long as I can remember.'

'That's bad luck. You won't find nowhere here though. Try the church.'

The man let go of his shoulder, giving him a gentle push. The black eyes were almost friendly and his hooked nose made Daniel think of the hawks he had seen from time to time during his forays into the countryside.

'Aye. I will.' Daniel backed away hurriedly, then turned to run.

'Hey boy!' The commanding voice pulled him up sharply, making him whirl around.

'Church's that way!' The man was pointing to St. Matthew's.

'I know, but I got to fetch my friend.'

The man waved his acknowledgement. 'Don't let me catch you back here again. Next time I'll throw you in the harbour. An' don't you tell anyone about seein' us or your throat'll get cut.'

Involuntarily, Daniel put a hand to his throat. Shuddering, he shook his head. 'I won't,' he promised feelingly.

Isabella was exactly where he had left her, hunched down in the doorway, shivering.

'The church's open. We can sleep in there tonight.' Daniel gripped her arm to help her to her feet.

Isabella looked miserably up at him. Tracks down her cheeks glistened where the hot tears had been turned to ice by the January wind. She shook her head. 'You go. I can't. I must stay here.'

'No! I'll not leave you.' Anger was starting to build. 'You must come wi' me to the church. If you stay here you'll be dead by mornin'!'

Isabella's face set stubbornly. 'I must be here in case my Mammy comes for me.'

'She will not come! She has gone for good!'

'No!' Instantly Isabella was on her feet, her eyes flashing angrily. 'Don't say that! She *will* come! I know she will. An' I'll *not* leave here until she does!' She stood with her feet apart, hands on her hips and for a long moment, they glared furiously at each other.

Defeated, Daniel sighed, his eyes lowered and his body sagged. 'Well, we'll have to find a way of gettin' in here then.' He looked at the outside of the house.

'I've tried the door, but it won't move.'

Daniel moved to the window and, tugging at the wooden slat, thought he felt a bit of movement. With a ripple of excitement in his chest, he turned to Isabella. 'I might be able to pull this off. Then we can get in the window.'

Putting his weight against the wood, he pulled back. It moved a little, then the nails held fast.

'It won't come. Help me pull it.'

Isabella moved to his side, gripping the far end of the slat and they pulled on it together, wriggling and twisting it all the time. Finally, it came loose, almost tipping the girl on her back. Staggering, she gave a cry of triumph.

Daniel put a warning finger to his lips. 'Hush. You'll have everyone out to see what's goin' on. Now you stay here whilst I go inside for a look.'

Pulling himself up, the boy wriggled through the tiny opening. There came a sudden frantic scratching, squeaking and scurrying from all around. Rats! He shuddered. Still, they were better than the cold. Rats, he could cope with. They might even be useful one day.

'Tis all right. You can come in. Bring the slat up wi' you so we can pull it against the window again.' Daniel leaned out to help her climb.

Once she was inside, he pulled the board in tight against the window, making the blackness in the room complete. 'Let's hope no one will know we're here.' He whispered.

'Mammy had her mattress over here.' Isabella groped for his hand, leading him, stumbling across the room she was so familiar with. Here it is. Oh! An' there's a blanket too.'

'Good. We'd best get to sleep now. In the mornin', we'll see if there's anythin' else she's left that we can use.'

Daniel awoke to the feel of warm fur brushing his face. With a cry of horror, he leapt from the mattress, wakening Isabella, who sat up, startled.

'What's wrong?'

'It was a rat. Against my face.' He shuddered, his stomach turning.

Wide-eyed, Isabella looked around. 'Where?' Her voice was husky.

'Gone now. Hidin'.'

'Is it mornin'?'

'Daniel moved to the window, and carefully lifting away the board, he peered out into the lane.

There was a faintly pink suffused light which illuminated, with a strange ghostliness, new snow that had fallen during the night and now lay, banked in corners.

Turning, Daniel said, 'I'll go an' see if I can find us some food.'

Isabella frowned, panicking suddenly. 'Are you comin' back?'

Daniel nodded, his unruly dark hair flying. 'Aye.' Then he scrambled through the tiny window and pushed the board back in place.

The harbour was starting to come to life in the pink greyness of the approaching dawn. Fishermen moved quietly about their business, with an occasional shouted instruction breaking the quietude of the scene.

Daniel stood listening to the dashing of the waves against the harbour, mingled with the scream of the seabirds. Looking towards the sea, the dawn was a blood-red smear, burning angrily through a long rent in the massed leaden snow clouds. On the slumbering water, each wave was tipped a pearly pink. The ragged, oblate sun rose through the clouds with agonizing deliberation.

A boat came in through the harbour mouth, Daniel idly watching its leisurely progress. Suddenly he recognised the large figure standing akimbo, feet spread for balance, in the prow. Quickly, he moved into the shadow of a building. It would not be wise, he thought, to let that man-mountain catch him hanging around the harbour again so soon.

Daniel wandered around the market but found nothing that would pass as edible. Too early, he thought. He kicked at the drifted soft snow, watching it arc out into the wind.

Returning to the alley, he let himself in through the window.

'I couldn't find anything', but I'll go back later when the shops an' the market are open.'

Isabella shook her head violently, her eyes filling with tears. 'You can't go thievin'!'.

Daniel sighed impatiently. 'We gotta get food an' in winter there's no other way to get it. I bin feedin' myself this way all my life. 'Tis easier in the summer 'cos you can go into the fields an' pinch some turnips or priddas.'

'That's still stealin', an, you know what'll happen if you get caught again.'

'Tis the only way to get food. I'll go out later.' Daniel was not to be put off. 'I promised I would look after you an' I will.'

'But what will I do if you get caught?'

'What will you do it we don't get any food?'

Isabella shrugged.

A search of the hovel produced another thin, ragged blanket Isabella's — from the loft, several stubs of candles, a handful of dried grass, a small pile of peat, a couple of battered buckets and a variety of cracked pieces of crockery.

'If we only had some sticks we could get a fire going an' warm the place up a bit.' Daniel rubbed his feet, again an unhealthy blue.

'Here.' Isabella handed him a blanket. 'Wrap this round your feet. It can't be good for them to be so cold all the time.'

Daniel accepted it gratefully and was relieved to feel the pain of the blood returning to his over-punished feet.

'Have you never had a Mammy or Daddy?'

Daniel thought about it for a moment. 'I had a Daddy once, but I don't remember him. I remember an Auntie when I was very, very young. She said my Mammy died in childbed — she was allus tellin' me I killed my Mammy. Said Mammy would still have been alive if it wasn't for me.'

'How awful. That must have upset you.'

Daniel shrugged sadly. 'Sometimes it did. But other times it just made me angry, 'cos it wasn't my fault my Mammy had me. I didn't ask her to. She must ha' wanted to, an' she must ha' known the danger o' it. But I think my Auntie just said it to make me feel guilty, so I would do things for her that she asked me to. Mostly she just said it when she'd drunk too much jough. She would come home from the alehouse wi' all her money spent an' not enough left to buy food for our belly's or peat for the fire, an' then she would want me to go an' steal them for her.'

'An' did you?'

'Aye. Well, mostly I did. There wasn't jus' me you see. There was my cousins too. Two o' them. One younger an' one older. The younger one was born when I was about three years old, an' I don't think my Auntie knew who his father was. Jus' someone she met in the ale house an' went into a field wi'. Then there was the older cousin, but he was an idiot. His eyes was always blank an' colourless an' starin'. Never knew what you was sayin' to him. Jus' stared, like a lizard — unblinkin'. An' he was always wettin' an messin' in his pants. Mos' o' the time I had to clean him up 'cos his Mammy was out in the ale house.'

Isabella stared at him for a long moment, horror clearly reflected in her blue eyes. 'How horrible,' was all she could think of to say.

Daniel chewed his bottom lip thoughtfully. 'I suppose it was. At first anyway. But I got used to it. Someone had to do it. I think my Auntie was all right when my Daddy was alive 'cos I remember her saying he used to bring enough money from the fishin' to feed us quite well. She didn't ha' to go to the alehouse then.'

'What happened to your Daddy then?'

'Some merchant from "across" asked him to go smugglin' for him. The money was good, so he did. But he got caught an' put in Whitehaven gaol. Next thing my Auntie heard o' him he'd died there. She thought he had been flogged to death 'cos he tried to escape.'

Isabella sat silent. There were no words she knew to properly express her feelings. 'What happened to your Auntie? Did she send you away?'

'No. She needed me there to find food an' look after her childher. No, she was taken wi' the smallpox.'

'An' your cousins? What happened to them?'

'Them too! They both died. I nursed them all. First the younger cousin took it. My Auntie stopped goin' to the alehouse then, because she did care about her boys really. I helped her nurse the baby while he burned wi' fever, covered wi' raw, weepin' spots. Before he was even dead, my Auntie caught the illness. When the baby lost his grip on life she seemed to give up hers an' died soon after. I thought my older cousin was goin' to miss it, but then I woke one mornin' an' he was burnin' wi' the fever too. He went into a deep, restless sleep an' never woke up. He didn't las' long though, his body jus' didn' seem to know how to fight the awful illness. Then I was alone. wi' only myself to care about — until now!'

'What age were you then?'

Daniel was thoughtful for a moment, counting backwards on his fingers. 'I would ha' bin 'bout six, I think!'

'Six!? How have you lived since then?'

'By my wits, an' by stealin', mostly. Sometimes, though, you find a kind soul who will gi' you a penny, or a bit o' bread, or a fisherman who'll throw you an odd piece o' stockfish.'

The tale seemed, to Isabella, hard to accept, yet, hearing it from Daniel, and spoken so matter-of-factly, she found it impossible to disbelieve.

Chapter 6

Daniel carefully examined the buckets. Choosing the least battered, he moved to the window. 'I'm goin' for some water. If we can't eat, at least we can drink.'

Pulling the board free, he looked carefully each way along the dirty, foul-smelling alley. Once he was certain that there was no one to see him, he slipped quickly to the ground.

Isabella stood just inside the window, nervous to see him go. 'Take care,' she pleaded.

Daniel nodded. 'I will. Now keep the board in place while I'm gone.' Turning, he strode quickly towards the bright strip of sky at the end of the alley.

A watery, patchy, pale sun struggled through its blanket of clouds from time to time but had not the strength to melt the snow, nor even warm the brisk chill breeze. Daniel rubbed his bare arms with cold hands, but felt no relief.

The tin pail clanged against the wall as he turned the corner by the harbour, startling a flock of seabirds who were wrestling and fighting, wings thrashing angrily, over some object on the ground. As one, panic spreading amongst them, they rose on wildly flapping wings, squawking and diving in all directions

At the moment the blanket of grey and white feathers rose from the ground, Daniel saw the object of their battle. A large fish lay in the dirt of the harbour, its flesh half torn away but still too heavy for the birds to lift. In an instant, he was across the pathway and had the fish safely in the bottom of his pail.

Several of the gulls swooped, and scolding angrily, made aggressive passes, with vicious looking beaks, at his greasy thatch of black hair.

Daniel swiped at them with his free hand until they admitted defeat and flew off, scolding, in search of easier pickings.

A few steps further on, his nostrils were invaded by the unmistakable smell of freshly baked bread. Sniffing deeply, he followed it to a shop. Stopping a little short of the doorway, he looked — innocently he hoped — towards the river inlet. From the corner of his eye, he surreptitiously studied the bakery.

There was only one customer. Daniel stepped back against the wall, laying his bucket on the ground beside him, to wait patiently. One was not enough. He wanted many people in the shop. It was easier to be lost in a crowd. It had been carelessness and impatience that had got him caught the last time.

Slowly the shop filled until Daniel saw seven ladies inside awaiting service. Heart thumping so he could feel his chest jump, he picked up his pail and slipped in through the doorway.

The baker was half turned away, talking and laughing with the lady he was serving. Daniel sidled up behind the queue of ladies towards a tray of steaming loaves at the end of the counter. Lowering the pail to the floor at his feet he looked at the baker and covertly watched the other customers. No one appeared even to have noticed him. Reaching the loaves, he turned with his back to the counter. He saw the baker had his back to him now.

One or two of the ladies were starting to shuffle a little irritably as the baker continued his flirting conversation with an attractive young customer.

Daniel reached carefully behind him, grasped one of the loaves and dropped it into the pail.

'Are you going to make us wait all day. Or do you intend to serve us at some time?' A large woman towards the front of the queue had finally run out of patience and voiced her question loudly.

The baker whirled to face her, his face thunderous with sudden anger. 'Sorry Ma'am, I'll be wi' you in a moment.' He managed to force a tight-lipped smile. As he turned away again his gaze landed on Daniel and he frowned suspiciously.

Daniel edged towards the nearest woman, smiling up at her, whilst she was apparently oblivious of his existence.

The baker glowered for a few seconds longer, then returned to his work.

Releasing his long-held breath, Daniel started to drift to the door. A lady, just a few feet away, studied him searchingly, almost, he felt, with a look of recognition. Her hand fluttered to her mouth, and the boy knew he had been discovered.

Stopping, he held the lady's gaze, his odd coloured eyes beseeching. Finally, he saw just a faint glimmer of a smile and knew he was safe. Heart pounding, he turned to hurry from the shop, noticing the lady craned to peer into his pail as he fled past her. Expecting a hue and cry to start at any moment, he ran as soon as he was out of the shop and didn't stop until he was well away. Finally, daring to breathe again, he hurried back to Isabella.

When he reached the cottage, Daniel quietly pulled the boards from the window. After looking around, carefully, he handed the pail with his spoils through the little window, climbing in quickly after it.

'We can eat well today,' Daniel told Isabella proudly.

Isabella lifted the loaf from the bucket, still warm, with an appetizing, crispy crust. Drawing a quick breath, she said, 'Oh, how lovely. Where did you get it?'

'From the bakehouse.'

'You stole it?'

'Aye.' Daniel nodded, unashamed.

Isabella sighed, shaking her head. Turning the bread over, she found it soggy at one end with the watery blood excretions from the fish.

'Ugh! What's that?' Her lips curled in distaste.

'A fish I took from the gulls.'

Daniel cut the fish into two pieces with a dirty, rusty knife he found on the corner of the floor, handing the larger lump to Isabella. Then they ripped the loaf in two, Daniel taking the blooded half

Isabella studied the fish doubtfully. 'I can't eat it raw.'

'Yes you can — an' you will.' Daniel told her decisively. ''Tis just as good for you raw as cooked. 'Tis good food an' not to be wasted. We must eat. Go on, try it. If you don't like it the first time you'll soon get used to it.'

Isabella took a tentative nibble, decided it didn't taste as bad as it looked and quickly wolfed it all. The bread lasted no longer.

'I'm thirsty now. You brought no water did you!' she accused.

'I was too busy gettin' food!' He protested. 'I'll go later, for water.'

Daniel slipped out. Along by the harbour, past Muckle's gate and up Big Well Hill, the pail clanking at his side. The square was crowded, the well a busy place. All around, women from the poorer homes were doing their washing, while people came and went all the time to fill pails at the well and take their water home.

Daniel waited his turn, rinsed fish juices from the bucket and filled it, while people jostled behind him. Shivering, he hurried back down the steep slope, battling to keep his bare feet gripping on the ice. *Tonight*, he thought, *I* must find a way to get a fire lit in the house.

As he hurried along the harbour he spied a familiar fishing boat, the *Louisa* at anchor. Also familiar was the giant figure standing, deeply held in conversation with a well-dressed man whom Daniel took to be a merchant. Lowering his head and turning his face away, Daniel scurried past and fled back to Isabella.

Later, after the light had gone from the day, Daniel stood up. 'I'm goin' to see if I can find wood.' He announced suddenly.

'Wood?' Isabella's face was blank.

'Aye, we must try to get a fire goin'. Warm this hovel up a bit.'

'No! Don't go tonight. Please don't!' Isabella's lips quivered. 'I'm afeared when you leave.'

Daniel shrugged lightly. 'Nothin' to be scared o'. No one knows you're here to come an' harm you.'

'I'm scared you won't come back.'

Daniel scowled. 'Of course, I'll come back. An' we'll be better off if we can get a fire goin' at night.'

'Where will you get wood, though?'

'Out o' town jus' a small way. There's some trees jus' west o' here.'

'But it's agin' the law. There's harsh punishments for cuttin' the trees!' Isabella cried. She clearly remembered her mother talking about it to one of her men. There were so few trees on the Island, and so many poor people prone to cut them down for fuel, that heavy penalties had been introduced against anyone caught so doing.

'I shan't be caught. I promise. So saying, he climbed through the window, said, 'I won't be away long,' replaced the board and was gone.

Locked, alone and frightened, in the little dark room once more, Isabella slumped on the straw mattress to wait. From nearby there came a scratching and scuffling. Terrified, she put a hand over her mouth to stifle a scream. Suddenly, in the one moment, something furry brushed against her cold, bare leg and another creature ran over her foot. Leaping up, she was across the room in an instant.

The candles! Where had they put them. She and Daniel had agreed that because they were only tiny stumps and they had little kindling, they would only use them when absolutely necessary. But Isabella decided this was an emergency. No longer could she sit in the dark with only vermin for company, and unable to see if they were coming for her.

Frantically the little girl peered into the gloom, thinking her way around the room until she remembered where she had put the candles for safety. With shaking hands she frantically struck the flints until the dry grass ignited. Having lit the first candle she laid hands upon, she stamped upon the burning grass.

Malevolent, glittering black diamonds glared at her from a multitude of furry faces in the corner. Whiskers twitched and white needles of teeth showed aggressively.

Isabella backed into the farthest corner from them.

Suddenly daring, sensing her fear, one or two of the braver creatures edged towards her, taking just one tentative step at a time, until they were close to her feet, glaring sneeringly up at her. With a sudden squeal of terror, Isabella kicked out, catching the largest animal straight under his chin, hurling him across the room to crash against the far wall.

There came a sudden flurry of activity from all around, and suddenly Isabella was alone in the room. All the tiny glittering candle reflections had turned tail and fled through a network of holes in the sod wall. The rat she had kicked, king of the pack, lay dead where he had fallen, his neck broken.

Wrapping the candle with her hand, to protect it from draughts, Isabella returned, weeping, trembling uncontrollably to the mattress.

*   *   *

On leaving their refuge, Daniel walked down the alley away from the harbour, turning left towards the west. The moon was at its fullest, shining in all its splendour, but the boy found the back end of the town, to his relief, to be deserted.

Passing behind Saint Matthew's Church, he headed out past Muckle's Gate towards the west, knowing, from past experience, of a copse of small trees near the Peel Road. Though his bare feet still pained him, he fancied the wind had swung round to the west and the cold was not so intense.

Only a fifteen-minute walk away Daniel saw, across a field, the gaunt, black shadows of the small gnarled beech trees. They stood, with their leaves gone and branches naked, like the skeletons of long-dead warriors reaching out to the night sky.

The field between the boy and the trees was lit by the wan, silvery light of the moon, whose mottled face hung, large and open-mouthed in a sky of swirling cloud. Looking up, Daniel could see it making a halo around a bank of thick black clouds which were building in the west. *Another storm is near,* he thought. *Better collect this wood and get home before the weather breaks.* Daniel strode swiftly across the field.

The trees were brittle with the cold, their branches easily snapped. In a very short time, he had a good-sized bundle of wood. Certainly, there was plenty to start a fire and keep the peat burning well for a couple of nights. Relieved to be finished, he started to bundle them together

Suddenly there was a demented howling close by. Daniel looked around, terrified. A cloud had moved across the moon, turning the world completely black. The boy backed away from the direction of the sound, finding his way blocked, eventually by an outcrop of rock.

The cry came again, a sound like the wailing of the damned. Daniel looked around desperately for a way of escape but could see none. Behind him the newly fallen snow clung to the rocks with an almost sentient tenacity, the only breaks being small rivulets of frozen water. Impossible to climb.

The sound was repeated. No closer than before, but this time, more like the cry of some animal crazed by pain.

Daniel went towards the cry, listening intently, moving stealthily, his pulse quickening with every step. The creature, whatever it was, was whimpering miserably now. The boy slowed his pace as he neared, fearful it might be a buggane trying to trap him. Not that he'd ever seen one, but he knew they were mischievous, evil fairies who were not above any trickery to get their way.

The sound was very close now and Daniel stopped, undecided. For an instant, the cloud cleared from the moon and in the sudden glimmer of light, he saw a dog on the ground, courageously gnawing at a leg which was caught in a viciously toothed rabbit trap. Hurrying forward, he stood looking down at the poor creature.

'What am I to do with you?' he asked aloud. The dog looked up, pleading.

'You'd gi' us a few good meals.'

The animal had ceased his whimpering and now lay looking up at the boy in silent, expectant, entreaty. Daniel felt around under the snow until his numb fingers found a large rock. 'I'm sorry about this, dog,' he said feelingly, raising the boulder above his head. Just as he was about to bring it crashing down on the animal's head, the moon cleared momentarily again and he found himself looking into two large, trusting brown eyes.

'Oh, all right then,' he said, sighing heavily. Tossing the rock away he took a stout stick from his bundle and forced it between the teeth of the trap, prising them open.

As soon as the pressure was released, the dog dragged himself free, leapt to his feet and disappeared into the woods, without a backward glance, on his three undamaged legs. A sad trail of blood followed him to mar the pristine snow.

Cursing himself for a sentimental fool, Daniel moved to collect his scattered sticks. There was no sound in the deserted woodland, but the mournful crying of the freezing wind.

As he started back to Douglas, Daniel felt the first few spots of icy-cold sleet. Soon it was slapping and buffeting, driving into him, soaking through his clothes with sudden fierce gusts.

Drenched, chin down he battled on, clinging grimly to his precious bundle.

Lightning flickered along the surrounding hilltops, cosmic flames, bursting like cannon-fire inside the clouds, emptying sleet and hail and hate down on the hapless boy. Guttering down the track it washed coldly around his feet. He stumbled on, determinedly, and the storm quickly blew itself out.

In front of him, to the east, banks of dark clouds, gravid with moisture and lightning scudded against the sky. Overhead, roiled remnants of thunderheads, the last flutterings of torn banners. To the west the sky was clear, the moon shining a frigid blue.

The larger branches he was dragging behind him made the trail home difficult. Catching on tufts of long grass and tangled undergrowth by the roadside, they held him back, making his arms ache long before he reached Douglas. The rain dripping from his hair and scant clothes weighed him down, made worse by rivulets running in the ruts of the road.

Isabella was still hunched on the mattress, her legs pulled up, arms wrapped tightly around them. Her wide, frightened eyes constantly roved for signs of life around the floor. The dead rat still lay where he had fallen. For a while his body had twitched, legs kicking spasmodically, while his nerves accepted death, then he had gone still.

Hearing the board being pulled away from the window, she looked towards it with a mixture of relief and fear. Her hand moved to snuff the candle, but then she heard Daniel's whisper. 'Isabella. Come here an' help me.'

Hurrying across the room, she pushed at the board until finally, it fell away. Daniel pushed the end of a tree branch through the window and between them they managed, after a struggle, to get all the wood into their cold dirty room.

'It rained an' the wood's wet, but I'll get it lit.' Daniel's teeth were chattering.

'I lit a candle 'cos it was awful dark an' there was rats runnin' over me. I was scared!' Isabella finished apologetically.

Daniel looked at the stub of candle on the floor, almost burned completely away and guttering now.

'We can use it to light the fire — if it lasts long enough.'

Daniel took the candle, moving it carefully to protect the struggling flame and placed it in the centre of the room. Breaking the tiniest twigs from the branches, he laid them gently over the candle flame. It guttered and choked then recovered and burned up miserably around the wood.

The flame, tiny at first, sizzled pale yellow and smoked profusely on the damp twigs. The black smoke wafted on the breeze from the window and the children, choking and coughing, were forced to turn their heads away. The orange light leapt and quivered, until it took hold, at last, on the slender branches.

With a sigh of relief, Daniel rose to pull the window board back into place, watching as the smoke then rose vertically to exit through the hole in the centre of the roof. Cheerfully he broke a few of the larger branches and piled them onto the fire. When these were well caught he placed a few sods of dry peat over them. Removing his wet clothes, he hung them close to the blaze, over the back of the broken chair, to dry. Wrapped in a blanket, he huddled as close to the fire as he comfortably could.

'I killed a rat!' Isabella shuddered at the memory.

Daniel's face lit up. 'Where is it?'

'Over there,' she nodded towards the corner. 'Where it died. I was scared to touch it to throw it out.'

Daniel smiled delightedly. 'Good. We can eat it.'

'The rat?!' Isabella's eyes widened in horror.

Daniel nodded enthusiastically. 'Aye. Now we have a fire we can cook it. They taste quite good,' he assured her, as she pulled a face.

Daniel found the broken, rusty knife and gutted the rat, cutting off its head, feet and tail. Then he pushed the body into the fire on a twig.

Isabella sat back, not wanting to watch, but finding her eyes drawn. Once it started to cook the smell was inviting and she moved closer to the fire.

When Daniel considered it well enough done, he removed it from the fire, peeled off the skin and handed half the animal to Isabella. She accepted it doubtfully, but when Daniel took a bite of his, she put it to her mouth, her stomach churning and nibbled tentatively. Finding it quite pleasant, she ate ravenously, feeling, afterward, better fed than she had for many a long day.

Chapter 7

Isabella was the first to waken, while Daniel slept on, exhausted by his adventures.

Little black eyes peered at her from behind twitching whiskers, but somehow they weren't so frightening when Daniel was there. When she moved to rise there was a sudden flurry of activity and in an instant, the room had emptied.

The fire was still glowing slightly, so Isabella stacked a few more twigs on it. What fuel they had wouldn't last long, but it was nice to be warm. She hunched close to it, starting slightly as the centre collapsed, sending out a sudden shower of sparks; then it settled again to a comfortable flicker.

The inedible parts of the rat lay on the earth floor where Daniel had thrown them. Stomach heaving, Isabella gingerly picked them up. Pulling the window board away, she peeped out carefully, then threw the rubbish into the street. Before it had landed the air was filled with noisy, angry seagulls, squabbling and fighting for the choicest pickings. With a grimace, she wiped her fingers on her dress and fixed the board back into place.

Daniel's eyes were open and he lay thoughtfully watching the smoke rising, swirling its way, like a gentle whirlwind, to the roof and out through the hole.

'We must let the fire die during the day an' only have it in the evenin', else we'll run out o' fuel in no time. We must try to make it last for several days.'

Isabella nodded, sighing. 'Your clothes are dry now.' She threw them to him and he discreetly slipped them on.

"Tis three days now since I left Castle Rushen,' the girl said thoughtfully. 'But it seems an awful lot longer. While you were in there did you ever see the ghos'?'

'What ghos'?'

'The one at the Castle.'

'Oh! Her! I heard some o' the guards talkin' about her once, but I never saw her. Did you?'

'No. But I heard her once. An' Jane saw her — an' some o' the other women did, too. They call her the white ghos''

'Do you know who she is — was?'

'Aye. There was a woman executed in the Castle once — a long time ago, for murderin' her baby, an' they say the ghos' is her. She jus' walks through walls, wherever she wants to go. She's even been seen outside the main gate. No one has ever dared speak to her though, an' if anybody dares go near she jus' disappears or melts through the wall.'

'I saw them rollin' a witch once; down Slieu Whallian.'

'What for?'

'Cos she was a witch, I s'pose. Least they thought she was. Only it turned out they was wrong!'

'What did they do to her?'

'Rolled her down the hill — right from top to bottom in a barrel wi' spikes on the inside.'

Isabella flinched, her fingers fluttering nervously to her mouth. 'Then what?'

'I could hear her screamin' quite a bit o' the way down, then she was quiet. When the barrel stopped rollin' — right down the bottom — they opened it up to take her out an' she was dead. All spiked an' cut to pieces. So then they knew she wasna' a witch after all.'

'How'd they know?'

"Cos if she was a witch she wouldn't ha' died in the barrel an' they would've had to kill her some other way. They used to burn witches at the stake. There were two — a woman an' her son — roasted in Castletown square, jus' outside o' the castle, las' century.'

Isabella shuddered. 'What'd they do wi' her then? The one they rolled?'

Daniel shrugged. 'Dunno. S'pose seein' she wasn't a witch they would've let her have a proper burial.'

Noticing Isabella was trembling, Daniel realised he had gone too far. Taking her hand, he said quietly, 'I didn' really see it. I was only jokin'. They used to do that to witches, but they haven' bin allowed for hundreds o' years.'

While Daniel battled to supply food and fuel, the weeks rolled past with glum, cold monotony. Occasionally he managed to beg a piece of coarse, damaged fish from one of the boats. He found that if he made enough of a nuisance of himself very often they would throw a piece Of cod, on the condition that he then left them alone.

An Englishman, one day, accompanied by a well-dressed lady, put a penny in his outstretched hand. Full of excitement, he bought two half penny rolls, still warm from the oven and rushed back to Isabella with the feast. Another time, seeing the same gentleman, alone, he held out his hand, looking as pathetic as he knew how, and was rewarded by a swift, sharp kick.

Every day he managed to find some food; mostly stolen at great risk.

During the first few days Isabella refused to move outside the house for any reason, fearing her mother would return while she was absent. Eventually she felt too caged and from then on she was the one to go up Big Well Hill for the water every day.

On occasions she went with Daniel to the woods and together they managed to keep the fire burning in the evenings. Though they tried to sneak in and out of the hovel without being seen, Daniel noticed, several times, the grubby curtains move in the neighbouring houses.

A sudden loud hammering on the door early one morning, brought the children leaping from their mattress in terror.

'Who is it?' Isabella asked huskily, her eyes wide and dark in the dim light.

Daniel shrugged. 'Dunno'. But if we keep quiet maybe they'll go away.'

'Come on out. I know you're in there. If you've not opened the door by the count o' ten I'll come in an' get you an' you'll be the sorrier.'

'It must be the landlord! What shall we do?'

'Stay quiet an' maybe he'll think we're not here.'

They pressed back into the darkest corner, clinging tremblingly together, while the loud voice outside the door counted upwards.

'Nine — ten! Right — that's it!'

There came a jangling of keys, followed by scraping sounds as one key after another was fitted in the lock. Finally, there was the sound of one grating as it reluctantly turned and the door flew open with a loud squeal, banging hard against the wall.

A large man stood in the doorway, his huge belly hanging over the front of his trousers. The bottom two buttons of his shirt had ceased trying to hold together and had ripped off. A piece of stout string substituted as a belt, for the waistband of his trousers no longer met.

He peered into the black interior, his eyes screwed up while they struggled to adjust. But at last, they did and he spotted Daniel and Isabella cowering in the corner.

'Come out here you two dirty urchins!' the man bellowed.

The children timorously approached the door, Daniel trying to keep himself between Isabella and the purple-faced demon.

'What the hell're you two little buggers doin' in my house?'

'It's my Mammy's house,' Isabella corrected, a trembling hand fluttering to her lips.

'Your Mammy's? Are you that slut's daughter? 'Tis my house, missy, an your Mammy went missin' from here owin' me near a month o' rent. What's you doin' here?'

'Waitin' for my Mammy'.

'Well she ain't here. Won't be comin' neither. She's long gone. An' you better be too. An' him!' he nodded curtly towards Daniel.

'Can't we jus' stay for a while? I know my Mammy will come back for me. An' she'll look here. I know she will.'

'You got any money for rent?'

Wordlessly Isabella shook her head. She felt her lips tremble and a tear stung her eye.

'Then you gotta leave. I can't afford to let brats stay in my house an' not pay no rent'

'You're not gettin' no rent wi' it locked up an' empty!' Daniel pointed out defiantly.

'Why you cheeky young beggar! You get out o' here this instant, 'fore I thrash the life out o' you!' The landlord's voice had risen in volume and now his entire large frame shook as if a violent storm raged within him. His face had grown darker than ever and frothy spittle flew from the glistening surface of his wet lips as he shouted. Grabbing Daniel's shoulder with one hand, he reached around, clutching a handful of Isabella's bodice. With a quick jerk, he swung them both round, throwing them down in the alley.

Daniel leapt quickly to his feet while Isabella, winded, sprawled full length in the slush.

'Now you two devils get out o' my sight 'fore I gi' you a good beatin'.' The voice was a shriek now, echoing off the walls of the narrow lane.

'Can we take our blankets, then?' Daniel asked, his mind working quickly on the essentials.

'Bring 'em out and let's ha' a look at them then.'

Daniel moved towards the door, noticing the alley was becoming quite crowded. It always amazed him how people appeared, as if by magic, whenever there was a bit of a commotion.

Stepping quickly into the gloom of the building, he collected the blankets and, as an afterthought, Isabella's shoes. At the door, the man snatched them from his hands. A quick look told him the tattered rags would be of no value to him and he thrust them, roughly back into the boy's hands.

'Take them an' be gone.'

'If you let us stay I could work for you to pay the rent.' Daniel had one last try.

'You? Work?' The landlord roared with angry laughter, making Isabella cringe.

Daniel held his head high, looking the man boldly in the eye.

'You hardly have the strength to stand. Work, indeed! I wouldn't dare turn my back on you for fear o' what you'd steal. Now get to hell the pair o' you.'

Daniel hesitated momentarily, then with a sigh, started towards Isabella. 'We'd best go.'

'Aye, you had! An' don't think you can come sneakin' back when I'm gone. If I see you aroun' here again I'll ha' the lock men take you off.' The man leaned menacingly over Daniel, his huge face quivering.

Grasping Isabella's elbow, Daniel steered her away and felt a lump swell and harden in his chest. A stillness eddied in the alley, the crowd parting to let them pass, and one or two quiet sniggers echoed from the dirty grey stone walls.

They wandered miserably down towards the harbour, where Isabella sat on a step to don and button her shoes.

'Where will we go now?'

Daniel shrugged uncertainly. 'Dunno'. Could try the church

for sleepin'. We can't stay there durin' the day though or we'll get thrown out.'

Aimlessly they wandered around the town, mostly the harbour area, blankets wrapped around them, keeping their blood circulating, as best they could, by continual motion.

At nights they crept into St. Matthew's, huddling together in a corner with their ragged blankets. Then they rose as soon as the morning light slanted in the narrow windows, to sneak, like robbers, back out into the bustle of the fishing town.

Winter slowly turned to spring and as the hours of daylight lengthened the sun started to give a little heat. Walks out past the Muckle's Gate and out into the country became more pleasant as the trees started to live again with spring buds.

Food became harder to find once they had lost their home. Daniel was more scared now of being caught stealing when he had Isabella along with him.

'Soon we'll eat better, now the snow has gone and there'll be food to be found around the countryside. There'll be turnips, priddas an' grain to be found in the fields. Eggs in nests an' even the leaves on the hawthorn trees an' dandelions.' Daniel glanced at Isabella's thin face, drawn and haggard now with fatigue, tinged almost a sickly yellow with hunger.

'Is it safe to eat those?' She trusted him completely now, and would willingly eat anything he gave her.

'Aye. I've eaten them often. An' many more. When you ha' to care for yoursel' you soon learn what's safe.'

Several times Daniel had the sensation of being watched, the hair on the nape of his neck creeping upwards. Then he would look round, to catch the big man — the one whom he took to be a smuggler — eyeing him with a look, almost, of puzzlement.

Most folks paid little attention to the two ragged children, for the streets of Douglas were alive with just such as they. But the shopkeepers in the town, and the farmers' wives at the market always kept a wary eye on the ragamuffins.

Daniel wandered beside a group of ladies in the market, edging closer to the vegetables on display He felt safer stealing fruit and vegetables because the greengrocers spread their wares out along the quayside. So, too, did the butchers, but meat was of little use now that they could no longer cook it, for Isabella steadfastly refused to eat it raw. The farmers' wives and daughters sold their eggs, butter and cheeses inside the market building, but Daniel felt it would be harder to escape from there if he were to be spotted.

So he dogged the women, just awaiting his chance. At last he found his way, unobtrusively he thought, beside a large turnip. With a surreptitious glance around, he whipped the vegetable up and under the cover of his blanket. Letting out the breath he had long been holding, he turned away.

There was a sudden shout and looking up, startled, Daniel found himself face to face with a large, furious farmer who had appeared from behind a building. Ducking nimbly under the man's outstretched hands, he took to his heels, fleeing along the quay.

'Stop thief!' a loud voice bellowed behind him. 'Catch that boy — he's stole me turnip!'

A few people stopped, surprised, to make a half-hearted grab at him, but he dodged them and sped on. With the pursuing mob growing larger and quickly gaining on him, Daniel shot across the road and up a narrow side lane, weaving and evading while the pursuers got in each others' way. As he ran on, desperation sweeping him along, his lungs were on fire, his legs pumping on their own, without his bidding. Once he tripped, staggered and almost fell, the breath lost inside him, but then he recovered. At last, under cover of a fish cart which almost filled the whole width of the lane, he nipped around a corner, hiding in a shadowy doorway. The mob squeezed past the cart, to run straight on up the alley.

Daniel waited a decent while, until he was fairly sure the crowd had dispersed, then he carefully made his way back to the corner by the market where he had left Isabella.

The girl was looking around worriedly, but her face lit up when she set eyes on him.

'I saw them all chasin' you an' I was feared you'd got caught. I couldn' bear it if you got birched an' transported.'

Daniel shrugged, laughing. 'I'm not so easily caught. But we'd best move off from here lest someone recognises me. I still have the turnip. so we'll find somewhere safe to eat it.

They were making their way jubilantly along the side of St. Matthew's Church, when suddenly the farmer appeared from around the corner at the top of the road.

'Run!' Daniel grabbed Isabella's arm, whirling her around and dragging her with him as he raced back down the street. Hesitating only momentarily, he rushed straight across the quay. to where he could see the masts of a boat. With the girl in tow, about half a pace behind, he reached the edge of the wharf.

'Jump!' he yelled and with hardly a break in their pace, they leapt from the dock. landing on the deck of a fishing boat. 'Under there.' Daniel ordered. pushing Isabella towards a sail that was spread in the sun to dry. In an instant, they were both hidden. motionless under the expanse of canvas.

From above came the sound of running feet and loud, angry voices.

'Them little beggars aren't going to get away again. I'll search all night if I ha' to — but I'll bloody find them!' the farmer roared.

Suddenly Daniel felt the vibration of heavy footfalls on the deck, and a great weight was placed on his back. forcing him down into the wooden planks

A foot! He was certain it was! The object moved, releasing the pressure slightly. Yes. He was sure now. Someone stood on the deck beside his head, with one foot resting on his back. He tried to breathe shallowly but was certain the person could not help but feel the pounding of his heart.

'What's the trouble?' a booming voice asked from straight above his head. It was a voice that held a ring of familiarity.

'We're lookin' for two urchins. Filthy little creatures. A boy an' a girl as far as I could tell. You seen anythin' o' the likes?'

Daniel recognised the farmer's voice. Beside him, he could feel Isabella trembling and prayed the movement would not show through the canvas.

'Can't say as I has. What's they done?'

'Stole some o' me turnips. They come this way. If you see 'em, grab em an' hold 'em for me.'

'I surely will.'

Daniel heard the sound of shuffling feet and voices receding. The foot was removed from his back, but its owner stood his ground beside the sail.

With startling suddenness, the sail was pulled back and the children found themselves blinking in the unexpected sunshine.

'Right! Now I think you two'd better come below an' explain jus' what you're doin' on my boat.'

Daniel's heart sank when he recognised the gigantic smuggler he had crossed swords with on the evening he had returned to Douglas. The man kept a tight hold on both their arms until he had them both safely shut below decks, his back against the door.

'Right now. First of all you can tell me who you are, an' why you're always hangin' aroun' my boat. I seem to have seen you aroun' an awful lot in recent weeks.' He looked piercingly at Daniel.

'I'm Daniel an' she's Isabella.' Daniel was unsure of how wise it was to tell this ferocious looking stranger too much.

Isabella, terrified of the man, stood dumbfounded. No doubt, once he had their stories he would hand them over to the authorities

— and what then? She didn't want to be transported! And she didn't want Daniel to be birched.

'Are those the only names you have? Were you not given surnames?' The man was still looking strangely at Daniel.

Isabella stole a glance at Daniel and seeing him staring at the floor, his lips clamped stubbornly together, she adopted a similar pose.

'I see. Lost your tongues have you? How do you expect me to help you if you won't talk to me?'

Daniel looked up, meeting the man's eyes squarely. 'We ask no help, save that you let us go free an' don't hand us to the lock men.'

'I? Give you to them? I have no sympathy for the lawmakers. I can see you are both starved an' ha' no warm clothing. I ha' watched you beg from the fishin' boats an' even pinch scraps from the seagulls. You have to steal to live so will surely end up in gaol. An' that's no pleasant place to be. My only wish is to help you. If I'd meant the authorities to have you I would have given you to that bad-tempered farmer.'

Daniel studied his feet, shuffling uncomfortably. The man had a ring of honesty about him and in spite of his scowling face and huge bulk, the boy could sense a warmness in him. But still, he stood, undecided.

'Well, what's it to be? Either you can talk to me and I can help you; put food in your bellies and warm clothes on your backs. Or I can turn you loose to starve and freeze and end up, one day, in gaol!' The smuggler looked searchingly at Daniel, sensing he was the spokesman.

Daniel sighed. 'What is it you want to know?'

'Your names, first of all. Then tell me where you came from and how you come to be in your present troubles.'

'My name's Quilliam an' Isabella's is Cain. We was in goal together at Castletown an' they put us out in only the clothes we stood up in.' Daniel related the whole miserable tale of their misadventures, watching the man's face go through a whole spectrum of expressions.

'So you're not brother an' sister then?' he asked finally, when the boy had finished his story.

Daniel shook his head. 'No we only met when they put us out o' the Castle. An' we thought it would be easier if we stayed together.'

'It shouldn't be permitted to happen. Childer shouldn' ha' to live like animals. I'm Joseph Cubbin. I'll look after you better 'n the authorities have. I can't gi' you anythin' fancy, mind, but I will gi' you warm clothes, decent food an' a roof over your heads. What's ye say?'

Daniel looked at Isabella, raising his eyebrows in question.

Isabella studied the smuggler thoughtfully. He seemed a genuine enough fellow.

'What would you want of us in return?' she asked timorously.

The man laughed. 'Nothin' too terrible. You would help my wife wi' the childer, an' the boy would work for me on the boat.'

'An' go out smugglin' wi' you?' Daniel asked eagerly.

'Who says I smuggle?' Joseph asked indignantly. He furrowed his eyebrows in a mock ferocious scowl.

Daniel reddened, shuffling uncomfortably.

'You're too young to sail wi' me yet, but no doubt you've the strength to scrub a deck or furl a sail. Now you'd better stay here till nightfall. I have work to do till then.' So saying, he ducked out of the cabin and the children heard the scrape of a key turning in the lock.

Chapter 8

At the rasp of the key, Daniel started to the door turning the knob frantically. It was locked solid. He tugged at it desperately, but to no avail.

From outside he heard a low chuckle.

'Make yourselves comfortable. If you're cold there's blankets on the bunk an' jerseys in the closet. An stay quiet. If my crew come aboard I don't want them to know you're here. I'll come for you after dark.'

'Why have you locked us in?' Daniel called nervously through the heavy door, but he got no reply.

'Why has he locked us in?' he repeated the question to Isabella, who shrugged fearfully.

They heard Joseph's heavy footsteps climbing the companionway and moving around the deck, working constantly.

Daniel looked around frantically. 'Maybe he's goin' to sell us as slaves! I don't like bein' locked in!' His eyes roved to the porthole. 'I wonder if we can get out there.' Unscrewing it, he struggled to lever it open.

Watching, Isabella was not at all sure she wanted to escape. She rather liked the idea of being part of a family. And she had trusted Joseph; was sure he would not sell them.

''Tis too small for me to fit through, but you might.'

Isabella shook her head. 'I don' wanna'. I like Joseph. I'm sure he means us no harm.'

Daniel stuck his head out the porthole. Below were many fathoms of cold, murky green water with, floating beneath its surface, strings of torn seaweed.

The harbour waters were choppy with a thousand cat's paws. Seagulls wheeled, bickering, ever watchful skimming the surface or, fat chested, riding the waves. Looking up, Daniel found himself gazing straight into Joseph's large amused face.

'There's no escape for you that way either, lad!' The man disappeared from view, laughing loudly and Daniel drew his head back into the cabin.

Through the porthole, the children, wrapped warmly in blankets to defeat the chill of coming evening, watched the end of the day draw in, the red globe of sun lowering like a swollen ember in a banked fire. The sky looked like cold ash, tinged with magenta and hot cinders around the sun's arc. And then it was gone, plunged suddenly into the blackness of the sea. Night stole over them so swiftly it seemed the sun had never been there at all. The smell of the sea mist wafted in from the darkness as the children, cosy now, started to doze. There was silence for a while, save for the moaning and occasional creak as the vessel wallowed on the swell.

Hearing a footfall on the companionway, Daniel was instantly wide awake and on his feet, akimbo, facing the door. When the door swung open he was on his toes, looking ready to attack, only his lack of stature betraying him

Isabella huddled wide-eyed behind him on the bunk, pressed as hard against the bulkhead as she could manage.

Joseph looked from one to the other, roaring with mirth. 'Well there's a fine show of trust, I must say. If I bring you two out of here to take you to my cottage can I count on you not to run from me?'

Isabella and Daniel exchanged a quick glance, the girl nodding almost imperceptibly. Now she was warm at last, and with a prospect of staying so, she was not prepared to throw the chance away lightly.

Daniel relaxed. 'You can trust us, sir.'

'Good!' Joseph turned, indicating with a jerk of his head that he wished them to follow.

As he stepped onto the deck he stopped, holding up a huge hand, and the children obediently waited on the companionway They could see Joseph's shadowy form as he peered out along the quay to ensure they were not being watched. Then the hand was raised, beckoning them to him. Crouched low, they darted across the deck to his side.

Jumping expertly over the rail, Joseph landed on a ledge partway up the harbour wall, 'Come. Quickly.'

Without delay he reached up, lifting first Isabella, then Daniel as though they were no weight at all, to place them on the ground beside him.

Daniel gazed around curiously. The ledge, he knew had been placed there so that the smaller vessels could more easily unload their cargoes, but the curious thing was that there was an opening in the harbour wall, and he knew them to be nowhere near the tunnel from the Market Hotel.

'Is this yet another smugglers tunnel?' he asked, awed.

'Smugglers again is it?' Joseph asked quietly. 'You seem to be obsessed wi' the breed!'

'Well you are one, aren't you? Else why were you loadin' your cargo under cover of darkness. An' why would you ha' bin so worried I might be a spy from the Customs?'

'You're too smart for your own good, lad. An' you're goin' to have to learn to keep your mouth shut.'

He led them in silence along a dark, damp passage, the walls alive with running water and cold slime, to a cellar, dimly lit with flickering oil lamps.

Isabella gazed about her, wide-eyed and open-mouthed. It was like Aladdin's cave. The whole cellar was piled high with barrels and boxes. Little feet scuffled and scratched around the floor, reminding her of her mother's house. Tiny round black eyes peeped at her from corners, glittering in the lamplight. Shuddering involuntarily, she realised Joseph was waiting at the far end of the storehouse, beckoning to her.

Obediently she hurried over to him. 'Whatever is in all those boxes an' kegs?'

Joseph surveyed her quizzically for a moment, then his gaze scanned the cellar with pride. 'In some o' the barrels there's brandy from France, an' others hold rum from the New World Colonies. Then there's tea, silks an' many other exotic things from Europe. Sugar an' spices come from India.'

'Is that what comes in the big ships we see often in the harbour?'

'Aye. We store it here for as short a time as possible, then load up an take it over to England or Scotland. We go most often to a point near Whitehaven, for that's where our merchant has most o' his contacts.'

'What's tea?' Isabella had fallen a little behind in the conversation.

'"Tis a drink, lass. Some sort o leaf. You stick it in a pot an' pour boilin' water over it, then put in a cup wi' some sugar an' milk — if you've a taste for it.'

'I don't think I've ever tasted it.'

'Nor are you likely to unless you ever marry a rich man, for only those with a fortune can afford to buy it. The cheapest you can buy is three shillin' a pound and it can go to as much as seven shillin' an' sixpence.'

Isabella felt shattered. Seven shillin' an' sixpence! She could live well for a year on that.

'It doesn't sound like a very nice drink anyway. I won't ever waste money on that!'

Joseph laughed, took a lamp from the wall and led them up a narrow, winding stairway, which brought them up through a trap door into a large, shabby, dusty room, piled as high as the cellar with boxes and large packages.

'This is where we keep the silks, sugars an' the likes. Anythin' the damp in the cellar will spoil. An' there's not so many rats up here either. '

They went up yet another flight of stairs, wider this time, then along a passage and out of a narrow doorway onto the street.

To the right and below them a little, Daniel could see St. Matthews Church. It's imposing bulk stood out blackly against the night sky, a cool, silvery moon hovering high above its spire.

The air was fresh and bright, scintillating with a chill brittleness which was not unpleasant, all the more enjoyable after the oppressiveness of the dark cellars. Below, in the harbour, the moon reflected from the water, a dark luminescent blue. Daniel gazed in awe. Nothing would ever exceed the grandeur and beauty of the sea in his eyes. Sometimes he felt he must have it in his blood. Something he had inherited from his father, perhaps. And his fascination with smuggling!

'C'mon lad. You're not goin' to stand there daydreamin' all day are you?'

Daniel turned. Joseph and Isabella were standing uphill from him, waiting, and without a word, he moved toward them.

Joseph led them up the steep hill then they ascended several flights of roughly hewn steps to a part of the town Daniel had not visited before, though he had heard it referred to as both Little Ireland and Little Hell. Its proper name, he knew, was Thornhill, and on arriving there he found it to be a congeries of little, shabby dwellings.

Joseph stopped beside the third cottage along. From the small, square window shone the dim, flickering light of a candle. Isabella heard the happy noises of children laughing, the gurgling, bubbling, infectious sound of very young children. A baby was whimpering and a woman crooning a lullaby, probably to soothe the infant.

Isabella hesitated, listening intently, enjoying the comfortable family sounds. Noises that made her think of home. Not home as she had ever known it. A proper home. A place where families were happy and comfortable together.

Joseph threw open the door, ducking his head to fit under the lintel.

Daniel and Isabella moved forward but lingered hesitantly in the doorway.

Peeping around the man's bulk, Isabella saw a young woman sitting huddled in a chair, a young baby clutched in her arms. Beyond her, in the corner, two little boys wrestled, giggling. They stopped when the door opened, to lie as though turned to stone, the grins frozen on their faces.

The woman looked startled at first, then relief lit her face.

'Joseph,' she sighed, 'Thank goodness you're home. 1 was startin' to worry.'

'You should know better by now. I'll not come to any harm. I've brought some young friends home wi' me.'

Joseph stepped aside indicating, with a sweep of his arm, the children standing apprehensively behind him.

'Catharine, meet Isabella an' Daniel.'

The woman stood up and smilingly beckoning the children to come forward.

Timorously they edged towards her.

Her eyes rested first on Isabella, then widened as they moved to Daniel. After a shocked, sudden intake of breath, she hoarsely whispered, 'Alexander!' so quietly they could hardly hear her.

When the realisation came that she was wrong, she shook her head sadly. To cover her confusion she said, 'My goodness.' What a state they're in!'

Her startled eyes rapidly took in the conglomeration of filth and the greasy hair, matted from months without washing.

'I thought they could stay wi' us for a while,' Joseph suggested tentatively.

'Who are they? Where have they come from?' Catharine looked as though she felt her eyes were betraying her.

'I found them on the boat — hidin' from a mob led by a farmer they'd stolen some vegetable from.' Joseph reached out quickly, grabbing the blanket from Daniel's grasp.

The turnip fell. It rolled across the floor.

Daniel stood, face reddening, head hanging, watching its uneven course on the dirt floor.

'I know you!' Catharine was studying the boy intently. 'You're the lad I saw in the baker's shop a while back. You stole a loaf o' bread right from under my nose!'

Daniel nodded miserably, recognising her as the lady who had turned a blind eye to his mischief.

'So you see,' Joseph continued, 'Already they have started to earn their keep. There can be turnip for supper.'

Briefly, he related the children's story and Isabella saw an unshed tear brighten Catharine's eyes.

'Oh you poor little creatures,' she said when the tale had been told. 'Of course you must stay here. We don't have much, but what we do have can be shared wi' another two. An' you can be a help to us. First, you must eat. You poor children look starved. How long is it since you had a proper meal?'

Daniel gave it some thought. 'Probably not since the rat. but that was jus' after we got out o' gaol.'

Catharine frowned. 'Rat?'

'We had to eat a rat, 'cos there was nothin' else.' Isabella enlightened.

With a shudder, Catharine said, 'Well there'll be no more rats for you from now on. There's a good, nourishing Manx broth for you tonight. Now sit you down an' let's eat.'

The baby had fallen asleep, so after placing it snugly in a basketweave crib, Catharine called the two little boys to the table from the corner where they'd huddled as they shyly watched the strangers.

Pushing together, each trying to hide behind the other, they edged to the table, finally making a sprint to hide behind their mother's skirts.

Laughingly, she pulled them forward. 'Stop bein' silly. Now these are Isabella an' Daniel. They're goin' to be livin' wi' us for a while. These here's James an' Thomas.' She nodded first towards the bigger boy, then the smaller.

'Hello.' Isabella smiled at James, who promptly hid his face in his mother's pinafore. Pulling him free, Catharine pushed him towards the table.

'They're not always this quiet,' Joseph said, laughing. 'Most o' the time you' re wishin' you could shut them up.'

They all sat on rickety chairs, round a scrubbed, rough, well-worn table. Joseph's two sons were on either side of Isabella and Daniel, perched precariously on the farthest away edges of their seats.

Isabella, at last, had time to study the room, taking in all she saw, its impression filling her with warmth. This was how she had always imagined a home would be — and a family. At last she had a family! Oh, how she hoped it would last! It must last. She would work hard at becoming a real member of the family. Already she felt a stirring of love for these warm, caring people. It was a lovely cottage. Cosy with its thick stone walls and small window to keep out most of the draughts. In one wall a huge fireplace was cut, with logs sending black smoke and huge flames billowing up the chimney. A huge swivel was fixed to the wall beside it, from which hung a large black pot above the hungry, licking flames. Steam emerged in merry bursts from the pot.

Several fowl scratched around the dirt floor, crooning and squawking as they searched fruitlessly for crumbs. In a gloomy corner behind the door, a black goat was tethered, looking heavy with milk. Isabella remembered her mother, during one of her more 'thinking' moments, telling her she should always really see the things around her. She had said she should look at every little thing as if she was seeing it for the first or the last time. This was how she looked now; emblazoning it on her memory. To her dying day, she would never forget this scene.

With a sweep of his arm, Joseph cleared a cockerel, screeching indignantly, from the table. With a taper lit from the fire, he then ignited a candle, rammed solidly into a dusty bottle, in the centre of the table. Swinging the pot away from over the fire, he lifted it from the hook, banging it down heftily on the table. When this was done, he filled a large kettle with water from a bucket, and hung it over the flames, in place of the pot.

Catharine laid out six good-sized bowls, into which she deftly ladled a thick broth.

'I hope you find it to your liking,' she said, handing it around.

It was the nicest food Isabella had ever tasted. She ate hungrily, though trying not to appear too greedy However Daniel, she noticed wolfed his down voraciously. When the broth was gone he wiped the bowl out thoroughly with a slice of crusty, home-made bread.

Joseph watched, smiling with satisfaction and without even asking, he rose to refill their bowls.

As the meal progressed James and Thomas grew to realise that the two strange, dirty, smelly creatures were quite harmless and they moved back to the centre of their chairs.

After the meal Catharine swung the kettle, on its swivel, from over the fire. Lifting it carefully from its chain with a protective piece of flannel, often folded, she filled a pail with hot water, which she placed on a shelf under the window. Gathering up the bowls and spoons, she carried them over, washing them out quickly in the pail. Drying them, she stacked them neatly away in the cupboard. Refilling the kettle, she hung it on the swivel, swinging it back over the fiery embers.

Isabella watched, enraptured

When Catharine was finished she looked up towards the roof. 'I'm afraid the only place I can offer you to sleep is the loft. But at least 'tis dry an' the cottage is warm.'

Isabella glanced at the fireplace, seeing the flames crackling and sparking and wondered from where they had fetched their wood. Her gaze travelled on upwards, toward the loft noticing, for the first time, the dark bulk of fishing nets hung in the rafters.

'So you fish as well?' she asked, surprised.

'As well as what?' Joseph asked mischievously.

'Smuggle?' Isabella blushed, flustered.

Joseph roared with laughter, startling his two little sons. She's getting' as bad as you now, boy!' he winked at Daniel, who joined his merriment.

'Stop teasin' the child,' Catharine chastised.

When the kettle had heated again Catharine fetched a tin bath from where it hung on a peg on the wall. With help from Joseph, she emptied the kettle into it, adding enough cold water from a bucket to make the temperature just right.

First Thomas was placed into the water and washed well, then James followed, Catharine seemingly unconcerned that the younger child had already piddled in it. Then, glowing pinkly with clean good health the boys were put into their nightgowns and tucked well up on mattresses in the far corner from the goat.

"Tis too late to heat enough for you two tonight, but in the mornin' fust thing, I'll ha' you two clean!' Catharine promised.

Daniel looked pleadingly at Joseph, who merely smiled, shrugged and raised his hands, palm up, in a gesture of helplessness.

Chapter 9

Isabella and Daniel found the rough, straw-filled mattresses heaven to lie on after the hard dirt floor they were accustomed to. The warmth in the loft, rising from the fire which was glowing heartily was like finding themselves in heaven.

In the morning Catharine, with grim determination, insisted on them going to the well for bucket after bucket of water, which she hung over the fire to warm, then poured into the little tin bath.

'Right who's going to be first?' she asked briskly when she had it ready.

Daniel backed off. 'Not me! I'm not havin' a bath!'

'Oh yes you are!' Catharine insisted firmly.

'No!' He shook his head, teeth clamped firmly, lips drawn in defiantly.

'Do you think you're goin' to like livin' here, Daniel?'

'Aye.'

'An' are you wantin' to stay?'

'Aye.'

'Then you must have a bath. An' wash all the muck out o' your hair!'

'Oh!' Daniel scowled, tutting impatiently. He looked hopefully at Joseph but he, good friend that he was, merely laughed and turned away.

'Well she can go first,' Daniel said finally, nodding towards Isabella

'I hope I'm not going to have all that silly nonsense from you too.' Hands on hips, Catharine glared at the girl.

Isabella shook her head. She had seen how much the little boys had enjoyed it the night before and a warm bath seemed like a nice idea to her. Without a moment's hesitation, she stripped off her clothes, dropping them in a heap on the floor and stepped into the little bath She sat with her legs folded, pressed up against her chest, enjoying the flood of comfortable warmth through her body.

'Oh — my! Look how skinny you are! There's no flesh on your little body at all!' Catharine was wide-eyed with horror. 'We must feed you well. I suppose you're no better.' She looked at Daniel, who was sulking in a corner.

He studiously ignored her.

It took a while, but at last, Isabella was scrubbed clean. There had been many pained squeals of protest along the way, but she finally emerged, glowing pinkly, her long curls glowing like burnished gold in the sunlight which streamed through the window.

'Well now, just look at our girl, Joseph. Isn't she pretty as a picture? Don't it make you proud to have her as a daughter?'

Joseph studied the girl appreciatively. Indeed she had scrubbed up very nicely. Something would have to be done, though, to put some covering on her ribs.

'Jus' wrap a blanket around you for the moment. We'll have to find you somethin' to wear, 'cos you can't put back on the dirty rags you came in. Now for you, young man!' Catharine looked threateningly at Daniel.

Realising his fate was inevitable, he dropped his clothes on the floor, waiting until Catharine had added some more hot water to the bath before he stepped in, sitting to squeeze his long legs into it.

Isabella collapsed in a fit of laughter when he finally emerged, scrubbed and shining as cleanly as she.

'Look at you!' she giggled. 'Look how shiny your hair is. It's so black it looks almost blue! An' look at your face and arms too!'

'What's wrong wi' 'em?' Daniel asked grumpily, looking down at his arms.

'You're all covered wi' freckles! I never knew you had freckles!' She dissolved into another fit of near hysterics.

'Come on now, that's enough,' Catharine told her, struggling not to laugh herself as she saw Daniel's discomfort.

Joseph tried without much success to hide his amusement and his choked snigger earned him a withering look from his wife.

With both children clean, the next problem was what they might be dressed in. Catharine, absolutely horrified with the skimpy, cold rags they had been sent from prison wearing, determined she would dress them always as warmly as she felt the day required.

'We must see if any of Alexander's clothes fit,' she said finally, and a look of deep sadness suddenly shadowed her face. 'Lift the trunk down from the loft will you Joseph,' she requested quietly.

Joseph studied her uncertainly for a moment. 'Are you sure?' he asked quietly

Catharine nodded 'Aye,' she said, and It was almost a whisper. 'Alexander doesn't need them. They would be best used for the living. Bring them please.'

Joseph nodded and went swiftly up the ladder to the loft. He well knew what it would mean to Catharine to give Alexander's clothing away. Ever since the diphtheria had taken him, she had kept the trunk full of his belongings up there, untouched. It was as though she had never really accepted he had died. She seemed to be ever waiting for him come back, glancing at the door as if she expected him to walk through it at any moment.

Catharine had been like a mother to Alexander. Had brought

him up, more like a mother than a sister, after their parents had died. When he had been taken ill she had fought for him, sat with him for days on end sponging him, loving him, begging him to live.

Remembering, Joseph saw it again so clearly. Catharine on her knees, head bowed over hands so tightly clenched the knuckles gleamed like polished marble. With tears gushing she had prayed, pleading with God to let Alexander live. Once he had heard her offer herself instead of the boy. Then in the final throes of the disease, when Alexander's throat had been closing tight and he was drowning in the thick, yellow mucous, choking, fighting for every little bit of air he could gasp in, still she would not stop fighting. Joseph had come home one day and found her with her mouth pressed tight to Alexander's, breathing for him, trying to blow air into his lungs. Even after Joseph was sure the child's heart had stopped, she had gone on blowing for a long time. Then he had dragged her away, sobbing hysterically, from Alexander's young body.

At the burial she had been completely distraught, almost to the point of collapse. A part of her seemed to have gone to the grave with the boy, refusing to let go. Not accepting he was dead.

Since then she had steadfastly refused to have his clothes taken away or even touched, so sure was she that one day Alexander would have need of them.

It had been Joseph's prayer that when she had children of her own to care for, her irrational feelings about Alexander would fade. But, though she was a wonderful mother and loved her children completely. Alexander had seemed to occupy a separate place in her mind and heart and remained an obsession. In a moment of bitterness, once, she had confessed to feeling guilty, of feeling she had betrayed her parents' confidence in her by allowing Alexander to die. And so his belongings had remained, untouched, in the loft.

Now, suddenly, with the arrival of Daniel and Isabella, acceptance seemed to have come and she was ready to give his clothes to those little urchins. Perhaps, Joseph thought, it was Daniel's uncanny likeness to Alexander — in particular, the odd eyes — and he wondered if Catharine might regard him as a reincarnation.

Suddenly he realised that so great was her acceptance, she had referred to Isabella as his daughter. His heart was lifting, Joseph hefted the trunk down from the loft, cheerfully throwing open the lid. Catharine sifted through the clothing, pulling out the items she considered most suitable.

'I'm afraid you're goin' to have to wear boys things until I can make you some frocks. But anything's better than what you was wearin' when you came.'

Daniel was easily fitted out, the clothes being only a fraction too large and the trousers only needing to be turned up once. The boots slid about a little, but never having worn anything on his feet before, two pairs of socks and the novelty made up for this.

Isabella was a little more difficult. Try as she would, Catharine could not find anything near her size. In the end, she had to settle for the least boyish amongst them, with the sleeves and trouser bottoms folded up several rolls. There were no boots to fit, so Joseph gave Catharine money to buy a pair.

Both children were given a thick gansey, hand knitted from the greasy wool of the Manx Loughtan sheep — again Isabella's being many sizes too large.

Catharine laughed, 'Well you look even more of a waif now than you did before, but at least you're clean an' warm an' comfortable. I'll start this mornin' to make you some frocks an' jerseys o' your own. Fus' we must milk the goat, she's about fit to bust. Haven't you men got some work you can be doin'?'

Joseph took the hint. He had been studying Isabella with a look of fond amusement, but now he pushed his chair away from the table, unwinding his long legs as he heaved himself to his feet.

'C'mon lad. We'll leave the women to their chores. There's much to be done on the boat.'

'What if the farmer's there?'

Joseph shook his head. ''Tis unlikely he'll be aroun', for there's no market today. Anyway, now you're clean an' look like a real person he'd never recognise you.' Laughing, he nudged the boy towards the door.

'We'd best go an' let the women get on wi' whatever they need to do.'

Isabella had a moment of irrational panic as she watched the door close behind Daniel, but it was short-lived.

The baby started to cry. Just a whinge at first, quickly growing to a lusty bad-tempered scream.

'Would you bring Elizabeth to me, please, Isabella. I'll feed her first, then I shall show you how to milk Jemima.'

'Jemima?'

'The goat! She should have been milked long since, but we are all behind today wi' havin' to bath you two. Daniel didn't like it at all, did he?'

They both giggled at the memory of the boy's fear and indignation.

Isabella carefully picked Elizabeth up. At the first touch, when she felt her covers being removed, the baby stopped her squawking and she opened huge blue, tearless eyes to gaze at Isabella. The arms and legs which had been flailing like windmill blades in a gale, were suddenly still and flopped limply. When she felt herself being lifted, her face lit in a beautiful, toothless smile.

Isabella fell in love immediately. Never had she seen anything so magical or bewitching. Picking the tiny body up, she was made nervous by the lightness and fragility. It awed and thrilled her that Catharine should trust her with such a precious bundle.

'She's so tiny!' She whispered, sighing with relief as she placed the child carefully in her mother's arms.

Catharine looked fondly into the tiny face, framed by a wispy, soft fair down. 'If you think she's tiny now, you should ha' seen her four months ago, when she was born.'

Catharine unbuttoned her bodice, while the baby fretted impatiently. The little eyes shut tight, head swaying slowly from side to side, mouth wide open in eager search. The tiny starfish fingers clutched and released, clutched and released, growing more frantic with every moment. Then she felt the nipple against her cheek, swung her head rapidly and swallowed it to the back of her throat, sucking avidly. For a moment she spluttered and coughed, as the milk started to flow, and her blue eyes flew wide open.

Shocked, Isabella feared the babe was going to choke. But then she shut her eyes again and she continued to feed greedily with an expression of sheer bliss.

'Well my Bess, that's what you get for being such a greedy little pig!' Catharine said laughingly.

When the baby was put against her mother's shoulder, on occasions, Isabella was quite startled at the unladylike belch she gave.

Once Elizabeth was fed and her hand-made napkin changed she was put back down to sleep, Catharine eyed Isabella speculatively.

'Well, young lady, I suppose with the rough life you've lived you won't have been taught much in the art of housekeeping.'

Isabella shrugged. As far as she knew, she had been taught none. 'I dunno,' was all she could think of to say.

'Well the first thing we must see to is Jemima.'

Isabella had noticed the goat becoming more restless and for the last few minutes she had been bleating quite pathetically.

Catharine drew a low, three-legged stool near to the goat. 'Come child. Watch how tis' done.'

Isabella sat on the dirt floor, absently scratching the animal's neck while watching, fascinated.

'See — you must pull and squeeze at the same time. Can you see how I'm doin' it?'

Isabella nodded wordlessly, fascinated with the way the rapid stream of milk from the udder sang when it hit the sides of the pail.

'Do you want to try?'

'Yes please.' Isabella sat on the stool, grasped the goat's udder just, she thought, as Catharine had done. She pulled, squeezed, almost wrung it out, but managed no more than a few drops.

Jemima repeatedly looked around at her with an expression of pained puzzlement.

It took several demonstrations, with Catharine holding Isabella's hand in just the right way, but eventually, she got the knack of it quite well. It was much harder work than she had imagined though, and her hands quickly grew stiff.

Later in the morning, Catharine bound Elizabeth firmly against her chest with a large shawl, then with Isabella at her side, set off down into the town.

'First, we must find some cloth to make you warm petticoats an' fine cotton for a good one. Then you will need two frocks. Something pretty an' dainty, I think, for you are such a pretty, dainty child.'

They trod carefully down the rough, weather-worn steps towards the harbour, Catharine with her purse clutched firmly in her hand. She felt she would enjoy making nice clothes for this angelic looking child. The girl appealed to her. She deserved to have nice things and to be cared for. It would make her happy, she thought, to care for Isabella — to be a mother to her.

Strolling together through Douglas, they were given some wary looks by passers-by. Isabella was conscious that she looked rather odd, in her oversized hand-me-down boy's clothing, and she so obviously a girl with her long, russet curls. She could not remember ever having had her hair cut and it reached almost to her knees now. When she noticed people turn in the street to look after her, she was unaware that their expressions were of admiration at the beauty of her gleaming halo.

In the fabric shop, she followed Catharine in awed silence. Never had she seen so many different materials, except perhaps those of the clothing worn by the fine ladies from "across" — the wives of the merchants who employed the smugglers.

Catharine quickly bought enough lengths of flannelette to make two warm petticoats and some fine cotton cambric for a 'best' one to go over them. Then sufficient pretty lace to edge them all. After that she went right through the shop, holding bale after bale of cloth against Isabella.

'I can not afford too much, but I wish you to have two dresses, so we must choose carefully an' make sure to get colours that will suit you well.'

In the end she chose a pretty cerise, with a tiny daisy flower pattern, because she said it showed Isabella's hair up well, then she bought, also, a cornflower blue which matched her eyes exactly, making them look bluer than ever.

Catharine managed to persuade the shopkeeper to lower her prices, because she was buying a good quantity, and with what she saved she was able to purchase enough wool for a jersey. After that there was only enough money left for the cheapest pair of boots the cobbler could produce.

When they had finished they stopped on the quay for a while, to sit in the sun. Elizabeth was still cosily asleep, so there was no need to rush home. Catharine sat on a bollard, while Isabella plonked herself on the ground, leaning comfortably on one outstretched arm. Gulls circled lazily, giving an occasional crooning wail. The early afternoon sun shone down, glinting like tourmaline on the tiny wave crests.

A little way along from them a huge merchantman from foreign climes was made fast. rising and falling gently with the lapping tide, its timbers creaking comfortably. Men trouped backward and forwards over the gangplanks, carrying barrels and crates of cargo. Amongst them, Isabella suddenly spotted the unmistakable bulky form of Joseph. Behind him, trotting proudly went Daniel.

'Oh — look'. Isabella pointed to them.

Catharine's eyes followed her finger. 'Oh, yes,' she said, nodding.

'Does Joseph work on the docks?'

'In a way, yes. 'Twill be contraband his merchants have ordered. When it comes he often helps them to unload.'

'In broad daylight?'

'Aye. There's no one will try to stop them. Nearly the whole Island is involved in smugglin' in one way or another. An' them that don't smuggle, drink. Drunkenness is an occupation most o' the Islanders follow these days. '

After a while the baby started to snuffle and become restless, screwing her face up, cramming her fingers into her mouth and rubbing her nose with a tiny, balled fist.

Catharine looked down on her, smiling fondly. 'All right, my Bess. Well go home now, then you can be fed as soon as you waken properly.' They rose, to toil up the steep slope to the hill overlooking the harbour. Isabella excitedly carried the great armful of parcels: more presents than she had ever known in the whole of her life.

While Catharine suckled the baby, Isabella was sent to tether the goat amongst the gorse on Shaw's Brow.

It was the most beautiful view from up there, and the most glorious day. The warmth of the sun brought with it a gentle inner peace. Isabella prayed it was not too much to hope this happiness would last forever.

Chapter 10

Daniel strode briskly down the hill alongside Joseph. The touch of the big man's hand resting lightly on his shoulder gave him a thrill like none he had ever experienced before. It gave him a sense of togetherness, companionship — of belonging. The way it must feel, he thought, to have a father. Now this man was taking him down to the harbour to help with men's work. Men's work, he had said! They had gone out together, leaving Isabella and Catharine to the women's work; looking after children; cleaning; cooking and all that sort of thing. And, both men together, they were off out to do men's work.

At the bottom of the steps, they wound their way through a maze of narrow, winding streets to the harbour. The boat, the *Louisa*, bobbed gently at her mooring, groaning quietly to welcome them as they went aboard.

Two men looked up from their tasks as the pair stepped onto the deck. One, Daniel had seen before, just once or twice around town, but the other was a complete stranger.

'We have a new man in the crew,' Joseph said in answer to their unspoken question. 'A street urchin who needed some work, some food an' warm clothes for his back.'

'A street urchin, you say?' The nearest man frowned disapprovingly.

'Aye. But he'll be more like a son. The lad'll be a great help to us at times. Name's Daniel. Here boy, don't be feared o' them.' He grabbed the boy's shoulder pulling him forward from where he was lingering timidly behind. 'Daniel, lad, this here's Philip Christian and him over there's William Quayle.'

The man working over by the rail, William Quayle, nodded, smiling.

'Welcome aboard boy. I think I've seen you aroun' a bit haven't I?'

Daniel nodded.

'Seen you pinchin' a bit at the market too, I do believe. Hard to be sure though, 'cos you're a mite cleaner now.

Daniel felt hot colour rise in his cheeks. It seemed just about everyone had seen him steal. And he had thought he was so good at it!

Philip Christian's face softened. 'So the boy thieves, does he? He might well fit in us after all then!'

At that moment a head popped up from below decks.

'Joseph, I heard…' Seeing the boy, he stopped short.

'An' Daniel, this is the last o' us, Arthur Keggin. He's half-owner o' the *Louisa*.'

'Only a quarter owner, but that should still give me a say in who gets brought aboard. Can I ha' a word wi' you, Joseph?'

The pair moved for'ard, talking rapidly, angrily perhaps, arms waving.

Then Joseph's voice boomed loudly, echoing around the rigging.

'No I won't be havin' him sailin' wi' us. You can have no fear o' that. The lad's too young to have his life risked. An' besides, until he's learned somethin' about sailin' he would be naught but a hindrance. But there's plenty he can do to be useful aroun' here. An' he can help unload the merchantmen when they come in.'

The man, Arthur Keggin, frowned and nodded, but still he chewed on his lip and looked doubtfully towards Daniel. 'What do you know about the boy? How do you know he's to be trusted?'

'I know he was in desperate need of help. I also know he would most likely not have survived much longer, the way he was goin'. Either he'd have starved to death, or got caught by the soldiers an' put back in Castle Russian an' near birched to death. Then he'd likely have been transported to the Americas. Then he'd most likely have died — or wished he had. Him an' the little girl. An' I saved him from that, so I have no doubt I can trust him. An' besides all that — I still have the biggest say in who comes on this boat!' Joseph finally pulled rank

Arthur shrugged, still looking a little disgruntled. 'Anyway, you might like to know there's a clipper comin' in this mornin' from the Colonies, got quite a bit on board for Mister Drinkwater.'

'Aye, right. Then wi' the lad here we'll have an extra pair o' hands to help us unload. Is Mister Drinkwater in the town this minute? If not we had better get a message to him, for we'll have a goodly cargo to take to Whitehaven for him this night.'

Daniel cheerfully buckled down to work on board the boat but was happy to stop when everyone else did, to watch the arrival of the clipper.

They lined the rail of the *Louisa*, watching in awe as the giant ship eased her way through the harbour mouth, gliding gracefully to her mooring at the quay. Faultlessly, her crew brought her in, to blend to the wharf with only the very slightest bump.

Daniel watched breathlessly, spellbound by the sheer grandeur of the magnificent vessel. He noticed a large crowd had gathered on the harbour to see her dock, each one looking as open-mouthed as he, himself, felt.

'She's beautiful!' He said in a dry whisper.

Joseph glanced down, smiling. The boy would make a good sailor one day. He was certain of that. The sea was in his blood. He had the instinctive love of a good ship.

'Would you like to come an' help us unload her?'

Daniel looked up, thrilled. Would he? There was nothing he could think of that he would like more. To actually go on board the mighty clipper!

'May I really?' He asked quietly, afraid to speak too loudly for fear he might wake up and the dream vanish. This last twenty-four hours just seemed too good to be real.

Daniel eagerly followed the four men along the quay, imitating, as far as he could, the way Joseph walked. The swing of his arms, the way he placed his feet, but he could not match the length of the big man's stride. For the first time in his life, he had found someone worthy of being his hero.

Excitedly he followed, the last of their group to cross the gangplank. Joseph stopped for a word with one of the crew, then nodding cheerfully, beckoned Daniel to join him.

'You can come an' help me wi' the cargo, lad.'

They hurried below decks, Daniel gazing in awe at all he saw. This was his first time on such a large vessel. The passages, he noticed, were all lit by black iron lanterns, wrought in open grills, the flames within them licking smokily at the surrounding gloom.

He hesitated for a moment in the hold, breathing deeply, his nostrils flaring to the steamy air, laden with the oily heaviness of the lamps, the sweet fragrances of man and the pungency of fresh spices and oils. Over it all came the heavy smell of sweat and the briny scent of the sea.

The air seemed thick with smoke, grease and burning tallow, yet it excited his senses like never before. Yes, this was the life for him!

Daniel thrilled to the slap of cargo continually being hefted, being unloaded onto the wharf. Knowing it would be hidden away, to be loaded, after dark onto the smaller boats and smuggled to England and Scotland. He heard the sharp slam of working doorways, the beckoning cries of the merchants — kings of the smuggling trade on the Island and the lilt of hoarse, monotonous work songs and sea-shanties.

All morning and well into the afternoon Daniel trotted behind Joseph, working as hard as he had the strength for. Feeling inches taller and miles prouder than he had as a street urchin. While they took a short break to eat, they sat on the wharf, alien islands in an ocean of moving bodies.

Fascinated, Daniel sat watching the scurrying workers, many bare-chested and bare-footed, with tattered trousers rolled halfway up their legs. Some were almost bent double under the immense weights they bore. They toiled endlessly with sweat streaming down their bodies. Many worked alone, others, like Daniel and Joseph, worked in pairs on the heavier cargo. Overseers screamed their instructions and barked their orders, while the wharf workers hurried to obey.

All about the clipper as he gazed around, Daniel saw movement, as men raced through the catwalk rigging, reefing the last of the unfurled sails, securing yards and lines.

Herring gulls swooped, screeching and swirling, overhead. or perched on the rails and rigging, ever hopeful that a crate of food might be dropped and break open.

The sun continued its quotidian trek across the sky, passing its zenith, marching down towards the western horizon. Shimmering off the surface of the water, its silver brilliance seemed, to Daniel an exciting omen of a bright future.

As the day wore on, the workers, tiring, slowed until at last the holds of the huge ship were empty, the cargo delivered to its owners and safely hidden away.

'We'll take a rest now, boy. Let's go home an' have some supper. Then after, we'll come down an' load the boat wi' the goods for Whitehaven.'

'Will you be goin' "across" tonight?'

'Oh aye. As soon as the boat's loaded. We've got brandy to take tonight'

'Can I come wi' you?'

Joseph shook his head. 'No, lad. Not till you're older. An' you to learn to sail first, else you'd put us all in danger.'

When they entered the cottage, after a long climb up the hill. They were met at the door by an avalanche of little boys.

'We went shoppin' this mornin' Daddy,' James grabbed his father's hand excitedly, hauling him to the centre of the room.

An' we bought lots o' things for Ishab,' continued Thomas, unable to say her name properly.

During supper, Daniel, thirsty for knowledge about the new life he was entering into, bombarded Joseph with question after question about smuggling.

'Why is smugglin' such a popular pastime?'

'Well, at the bottom o' it all is the British Government's theory that the nation's wealth depends on the amount o' gold held by the exchequer. If too many goods are imported from other countries it means that gold is goin' out o' Britain. So to stop that, an' to encourage home manufacturers an' exporters, they introduced a system of bounties. These people were offered inducements to encourage the economic growth o' the country. Do you understand all that?'

'I think so. The English Government paid the people to make all they needed an' to export as much as possible to bring money into the country.'

Joseph nodded enthusiastically. 'Aye. Well, to help this along, they put high duties on goods bein' imported from foreign countries, to put people off buyin' them, an' to stop money goin' out o' Britain. On the island, here, the rate o' the Manx Custom's duty is much lower, so foreign things can be bought more cheaply.'

'So people buy what they want here an' take it over to the mainland?'

'More or less. But there are a lot o' rich merchants from "across" livin' on the Island now. They were very quick to see how a fast penny could be made, an' lots moved over here so they could run their operations better.'

'Is that why there's so many wealthy English, Irish an' Scotsmen here now?'

'Aye. That's why, boy.'

'Why is it, though, a foreign ship can come into Douglas in broad daylight an' unload, as this one did today, quite openly, wi' no one to bother it. Is that not dangerous?'

Joseph shook his head emphatically. 'Not at all. You see, the goods are brought in here quite legally, wi' Manx duties paid -which are very low. 'Tis when we take them "across" the danger comes in. For then we have the British Custom's cruisers to dodge.'

Seeing Catharine's sudden look of fear, he quickly added, 'But that's not too difficult, for they only ha' them every six miles aroun' the coast.'

'Six miles? That leaves a big space for you to slip through.'

'Aye. Not one in a hundred of our boats involved in smugglin' is ever taken at sea, or even seized afterwards.'

'You'd think the Crown would put out more cruisers.'

'I suppose they have not enough o' them, for they ha' the whole o' their coast to watch, not just the stretch between the Isle of Man an' the mainland.'

'Then we cannot be stopped?'

'The British are tryin' to find ways. Perhaps one day they will succeed. As long ago as 1727 the British treasury was given the power, by an Act o' Parliament, to buy the rights o' the Lordship o' Man. But our Earl, James Stanley, Lord o' Man, refused outright to sell.'

Daniel, leaning forward, elbows on the table, listening intently, nodded his approval. 'Then what?'

'Then in 1736, when his son became our Lord, the English reopened negotiations. He, it seems, has been a little more forthcomin', but still has not sold.'

'I hope he never does,' Isabella said with feeling. 'I wouldn't like the Island to jus' be a part o' England.'

'We mus' hope that never happens,' Joseph agreed. 'Anyway a few years ago, 1751 it was, there was a call for the Isle o' Man to be annexed to the Crown o' Great Britain, but his Lordship, who wished to will it to his heirs refused to deal. So as long as he lives I think our Island will be safe from the English.'

"Tis said,' Catharine interjected, 'That most o' the Lord's revenue comes from the duties charged on the Island for prohibited goods.'

'That's not really right,' Joseph corrected her, 'Because the goods are not prohibited on the Island, but only "across", in the Three Kingdoms. 'Tis only the English Treasury what calls 'em prohibited. They are legal imports here.'

'I still worry when you're out,' Catharine frowned.

'There's little to fear, for the English Customs' vessels can neither search nor seize a vessel in a Manx harbour, nor even within three miles o' our shore. An' "across", wi' our craft bein' smaller, we can sail into shallower water than their cruisers an' lose 'em that way.'

'It all sounds so exciting,' Daniel's eyes were sparkling.

'Aye.' Suddenly Joseph laughed. It started as a low rumble, building up into a roar, his shoulders shaking.

'Do you remember Captain Dow, Catharine?'

Catharine giggled. 'How could I forget? Who will ever forget.'

'Who was Captain Dow?' Isabella and Daniel spoke as one.

'He was the Captain o' a Custom's cruiser name o' *Sincerity*. The cruiser had delivered Bishop Wilson back to the Island some days previously and, for some reason unknown to us, had remained in Douglas harbour.'

'Now that mornin', 26th o' June 1750 as I remember it, two Irish wherries arrived in Douglas. One o' them was let to pass safely into the harbour, but the other, in the small space, accidentally bumped against the *Sincerity* in passin'. Harsh words passed between both vessels, sending Captain Dow into a rage. In his fury, he sent a number of armed men on board the wherry to seize an' search her. On findin' there was no cargo on board the wherry, the customs' men, in their anger, stripped the clothes from the crew and robbed a passenger of twenty-five guineas.'

Isabella gasped. Twenty-five guineas! Such riches were unbelievable to her young mind.

'When the Customs men returned to their vessel,' Joseph continued, 'They took wi' them several members of the crew o' the wherry, what was tied up alongside the *Sincerity*. Captain Dow had a mind to set sail when the tide was favourable and take his prisoners home to Whitehaven wi' him.'

'Could they do that?' This was a rich tale indeed to Daniel's young ears.

'Not in a Manx harbour, he couldn't. 'Twas piracy. The Captain o' Douglas, Paul Bridson, received a petition from the Master o' the wherry an' his passenger who was robbed, askin' for the release o' the prisoners an' the arrest o' Captain Dow. Mister Bridson, as was his duty, went aboard the cruiser an' although he managed to have the prisoners freed, he was ill-used an' badly abused by the crew o' the Customs' vessel.'

'So he didn't get to arrest Captain Dow?'

'No. But a huge crowd had gathered by then an' saw how our Town Officer was treated by these foreigners. The mood became ugly when the *Sincerity* tried to escape justice by puttin' to sea, her crew firin' blunderbusses at the mob on the harbour. Once out in the bay, Captain Dow trained his eye on a Dutch dogger, The *Hope*, what was on its way to Douglas wi' a cargo o' tea an' brandies from Rotterdam.'

'Did they catch her?' Isabella was now as enthralled as Daniel, hanging on every one of Joseph's words.

'The *Hope* saw them comin' to intercept and withdrew from the bay, makin' for Ramsey with the cruiser in pursuit. The dogger, unfortunately, ran aground on a bank at the entrance to Ramsey Harbour an', having her helpless, the Customs' men boarded her.'

Daniel leaned forward, his face supported by his hands and his mouth half-open in awe.

'Word o' the goin's on at Douglas had reached Ramsey by a horseman, before the ships arrived, an' Captain Christian, who was Captain o' Ramsey, had instructions to serve a summons on Captain Dow for the theft o' the twenty-five guineas from the passenger on the wherry. Captain Christian went aboard the Dutch dogger, wi' an armed escort, an' arrested the Customs' men who were plundering her. They were taken off then to Castletown, for imprisonment, an' Dow was left wi' only two men an' a boy to look after his ship.'

'What happened after that? Captain Dow surely couldn't sail his ship with so few crew.'

Joseph shook his head. Pushing his chair back from the table, he rose to stoke some more logs on the fire. The children's' eyes followed his every movement.

'No. Several days later, feeling the *Sincerity* might be in danger, Bishop Wilson, who was a great friend of the Customs Officials, asked the Deputy Governor that a few of the crew of the *Sincerity* be released to give assistance. This request was granted an' six members o' the crew was sent to Ramsey.

'What happened to the rest o' the crew then?'

'Well, when they came to trial the court was told they had done only as their Captain had instructed. But Dow had not the courage to attend the trial, so the court could only find that the men were pirates an' send them to prison. From that day forward Captain

Dow swore vengeance an' carried out a private war against the Manx.'

Daniel and Isabella waited, agog, for him to continue, but after a moment he stepped away from them. 'Tis time to load the boat an' be away.'

Daniel jumped to his feet. 'Can I come wi' you?'

'You can help wi' the loadin', but not to sail.'

Daniel nodded excitedly. Well, that was better than nothing. For the moment it would have to be enough, but one day, he determined, he would be one of the Crew.

Chapter 11

Daniel stepped out proudly down the hill beside Joseph with powerful waves of excitement surging through him. At last! At long last, something worthwhile was happening in his life Finally, he was going to be someone. Someday, he vowed, he would be the greatest smuggler of all time. He would be a name every Manxman would remember and talk about for all time.

For the moment, however, he would be satisfied with being Joseph Cubbin's right-hand man. For now, he would just be happy to learn the trade. He wanted to skip with joy, but decided that would be childish behaviour for someone in his position.

The sea smell was very strong when they got down towards the harbour and Daniel could distinctly hear the lapping of the sea sloughing against the wooden wharf.

A fine rain began to fall, sighing amongst the rigging of the tall ships, misting around the furled sails, blown on a gentle evening breeze. It drizzled around them as they made their way, cautiously, to the rear entrance of the Market Hotel.

Philip, Arthur and William were there already, sitting on benches by the fireplace, joking with another man, well dressed and English looking. They all stood up when Joseph and Daniel entered, all four nodding their acknowledgment as if one single string controlled all four heads.

'What's it to be tonight?' Joseph asked without any further ado.

The stranger hesitated, frowning pointedly towards Daniel.

'This is my friend, Daniel,' Joseph explained. 'Daniel, this is Charles Drinkwater. He's the merchant from "across". Most o' the goods we run are for him.'

Charles scowl deepened. 'Careful wi' your tongue, Joseph. Don't say too much in front of the boy. Who is he anyway?'

'I told you,' Joseph replied sharply. 'He's my friend. An' he's safe to know our secrets. He'll be as close to me as my own two sons one day.'

Daniel felt himself swell with pride, and after another wary look at him, the Merchant said no more. After a quick jar of ale, with Daniel watching, wishing he would soon be old enough to drink it, they all made their way to the *Louisa*.

The rain had become quite heavy by now and beat against Daniel, running down his face as he hurried to keep pace with the long strides of the men. He blinked, wiping one hand across his face to clear his vision. When they reached the boat he saw the rain beading and running, as though alive, down the rigging and the superstructure. A lone seagull sat miserably on the yardarm.

Charles Drinkwater climbed down to the lower platform of the wharf with them, following Joseph through the dimly-lit, rat-infested tunnel to the cellar. Quickly he paced, pointing out the barrels that he wanted shipping that night.

'Only brandy? Nothin' else?' Joseph asked.

The man nodded. 'That's all. Deliver it to St. Bees Head. And bury it in the usual place. My agents will collect it from there.'

Immediately they set to work, rolling the brandy kegs to the side of the *Louisa*, where they were quickly lifted aboard and disappeared below deck with unbelievable rapidity. In less than thirty minutes the ship was loaded to the gunwales with about twelve thousand gallons of French brandy, and was ready to sail.

'Well, that's it, boy,' Joseph said, finally. 'You'd best go home now.'

'Can't I please come wi' you? I'll stay out o' your way. I promise.'

Joseph shook his head without a moment's hesitation. 'No! I told you, boy, not until you're much older. Havin' you along would put us all in more danger if we got in any trouble. Now, get off home wi' you.'

'May I stay an' watch you sail then?'

Joseph relented. He didn't want to discourage the boy's enthusiasm 'Aye. If you'll promise to go straight home after. There's some rogues abroad at night.'

Daniel nodded. 'Aye. I will.' Reluctantly he dragged himself ashore, to stand close to the edge of the quay beside Charles Drinkwater. ''Tis a poor night to put to sea,' Daniel commented.

Charles gazed around thoughtfully, looking finally to the sky, with its cover of scudding clouds. 'Not too bad. The wind is strong, but not dangerously so. It should speed their progress, especially if they should be spotted by a Custom's vessel.'

The merchant took a last look around, then turning abruptly he walked away without as much as a farewell.

Daniel watched him go for a moment, then returned his attention to the harbour. It appeared to be bustling with more activity than it ever did during the day. Everywhere he looked people were scurrying on board boats of all different tonnages, carrying barrels, crates and bales of cloth. The whole place looked like an anthill. Suddenly he became aware his name was being called. Looking up, startled, he saw Joseph at the stern of the *Louisa*, signaling to him. Putting a hand behind his ear, he strained his head forward.

'Cast off for'ard,' Joseph shouted. With a quick nod, Daniel strode to the bollard, unwinding the rope with as much speed as he could. Joseph smiled his acknowledgment, then waved cheerfully as the boat started to drift away from the harbour wall.

Daniel watched as a sail unfurled, creeping slowly up the mast. The *Louisa* glided away into the clearing night, ahead of a fresh, strong sea breeze. He smelled the sea, as the blackness of the night engulfed the boat. Then he caught another glimpse of her, gleaming in the silver light of the moon, which momentarily slipped its cloud cover. Another black cloud came and the *Louisa* disappeared like a ghost in the night.

For much longer than he had intended, Daniel stood on the wharf watching the other vessels quite openly loading their contraband, making their preparations and sailing out into the night in the wake of the *Louisa*. Altogether he counted over twenty, but then he ran out of digits.

'Well,' he thought, '*if the Customs' cruisers are on the prowl tonight, they'll ha' their work cut out.*' He saw no man of the Island's Customs come near while he stood there. Neither did any person challenge his right to be watching, so confident were the smugglers of their security on the Island.

The weather turned ever more hostile, with cold, heavy gusting rain and a high wind that rapidly became a hard north-easterly gale. He saw dark thunderheads piling up in the north-east, writhing their way rapidly southwards, and the rain quickly changed to ever-thickening sleet.

The activity on the water-front died and Daniel, deciding it was time to return home, turned his footsteps towards *Little Ireland*.

With his head lowered into the driving rain, he was moving towards the first of the narrow twisting roadways. Suddenly, from a darkened doorway, a hand reached up to grasp his ankle.

Stumbling, he lurched against the wall, bruising his shoulder and he only just managed to keep his footing. Looking down, he saw a man, ugly and unkempt, half sitting, half lying against the door. Horror and revulsion flooding through him, he pulled against the man, but his grip was like iron.

'You got money, boy?' the voice was coarse and gravelly.

Daniel shook his head, panicking. 'No. I have nothin' o' value.'

'You mus' ha' somethin' you can gi' me? Jus' the price o' a jug o' ale's all I want. Fine upstandin' boy like you mus' ha' that much.'

Daniel shook his head again, still desperately trying to jerk his ankle free.

'If you don' gi' me nothin' I'll sell you to the white slave traders.' Another hand reached towards him and in a moment of blind terror, unable to free himself, Daniel lifted his free foot, kicking with all his strength towards the man's face.

There was a sickening crunch of crumbling bone.

The man screamed and clutching at his face, he released his grip on the boy's ankle.

Daniel froze, terrified, for a moment, seeing the man, looking inhuman now, holding his face as though he was trying to push back into it the blood that was gushing out. The front of his clothes reddened, a pool started to form in the dirt and suddenly Daniel came out of his trance. Turning, he fled blindly along the alley, leaping up the steep steps two at a time. Finally, he burst into the cottage in *Little Ireland* sobbing, shaking and gasping painfully for breath.

Catharine jumped to her feet, running to put her arms around him. 'Whatever has happened?' She felt she had never seen such terror written on the face of a human being.

Daniel told his story, feeling his supper surge to his throat when he told of the awful sound of breaking bone.

'There was blood everywhere. I killed him! I know I did. I must 've.'

'No, you haven't. People don't die of a broken nose. They just has a lot o' pain. An' serve him right too.'

'But the blood — .' Daniel insisted, shuddering. 'There was so much blood. A person can't live wi' so much blood gone. They'll be after me for murder by now.' His voice broke and in the next moment he was weeping. Struggling for control, he brushed the tears from his cheeks with his sleeve.

'Hush now. A bang on the nose always bleeds a lot. Always looks wors'n it really is. An' if he is dead 'tis his own fault. No one will ever think it was a child what done it. They'll think it was some brigand out to rob him. Now you just put it out o' your mind.'

Daniel tried, but it was no easy task. Lying on his mattress later, the scene replayed and seemed to grow and grow in his mind. Every time the vision came back to him, the crunch of breaking bone was louder, the flow of blood more prolific. He held a shaking hand to his eyes as though the gesture would blot out the nightmare that played in his mind. What if Catharine was wrong and the man was dead?

Outside, the wind was rising, increasing in intensity, plucking at the thatch of the roof above his head. Below him, Daniel could hear Catharine tossing restlessly in her bed.

It was an awful night to be at sea, he thought, *and just as bad to be at home knowing someone you loved was out in such a storm.* He was annoyed with himself, then, for having caused Catharine extra worry.

Finally, he fell into a restless sleep and when he woke again morning had come.

Opening his eyes, he turned on his back, looking upward, painful memories slowly flooding back. Somehow this morning he must find out if a man had been murdered during the night. He looked above him to the timber roof beams and the darkness beyond. A darkness broken here and there with speckles of diamonds where tiny holes in the thatch let in the early morning light.

Turning on his stomach to look over the edge of the loft, he saw Catharine was already about and washing some clothes. She heard his movement and looked up, smiling.

'Are you feelin' better this mornin', Daniel?'

'Aye. A bit.'

'You had a restless night, I think.'

'Aye. Whenever I closed my eyes I could see that man an' all his blood runnin' out o' him. I heard you tossin' a lot in your bed too.'

'I never sleep well when Joseph is away. 'Specially when the weather is so wild.'

'Will he be all right, do you think?'

'Aye. He's been out in far worse storms than this an' come home unharmed. An' 'tis not so very far to Whitehaven.'

'Do they sail into the harbour there?'

'No. No, never. The Custom's men would love it if they did, for they would be within their rights to arrest them in an English harbour. 'Tis only in Manx waters they're safe.'

'I must see if I can find out, this mornin' if that man died last night.'

Catharine nodded. 'You can come wi' me when I fetch the water from the well. Isabella can care for the little ones for a while, an' we'll see if we can hear anythin' about him. The well's a good place for that, 'cos that's where all the gossip's spread.'

Daniel studied his new home while he tucked into a large bowl of porridge and goat's milk. Jemima bleated quietly from time to time, shifting her weight constantly as milking time came nearer and she grew more uncomfortable.

Catharine had stoked the fire with peat this morning, so it glowed a cosy red instead of its usual leaping, spitting, noisy flare. Its smoke had the sweet smell of burning moorland. In the corner farthest from the bed stood a large crock, in which he knew would be stored salted herring. At this end of the winter it was sure to be almost empty.

The two little boys were still sleeping soundly, while the baby, Elizabeth, made snuffling, sucking noises as she stirred in her crib.

When the rest of the household had awakened and been fed, Catharine tied the baby firmly to her chest, making sure she was well protected from the biting wind.

'Are you happy to be left wi' the boys to care for?' she asked Isabella.

'Aye.' The girl was aglow. Thrilled to be so entrusted.

'Good. Then if you bring those two pails by the door, Daniel, we'll go to the well an' see what gossip we can hear.'

When Daniel lifted the latch, the door was wrenched from his hand, bursting in against him, engulfing him in the fierce bite of the high wind

Though the rain had stopped the sky was alive with roiling, tumbling banks of black cloud. Stepping through the doorway, he found himself almost blown away. Putting both buckets in the one hand. he used the other to steady Catharine as she stepped out into the teeth of the gale.

They struggled, huddled together, down the hill and across to the well. The number of people there surprised Daniel, though he supposed people must have their water, no matter what the weather.

Most of the talk was of the smuggling fleet. The vast number of craft that had gone out the previous night — before the storm had broken. Everyone wondered how they would have fared. Women worried for their husbands and sons. Children worried for their brothers.

Every eye, from time to time, turned to gaze out over the angry sea.

Catharine and Daniel moved quietly around the fringes of the groups, saying little, but constantly listening.

'The hussey's got no wuss than she deserves,' One old hag was saying spitefully. ''Tis my bettin' none o' them children's her husband's. 'Bout time he gave her a good thrashin' in my recknin.'

'Aye. That one's no better'n she should be,' agreed her companion.

Catharine shook her head, smiling, and passed on.

'Did you hear what come about 'cos o' the Clague marriage?'

'Clague? No. Don't think so. She's the one as had to wed in a bit o' a rush, like isn't she?'

'Aye. Well, 'cos o' that they got one o' them, Non-Conformist minister fellows, to say the words over them. Then 'cos o' that new law everyone got in a heap o' trouble when the proper church got to hear o' it.'

'Which new law? What new law's this?' The listener was agog now leaning forward eagerly, keen to know everything.

Catharine, finding herself curious, edged nearer the narrator

'Well. It seems Tynwald brought in this new law las' year that if a Non-Conformist minister conducted a marriage ceremony, or if one was performed, by any minister wi'out the banns first bein' called, he could be made to suffer the most awful punishment. An' this fellow who did the Clague weddin' was Non-Conformist — and he didn't call the banns neither!'

'So what happened to him then? What punishment did he get?'

Catharine moved even closer, her ears working hard. She knew this Clague girl, Agnes, quite well and had heard the rumours concerning her rushed marriage. From the start, people had been counting the weeks on their fingers.

'Well, lucky for the minister he was a Manxman an' he was only transported for fourteen years. But if he'd been from off the Island he'd ha' fared wuss.'

'Fourteen years is bad enough. What could be wuss than that?'

'Well, if he'd been from off the Island he'd ha' bin pilloried wi' his ears nailed to it, then cut off afterward, an' he'd ha' bin fined an' put in gaol.'

Catharine, looking at Daniel in wide-eyed horror, saw he was looking a little green.

'Anyway, the minister's to be transported, an one or two others wi' him who knew there'd bin no Banns declared. An' Agnes' brother, Francis, got his ears cut off for helpin' to arrange it. On top o' all that, 'twas all for nothin', for now the marriage has bin made void. So now they's livin' together in sin.'

Catharine shook her head sadly, then moved on the next group of women.

'Life can be so terribly cruel, sometimes, Daniel,' she said quietly. 'Yon's a nice, kind, friendly lass they was talkin' about. Francis is a good lad, too, an' only young. An' them women was gettin' so much pleasure from their terrible bad luck.'

'Did you hear what happened to yon ol' drunk? You know him. The one what hangs aroun' tryin' to scare good folks into buyin' his ale for 'im?' An old lady with a face, Daniel thought, like a witch, was clearly eager to impart her news to anyone who would listen.

'Aye. I knows 'im! What happened to 'im d'you say?'

'Was foun' wanderin' in a daze las' night — or early this mornin' I think it was.'

Catharine had stopped behind the women, ostensibly seeing to Elizabeth's wrappings, but listening carefully, looking intently into Daniel's frightened, brown/green eyes.

'Covered in blood, he was. His nose is busted bad an' his face all black an' blue. I heard he's got both eyes blackened as though someone has given him a good beatin'.'

'What happened to 'im d'you know? Was he thrashed?'

'Dunno. Told the soldier what found 'im that he'd tripped an' fell and hit his face against a wall. 'Tis my reckonin' he picked on the wrong person this time an' got hisself a beatin'. An' not before time neither.'

'Serve 'im right, I say. Might stop him scarin' decent folk. For a while anyway.'

Catharine smiled at Daniel, who nodded and grinned back. The utter relief on his face amused her.

It was in a much more lighthearted mood they returned to the cottage on the hill.

Isabella had enjoyed herself with the boys. Young enough to bring herself to their level, she had wrestled, rolling on the floor with them, her giggles matching theirs. That was the scene Catharine and Daniel found when they were blown back in through the cottage door some time later, feeling as cheerful and excited as Isabella and the boys.

Isabella leapt to her feet as they entered. 'Did you find anythin' out?'

'Aye. The bugger's not dead. Just sore an' bruised, wi' a broken nose. He didn't even dare tell the soldiers he'd bin' kicked. Told them he hurt hissel' fallin'.'

Jemima was milked, then Daniel offered to take her to tether on Shaw's brow. He considered the day too wild for the womenfolk to venture out.

The wind having eased a little, he decided to walk farther on up the hill, to look out over the bay and see if he could spot if the *Louisa* was in sight anywhere.

From high on the brow he looked out towards the north-east, from whence Joseph should come.

There were several boats in his view, mostly just small black dots on the shimmering grey sea. The ones close enough to make out were not the *Louisa*.

Then suddenly his eyes were drawn to the rocks in Douglas Bay. A ship lay there on its side, partly broken up, with waves breaking over it. On the highest point of the rocks two figures clung, being washed and tugged by the boiling sea.

Daniel stared at the scene, a hand to his brow to aid his vision, but because the ship lay deck towards him, he was unable to get a proper view of it.

Heart leaping he spun and raced down the hill. Jemima looked up, startled, at his rapid approach, jumping nimbly out of his way. A flock of sleepy seagulls took flight, squawking angrily.

When he burst into the cottage a few minutes later, like a blast of cannon-fire, the four people inside froze in alarm. He had an impression of Catharine and Isabella, heads turned from where they had been bent over the frock they were cutting out, eyes popping in fright.

James and Thomas who, when he entered, were prodding the tail end of a beetle to make it run faster, raised startled eyes towards the door. The poor, frightened creature seized its opportunity and disappeared rapidly into a crack in the wall.

Daniel stood inside the door, his back to it, gasping for breath, his eyes wild.

'What's happened?' Catharine was on her feet, moving anxiously towards him.

'There's a boat,' he blurted. 'Wrecked on Conister Rock!'

'Is it the *Louisa*?'

Daniel shook his head helplessly. 'I dunno. She's on her side wi' the deck facin', so I couldn't see her well. But the size looks about right.'

Catharine grabbed her shawl. 'Look after the childher for me please Isabella. I must find out.'

Isabella nodded, her eyes wide and fearful.

'You come wi' me, if you will, Daniel.'

Side by the side they rushed down the steps and through the maze of narrow streets to the harbour.

The news had spread like magic and people were flocking from every direction.

'Do you know what boat it is?' everyone was asking. But no one seemed to have any idea.

At last they were as near as they could get, hovering on the fringe of a huge crowd. They could see only the shattered deck of the stricken vessel, its masts torn off, rapidly breaking up on the rocks.

A boat had managed to snatch the two seamen from Conister Rock and, though Catharine and Daniel could not tell who they were it was quite clear, to their dismay, neither was large enough to be Joseph. They watched with bated breath as the rescue boat came around to enter through the harbour mouth. It was not until the craft was quite close to the quay they were able to see the men were not from the *Louisa*.

'Thank God!' Catharine breathed and Daniel, holding her arm, felt she was trembling like a leaf in a winter storm.

Fear had enervated them and it was with great effort they climbed unsteadily back up the hill.

Isabella looked up, wide-eyed as they dragged themselves through the door.

'Twas not the *Louisa*,' Catharine said quietly, then burst into tears.

SEPTEMBER 1763

Chapter 12

Catharine, seeming to put the scare from her mind sat, in the afternoon, to start teaching Isabella how to sew. Daniel watched, from time to time, quite amazed at how tiny and neat Catharine made her stitches.

Isabella did not do quite so well, but he supposed that as she had never sewn before, she wasn't doing too bad a job of it. How they managed to put the thread through the tiny eye of the needle was quite beyond him.

Unable to settle he played, at times, with James and Thomas. Several times he toiled to the top of Shaw's Brow, and on up higher, peering longingly towards the English coast. Then, no more contented wandered home again.

Home! What a wonderful feel that had, he thought. It was the first real home he'd had in his life. And Isabella's. He was relieved he no longer had the responsibility for her. Glad they were still together though!

The day warmed later in the afternoon, as the wind dropped. But then it turned quite chill as black, gravid, billowing clouds obscured the face of the sun, blotting out its warmth.

The sea changed colour rapidly, becoming slate grey. Here and there white horses rode the waves.

One step only, Daniel had taken down the hill, when he thought he glimpsed a speck well out to the northwest. Stopping, staring seaward, hand raised to shield his eyes from the sky's glare, he tried to make out what he had seen. There *was* a ship, far out. Too far to be able to tell yet. He stood watching, for a good half hour as the speck grew slowly larger until at last, he was able to recognise the boat and even the huge man standing at the prow.

Daniel felt his heart surge with joy. Like the onrush of a spring waterfall, sending dazzling rainbows in a sun shower, a whole score of emotions seemed to dart around his mind. His spine tingled with excitement and the release of the fear he had held all day. For a long moment, he felt unable to move or speak, then with a great yell of joy he hurtled down the slope, slipping and sliding tearing the skin from his hands on gorse bushes. Losing his footing on a steep part, he crashed ahead of a small avalanche, legs and arms flailing, threshing, to thud full length against a jutting rock.

A flock of jackdaws, rooting for grubs on the barren hillside, leapt nervously into the air, with a wild fluttering of wings, scolding noisily. He lay full length for a few moments, spread-eagled and winded against the boulder before he dared move. A sharp pain shot through his ankle when he moved it, but when he stood up to test it under his weight it held all right. A little more sedately, he made his way back to the cottage, limping slightly.

Sticking his head round the door, his eyes encompassed the scene inside. Thomas and James had played themselves to exhaustion and now lay dozing on the mattress in the corner. Baby Elizabeth was firmly attached to Catharine's breast and sucking greedily, snuffling and coughing in her haste. Catharine watched fondly while Isabella painstakingly stitched the cornflower blue dress.

His mind, contented, Daniel thought what a comfortable, warm and homely scene it was.

'*Louisa's* comin' in,' he said jubilantly. 'I saw her from the hilltop.'

Daniel saw the immediate relief light up Catharine's face, but she said nothing. 'May I go down to the harbour an' meet her?'

Catharine nodded, smiling. 'Aye. An' I'll put the broth on to boil.' So saying, she rose and, grasping the swivel, swung the pot on it's chain over the fire. A few more logs were added to put more heat in the embers.

Elizabeth grumbled mildly at the disturbance, then returned enthusiastically to her feed.

Daniel backed out and, shutting the door behind him, hurried towards the harbour.

There were several boats in view now, at varying distances and fanned in every direction, but the *Louisa* was nearest, just passing Conister Rock when Daniel reached the quay. Very soon she was edging in between the harbour walls. Joseph stood tall and proud at the helm, while the other three men moved busily about the deck preparing to dock. Sails were being furled and stashed, rigging lashed. They all stopped working for a few moments to look at the wreck on the rocks, but it was almost completely broken up now, drifting off the ragged rock to sink to its watery grave.

As the *Louisa* moved slowly towards her berth, Daniel walked alongside her on the quay. Seeing him there, Joseph smiled broadly and waved. Daniel thought how tired he looked, and so much in need of a shave. He looked a real vagabond with the stubble shadow on his chin. Joseph became more alert as the *Louisa* neared the side, then Daniel heard a brief command and a slight burp as the boat touched the creaking timbers of the long wharf.

A line was thrown to Daniel and he made it secure. All the time he listened to the four men on the boat, longing for the day when he would be deemed old enough to sail with them. To join in the laughter and bustle of docking and the thrill of relief at being home safely once more.

The moment the ship was secured, Daniel scrambled aboard.

He had an urge to run to Joseph and throw his arms around him to welcome home, but restrained himself, feeling that might be thought too childish.

Philip and Arthur moved to stand on either side of Joseph, dwarfed by his bulk.

'That's a voyage well over wi'.' Philip said.

'Aye. But we've known worse.' Joseph agreed, thinking only briefly of the adventures they had faced. With the deck now stilled beneath his feet, and the winds of home in his face, he had forgotten all apprehension in the unfailing joy of homecoming. No matter how short their time away had been, it always seemed to him a long separation by the time they returned to Douglas.

'What happened?' Daniel longed to hear of what dangers they had faced.

'Later,' Joseph said absently. 'I'll tell you about it later. 'First I must find what ship it was wrecked on Conister, an' how her crew fared. Do you know, boy?'

Daniel shook his head, wishing he had taken the trouble to enquire. He was sure it would have pleased Joseph well if he'd been able to give him the news he desired.

With the ship secured, Joseph leapt to the wharf, heading straight for an alehouse, with Daniel scrambling in his wake.

There was a group of men around a table, lit only by a single flickering candle, all gaunt-looking with sombre faces. Joseph sat with them, his movement making the tiny flame shiver, throwing pinpoints of light across their faces.

Feeling like an intruder, Daniel edged to stand in the gloom a pace or so behind his friend.

'What ship was lost on the rock, does anyone know?'

The other men at the table looked up mournfully. 'Aye. Twas the *Mary Ann.*'

'John Cannell's?'

'Aye.'

'Were they found safe?'

The men at the table all silently shook their heads. One, a thin, very old looking man said, 'They got chased by the Custom's cruiser. Twas firm' on 'em an' they was runnin' afore it to make shallow water, but the storm was so bad an' they caught a rip what turned the boat on its side. It righted itself, but John an' his boy Robert got swept overboard an' wi' the sea bein' so rough the crew couldn't see them nowhere.'

'The Custom's vessel was closin' fast, so the men had to keep on runnin' for the coast,' another man took up the story. 'They managed to get clean away in the end, but then they tried to bring the boat into Douglas by themselves this mornin' and got run onto the Rock.'

'John Cannell — dead?' Joseph had the look of a man in deep shock.

'Aye. An' his boy, Robert!'

'Was that the little fellow wi' the squint in his eye?'

'No. The bigger one than him. The one that had eyebrows so arched he always looked surprised.'

'Oh aye. I know the one you mean. Nice friendly lad. Not very bright, but a good worker.'

The men around the table all nodded their agreement.

'Got about another ten young 'uns at home an' another due any day now.' The alehouse keeper, delivering Joseph's drink, joined in the conversation.

'Aye,' Joseph said thoughtfully. 'The sea's a greedy master. Makes more widows than she's a right to.'

'Aye an' orphans.' agreed the landlord.

'The Customs men helps her evil task!' One of the other men finished darkly.

After the initial conversation about the wreck, there was a

strange quietude in the alehouse that evening. Daniel had been aware of it in other places, at other times in the past.

The wreck of a ship always had a sobering effect on a seafaring community, but more so when the vessel sunk was from that port. A good friend was dead! Looking around the shocked faces, Daniel realised they were all thinking it might just as easily have been them. There would be many men awaken, sweating in the nights to come, their dreams filled with the secret terrors of a terrible nightmare.

Joseph stayed only long enough to finish his ale.

'C'mon, lad, we'd best get home,' he said quietly, unwinding himself the bench. Daniel stepped back to let him lead, then followed him from the alehouse.

Close to the foot of the steps to Little Ireland they came upon a woman, dressed in filthy clothes sitting in the dust of the street, a screaming baby clutched in the crook of one arm. Her sad, pain filled eyes caught and held Joseph's and she hopefully held out a grimy hand, nails torn and black with dirt, palm turned upwards.

Joseph stopped to look at her then, shaking his head unhappily, reached in his pocket, pulling out a penny which he pressed in her hand.

'I pray to God John Cannell's missus never ends up in such straits,' he said feelingly as they started up the steps. Looking up at him, Daniel saw tears standing at the corners of his eyes.

*   *   *

When they were all nicely filled with thick broth, and Joseph relaxing comfortably before the fire, Daniel asked him, again, to tell him of the *Louisa's* escapades.

Joseph looked into the odd coloured eyes, smiling. The boy's excitement and enthusiasm were infectious.

'Soon after we sailed,' he began, 'The wind picked up an' buffeted the boat. It strained the sail. Already the weather was changing, the air wetter than before and because of it the cold seemed fiercer, creeping beneath the skin into flesh and bone.'

'Aye. It turned wild here soon after you sailed.' Daniel agreed.

'The air became heavier still, leaden in spite o' the strength o' the wind. A fine drizzle started and soon it was freezin', turnin' to sleet and hail, hammerin' unmercifully at the sails. The waves heightened, makin' the boat yaw badly and hard to control. The nearer we got to the coast o' Englan', the wuss the storm seemed to grow.'

'Aye. It was wild here, too. We was real worried about you. 'Specially when we heard there was a ship on Conister. Daniel an' me went down to ha' a look, but we couldn't see what one it was. Managed to find out it wasn't the *Louisa* though.' Catharine was well controlled but clearly upset.

'The storm continued all the way across, an' so wild was it that we didn't dare get too close to shore, so had to lie up an' wait for it to calm a bit. After a while the rain an' sleet stopped an' it was so cold then that our whiskers an' eyebrows was rimed wi' frost, our hands so cold we couldn't feel nothin' wi' them.'

Isabella shuddered, remembering suddenly the night she and Daniel had had to hide in a haystack from the storm and snow.

'The clouds started to break up a little an', as the spells o' moonlight grew longer, the wind weakened. We was just about to get under way again, when Arthur Keggin thought he saw a boat, not too far off. Jus' at that moment dense clouds rode across the moon's face an' in the uncertain light we was unable to make out what the other vessel was. Then the cloud passed, the moon shone an' we saw, much nearer now — a customs' cutter.'

Daniel's eyes widened and he leaned forward in his seat.

'We set sail immediately, of course, but they was outrunnin' us an' closin' fast. Then they started firin' on us, so we was left wi' no choice but to run for shallower water. Once or twice we felt the keel catch, an' the boat went near over on her side. Luckily the waves was jus' strong enough, an' caught us right, so she came off the shoal an' righted hersel'. We was lucky, though, 'cos we had a big load on, much o' it lashed on deck an' we didn't lose a single barrel o' the brandy.'

'You got away from the Customs all right then?' Daniel was completely rapt.

'Aye. We got in such shallow water that they couldn't follow wi'out puttin' themselves in danger. In the end we jus' lost sight o' them. Could ha' bin them what went after John Cannell. I shouldn't think there'd be more'n one Customs' cutter in the one area.'

'I wonder if it might ha' been Captain Dow?' Catharine asked reflectively.

'It well might ha' bin,' Joseph nodded. 'The way that cutter was firin' on us, an' Dow has vowed to make the Manx pay. Anyway, once we'd made our escape, we hove to in shallow water to wait until there was enough light in the day to make Bees' Head. Finally, daylight came. There was a slight mist, but not so much that we couldn't see, so we very quickly made our way north to the landin' place.'

'Were you far from it, then?'

Thomas had wandered over and now climbed on his father's knee.

'No. Not too far,' Joseph continued. 'First, we put a man ashore, to check carefully there was no one to see us, but he found the merchant's men already there. Because of our delay, they had been there all night waitin' for us. So we had help unloadin' the boat and did not have a need to bury the brandy kegs. They were put straight onto a cart an' taken quickly away in case any foot-soldiers should happen along. The British Government is puttin' more an' more o' them aroun' the coast to try an' stop our trade.'

'I wish I'd bin wi' you!' Daniel said enviously.

'Well, I'm glad you wasn't, boy. There was enough to worry about wi'out havin' a youngster along. Look what happened to young Robert Cannell an' he was about your age. Our troubles wasn't over when we'd passed on the contraband, though.'

'Why what happened then?' Catharine was starting to look quite worn.

'We set sail again, an' were only about half an hour on our way when Philip saw a ship right on the horizon. We weren't about to take any chances, so we set sail, full speed, for home. The other ship started slowly to overhaul us, an' soon we could see she was a Customs' cutter. She let off several shots at us, which fell well short. I think they were jus' tryin' to scare us into heavin' to, but we kept on runnin'. Luckily we were less than three miles from the Island by the time she drew near enough to fire on us.'

'You didn't get hit did you?' Isabella was looking pale and anxious now.

'No. By that time the boat was close enough for us to see t'was the *Sincerity*. They fired a couple o' shots across our bows to try to intimidate us, but I wasn't about to let Captain Dow get his hands on me — or my boat. So we kept on comin' an' they turned away an' went off huntin' again. Dow wouldn't risk comin' too close to the Island after the affair in fifty.'

Catharine shook her head despairingly. 'I wish you would give up the smugglin' an go back to fishin'.'

Joseph shook his head stubbornly. 'There's no money in fishin'. You know that as well as anyone. I've promised some day I'll buy you an' the childher a good big house in a better part o' town. An' I'll never get the money for that from the fishin'.'

Catharine sighed sadly, her heart going out to Mary Cannell.

'Don't look so worried, lass,' Joseph said kindly, "Twould take a better man than George Dow to capture me.'

Chapter 13

Isabella watched anxiously as Catharine hoisted herself laboriously from the chair. Moving uncomfortably, she ambled to the fireplace to stir the pot of broth.

'Leave that. I'll see to it. You sit down.' Isabella. now nearly fifteen, fussed about Catharine, enjoying the chance to mother her.

Catharine laughed. 'I spend all my life sittin' down these days. I have to get up an' move some time or I'll stiffen up an' turn into a rock here.'

'You'll ha' plenty o' movin' aroun' to do after the baby comes. Now you must rest. The doctor said so last time he came didn't he? He said you was workin too hard an' worryin' too much an' if you kept it up you'd only do yourself a mischief — an' the little one wi' you.'

'Aye. But I worry even more if I ha' to sit here doin' nothin' when Joseph is carrying contraband "across".'

'Well, it can't be for much longer. You're near three weeks past your time already. The little one can't hang on much longer.'

Catharine sighed, nodded and shuffled gratefully back to her seat. She felt to have waited forever for this baby, growing larger than she had ever been before, more and more tired daily. It was now she was most thankful Joseph had brought Isabella home to her, though she had loved her from the first moment she had set eyes on her. *An' Daniel too*, she thought guiltily, but Isabella most of all.

Isabella stirred the broth, set bowls on the table for when the men came home. Kept a watchful eye on the three younger children and loved them even more than a true sister could.

Catharine watched her fondly from the chair as she gently chastised little Sarah. Isabella had been a tower of strength at Sarah's birth, she remembered, doing more to help her than the midwife herself.

Isabella looked towards the door as she heard male voices approaching, her face lighting as the door opened with a bang and James came rushing in, clutching an armful of twigs. Close on his heels came Joseph and Daniel, a huge bundle of wood carried between them.

'We got a real stack o' wood!' James said unnecessarily.

'We thought we'd best get a good stock. since the weather is closing in an' your confinement must be near now.' Joseph explained

Catharine shook head, sighing irritably. 'I wish you wouldn't go cutting wood. You'll get gaoled if you get caught — maybe even transported. Then where would me an' the childher be? Between smugglin' and pinchin' wood I despair o' you sometimes. An' takin' the boy wi' you to get him into trouble an' all! An' in broad daylight too!' she finished petulantly.

'Where else am to find fuel? Even if could find coal to be bought, we haven't the kind o' money to pay for it. An' I can't ha' you goin' cold at a time like this. Wi' winter comin' on the new little one will need a warm house when it comes.'

'If it ever comes,' Catharine sighed tiredly.

'I was talkin to Agnes Quirk on the way home. She was tellin' me her Henry got put in gaol yesterday for not payin' his dog tax.'

'What dog tax? There's no tax on dogs!' Catharine frowned.

'Aye, there is now. They made a new law this year. Now if you've a dog you have to pay a tax on it. Now there's more carriages on the roads they need money to make better roads. So they've put a tax on dogs to help pay for new roads.'

'What if you've got a dog an' you don't use the roads?' James suggested.

'You still has to pay. Everyone uses the roads,' said Joseph. 'Anyway, poor old Henry got ten days in gaol for not payin' his. I'd guess he'll get rid o' his dog now.'

'Well I think all the Members of Keys must be mad to make an unfair law like that. They all need stringin' up by their thumbs!' Daniel jabbed both thumbs forward aggressively to emphasise his point.

Joseph rounded on him suddenly, his face contorted with fury. 'Don't you ever talk like that about any Member o' the House again — or any of the chief officers of the Island for that matter.'

There was a stunned silence in the cottage for a few moments. Catharine was the first to find her voice.

'There's no need to shout at the boy,' she said angrily. 'When did you suddenly become so fond of our politicians?'

Joseph shook his head in momentary confusion. 'I have no liking for politicians at all. I'm sorry, Daniel, I had no right to shout. But you must never talk like that, the penalties are too severe if you are overheard.'

'Are there laws now against speakin' your own mind?' Catherine snapped.

'Aye. If you speak it about the wrong people. 'Tis not a new law, though. This one has been about for hundreds of years, but it was discussed again this year an' the decision was made to keep it. So they will likely be more stringent about upholdin' it. There's a lot o' laws we don't fancy, but we jus' ha' to live wi' 'em an' say nothin', whether we like 'em not. Like that one what had Agnes Quirk, Clague that was, livin' in sin until her an' Robert foun' another minister an' got married proper. So jus' watch your tongue boy. An' that goes for the rest o' you too.'

'What is the punishment for it, then?' Daniel asked a little nervously.

'If you speak slanderously of any o' the folks I mentioned, an' you're caught at it, they chop off your ears — an' fine you ten pounds into the bargain!'

Isabella gasped, blanching.

'So you ha' to hold your tongue or lose your ears!' James quipped and got a swift, though gentle, cuff across the back of his head from his father.

'I've bin thinkin' Daniel,' Joseph said, as they relaxed after supper, 'That perhaps the time has come for you to come out wi' us at night.'

For a moment Daniel was numb, unable to believe what he was hearing. Then he jumped to his feet, eyes sparkling, heart racing with boundless excitement. Rushing over he stood before Joseph. 'To come smugglin' wi' you, you mean?'

Joseph nodded, laughing. 'Aye. Well, you bin out sailin' wi' us often enough now, an' you've learned well how to handle the *Louisa*. An' you're near seventeen now aren't you? There's many a lad started to the trade much younger'n you.'

'Oh, no! He's only a boy!' Catharine protested.

Daniel turned, fixing her with a pleading look. 'I'm old enough. Please don't stop me.'

'He'll be all right. Don't be worryin', Missus. He's nearly a man now, an' Arthur wants to give up. His rheumatics is gettin' real bad now an' he's gettin' too slow to be safe. Puttin' us all in danger he is. An' he knows it. The boy's quick, an' he handles the boat well. We'll all be much safer wi' him along.'

Wordlessly Catharine shrugged, averting her eyes. Joseph's mind was made up and she knew it would be useless to argue with him. As ever, she would just have to suffer in silence.

In the morning, early, Joseph left with Daniel, now feeling ten feet tall, striding at his side.

Catharine shook her head sadly as she watched them depart. 'I don't like it at all,' she said quietly to Isabella. 'If he's goin' to take Daniel wi' him I wish he'd jus' go back to fishin'.'

'Hush now,' Isabella consoled. 'They'll be all right. Daniel's full grown now. He can take care o' hisself.'

Truth be told, Isabella liked it not one little bit either, but she did not want Catharine worried any more than she had to be right now.

Quickly she got the three older children breakfasted and ready for school. It had been her suggestion originally, on learning there was a minister teaching education in St. Matthew's Hall, that the children should attend. By law, they were all supposed to go until they could read and write, but it was not enforced very rigidly.

Catharine had been easy to persuade for, like Isabella, she would dearly have loved to be able to read and write.

Joseph scoffed a bit at first, saying learning was only for the rich and posh. He told the women it wouldn't pay for them to try to put themselves above their station. But in the end, he had shrugged and told them they could send the children to school if that was what would please them.

Isabella had rushed down to the hall to enrol them and each one had started school the minute he — or she — turned six years of age.

When she had packed them all off down the hill to school, Isabella turned her attention to washing and dressing little Sarah. Of course, she loved them all, they were her family. But Sarah was special, she had a real way of twisting the heartstrings. Often Isabella felt almost as though she were really her own child. Perhaps, she thought it was because she had been there at her birth — had helped her into the world. Had watched her blue little face gulp in that first breath of air.

It had been to Isabella that the midwife had handed Sarah. She who had drained the mucus from the rosebud mouth, cleaned the tiny eyes so tenderly, washed away the grease that had protected her in the womb. And Isabella's face was the first those sparkling hazel eyes had looked upon. From the first Sarah had almost become a part of her.

'Isabella. 'Tis time. The baby is comin' at last.'

Isabella froze. Catharine had spoken so quietly and calmly that for a moment she wondered if she had heard correctly Turning her head. she looked searchingly at the woman she had come to regard as a mother

Catharine smiled back. 'Aye, Isabella. Time.' Though she appeared placid on the surface, the girl sensed her undercurrent of excitement — perhaps tinged a little with fear.

Isabella leapt to her feet, rushing to Catharine's side. 'Here. let me help you to the bed.' Took a hold of her arm.

Laughing, Catharine wrested her arm free. 'Not yet, love. 'Tis too early yet. There'll be time enough for me to lie abed when I have to.'

'I'll take Sarah to Agnes an' ask her to go down an' tell the midwife. Will you be alright alone for two or three minutes?' Isabella tried to echo Catharine's calmness but could feel her heart crashing against her ribs.

'Aye.' Catharine laughed, holding on to her huge belly, wincing.

'But best tell them 'tis early times. Little 'un won't come for hours yet.'

Isabella snatched Sarah from where she played on the floor. Wrapping a cape around her, she sped to the next cottage. After a quick rap, she lifted the latch and let herself in.

Agnes looked up from her sewing, smiling, and half rose from the table.

'Catharine's time has come. Can you care for Sarah for me, please?

An' would you run down an' ask the midwife to come. Catharine says the baby won't be here for hours yet, but ask the midwife if she would come as soon as possible to take a look at her.'

'Aye.' Agnes grabbed her cloak from the hook. 'I'll go right away. 'Come Maria, we must go out.' Turning, she spoke to her daughter, who played on the floor by the fire.

'An' can you keep an eye open for the childher comin' home an' take them in, please, Agnes. Jus' in case their mother's in the thick o' it then. You could send James to sit on the doorstep in case I have need o' him to run a message.'

They left Agnes's house together, Agnes hurrying off down the steps, while Isabella scuttled home.

Catharine was still in the chair and determined to stay there as long as possible.

Isabella scrubbed out the huge black pot they cooked almost everything in, then filled it with water and swung it over the fire to boil. She wasn't sure quite why, but she remembered having to boil vast quantities of water when Sarah was being born, though she had no memory of very much of it ever being used.

Catharine sat calmly watching. 'You are a good girl, Isabella. I could never have wished for a better daughter. I bless the day Joseph brought you home to me.' Suddenly she giggled, but broke off abruptly, wincing, as another wave of pain broke over her.

Isabella rushed to kneel at her feet, looking anxiously up into her eyes. 'Are you alright?'

Catharine smiled gently. 'Bless you, yes. Jus' a little pain. You can't have a baby without a bit o' pain. But they're worth it all once they've come. I was jus' thinkin' about the day Joseph brought you home. You an Daniel, You were such a poor, skinny, filthy pair. A fine pair o' urchins I thought when I first set eyes on you. I wondered what that man o' mine was thinkin' o' bringing home a brace like you.'

Isabella remembered it well. The look on Catharine's face. 'I thought

You was goin' to faint right away wi' shock. At first, you looked so horrified. Then your face softened an' all I could see was compassion.'

'Oh, I *was* horrified!' Catharine admitted. 'Completely shocked. Your hair was so filled wi' muck I thought it might crawl right off your little head on its own. Couldn't even tell what colour it was. I wondered whatever could ha' possessed Joseph to bring such creatures into my house. Then I saw how skinny you both were, an' thinly clothed, an' Daniel wi' no shoes even, an' it the middle o' winter, an' him lookin' so much like my dead brother, Alexander. Then I knew why Joseph had brought you, an' it didn't matter from where. Now I know 'twas the best present he ever gave me.'

'Aye. An' you an' Joseph's the best thing that ever could ha' happened to me — an Daniel. I never knew what it was to be happy until that first night I came here. I thought all Mammies were like mine.'

* * *

The midwife came quite a long time later, long after Isabella had become worried about her absence. Throwing open the door without as much as a knock, she marched briskly into the room, ordering Catharine straight into bed.

'Come on girl. Off that chair an' into bed this minute!' she commanded.

Catharine tried to protest, but was overridden by the bossy, rather large lady.

'Don't argue, madame. I want you on the bed. The baby can't make its way into the world wi' you sittin' in a chair.'

With a sigh of defeat, Catharine tried to struggle from the chair. Isabella rushed to grasp her arm and help her. She had to stop for a few moments before they reached the bed, for a pain to pass. All the while the midwife looked on, nodding in satisfaction.

'There now! How do you suppose you would have managed that if your labour had been further on?' she asked smugly.

Having arranged Catharine, in great discomfort, on her back, the woman prodded her around a bit and timed her pains. For a while she fussed about checking all was in order, seeming satisfied with the quantity of boiling water. Then, as abruptly as she had arrived, she announced that she was leaving.

'Leavin?' Isabella was appalled.

'But you can't! We ha' need o' you here!'

'Yon baby won't come for many hours yet. An' there's another comin' today down the hill. I'll be needed there.'

'But *we* need you here!' Isabella's eyes were wild, lips trembling.

'The other one will likely come first an' I'll be back here in time for yours. Anyway, this is the other lady's first, an' Catharine has had enough to be able to pop hers out on her own.'

Then she was gone and Isabella, terrified, was left alone with Catharine.

Catharine's labour strengthened as the afternoon wore on, but there was no sign of the midwife returning. Finally, to Isabella's relief, a knock came on the door. Rushing over, she threw it open, to find a young boy on the doorstep.

'Missus Cubbin?'

'No. Have you a message for her?'

'Aye. Her husband says to tell her he won't be home this night for he's gone on a bumboat run.'

'No! He can' t! He can't go tonight! Run back down an' tell him he can't sail tonight.'

'I can't, Missus.'

'What do you mean, you can't? Of course you can. You must! Go an' tell him his wife is havin' the baby an' the midwife's not here. Tell him he cannot sail tonight.'

'Tis too late, Missus. He's gone already. They were near loaded an' ready to sail when he gave me the message. But that was a while ago, for he didn't say there was any rush, so I stopped to spend the thruppence he gave me for bringing the message.'

'Gone?' Isabella stood, stunned, for a long moment. 'Gone? Dear God, no! Since you took so long to come, will you now run next door an' ask Mrs Quirk to come through. Tell her 'tis urgent.'

Agnes arrived at a run just moments later. 'Has that woman not come back yet?'

Isabella shook her head worriedly. 'Catharine seems to be havin' jus' one pain after another. She seems to be in a terrible agony sometimes, yet the baby never seems to come any nearer. I'm certain there's somethin' badly wrong.'

Agnes stamped her foot angrily. 'Oh, that awful woman! Surely the other mother must ha' given birth by now I'll go down an' get her. I'll get back wi' her as soon as possible. An' the doctor. It might be a good idea if he has a look at her too. Ha' you plenty of money to pay him?'

'Aye. If we haven't Joseph will soon find some.'

'My brother, Francis, stopped by, so I'll see if he can sail an' try to find Joseph. If there is to be trouble he should be here.'

'Thanks Agnes.'

At that moment Catharine cried out.

Isabella ran to her and Agnes darted out. It seemed hours before she returned, distraught.

'Oh, Isabella, what are we to do? I went to the midwife's house, an' they told me there that she was at *The Brig* — you know, that big house down near the church; the one wi' the steps up an' the hitchin' post for the gentlemen's horse?'

'Well didn't you go for her there? You should ha' gone an' told her things was gettin' desperate here an' we ha' great need o' her!'

'Oh, I did! I did, Isabella! Of course, I did! But she said she was needed more there. Said she'd come as soon as she could, but not until the little one at *The Brig* had been delivered.'

Isabella hung her head, covering her face with her hands. 'If you want my opinion I think 'tis jus' money. They got more to pay her at the big house than we have.'

Catharine screamed and, looking round, Isabella saw her writhing on the bed in the grip of a terrible agony.

'Oh, Agnes, I must have help. I cannot manage on my own. I shan't know what to do if things go wrong. Can you fetch the doctor?'

'I went to his house too, but he is out on a call in the country somewhere an' they don't know what time he will be back. They took a message an' said they would ask him to call as quickly as he can. I told Francis too, an' he is goin' after Joseph. It is probably too late, for he has been gone so long, but Francis says if he finds him he'll bring him straight back.'

'Many thanks, Agnes, but what am I to do?' Isabella wrung her hands and gnawed her bottom lip.

'I'll take the little 'uns to my mammy, meet your other three from school an' send them there too, then I'll come back an' do what I can to help here.'

'No. Send James home. We may ha' need o' him. He can sit outside.' Agnes rushed away, while Isabella went to Catharine, to sit, holding her hand and helplessly wiping the perspiration from her brow.

It had not been like this with Sarah, who's birth, in Isabella's memory, had been a beautiful occasion. She remembered Catharine had seemed to suffer very little pain.

Suddenly Catharine started screaming, her back arching, lifting well clear of the bed. Then she collapsed, as the pain passed, to lie exhausted and only semi-conscious.

'Tis tryin' to come!' she gasped. 'I can feel it tryin', but 'tis stuck!'

Isabella lifted the end of the sheet to look. There was something in sight — a part of the baby — but she sagged in horror as she realised it was not the head she was seeing!

Chapter 14

Daniel had never felt as excited as he did that morning, striding down to the harbour at Joseph's side. He was a man now. Had Joseph not as good as said so? He had insisted Daniel was old enough to go smuggling with him.

That was as good as saying he was a man. Of course, Daniel himself had known it for a long time. Had suffered (was that the right word?) yes, suffered normal, pleasant though embarrassing grown-up male reactions on too many occasions not to know he was a man.

But now that Joseph had confirmed it, Daniel felt even more of a man. 'How soon will you be takin' me out?' He desperately wanted to show what he was made of and his impatience was hard to control.

'Next time we ha' contraband to deliver. Arthur asked to be let out o' it as soon as possible, so he might as well go now. I'll be glad to be rid o' him really, for he's gettin' too old an' slow an' a danger to himself an' the rest of us. It shouldn't be too long before you get a run. Don't say too much about it at home, though, at least not until after the baby comes. No need to worry Catharine any more than we ha' to.'

Daniel had just finished scrubbing the decks and was standing with Joseph, discussing his next task, when the merchant, Charles Drinkwater called to them from the shore.

'Have you a busy day, Joseph?'

'No. Jus' cleanin' the boat an' checkin' the sails an' riggin'. We're not goin' out.'

'I was wondering if you could take a cargo for me today?'

Joseph frowned doubtfully. 'I think perhaps not tonight. My missus has a little 'un three weeks overdue now, an' startin' to worry more than's reasonable about things — you know how they gets. I think maybe 'twould be best if I wasn't away a night. Ask Richard Curphey, he'd likely be glad o' the money.'

Charles looked doubtful, chewing the inside of his cheek. Rubbing his chin thoughtfully between thumb and forefinger, he shook his head. 'I think perhaps not. I'm not too keen on Richard. Gets a bit big for his boots — an' a bit greedy for my liking. You'd be back afore night, I promise. It's a bumboat run. Should only take a few hours.'

Joseph thought carefully about it. Certainly he could use the extra money. What with a new baby to provide for. An' the doctor an' midwife to pay. For sure it was tempting.

'Come on, Joseph. Let's do it. Please?' Daniel pleaded, scared lest Joseph should turn down his first chance to prove his worth as a smuggler.

'Please?' he repeated, more strongly.

'What's the cargo, Charles?' Joseph's resolve was weakening.

'Brandy and rum.'

'Where's it to be delivered?'

'A collier from Ireland. *Mermaid* by name. It'll meet you two miles off the Point of Ayre for the transfer.'

'What time?'

'About four of the clock.'

Joseph gazed thoughtfully at the gathering clouds for several moments, then nodded his head slowly. 'Aye. All right. We'll do it.'

'Yippee!' Daniel gave out a great yell, leaping triumphantly into the air, then hanging his head in red-faced embarrassment.

Joseph laughed, explaining to Charles that this was to be the boy's initiation into smuggling.

'This urchin of mine is going to prove his worth,' he added.

Charles laughed. He had been wary of the boy at first, but over the years he had watched him work. Had seen him develop into a worthwhile young man. Joseph had shown good sense, he realised, when he had given a home to this child of the streets.

They moved the boat to the section of the quay across from the Market Hotel and while Daniel leapt ashore to secure the painter. Joseph, Philip, and William hurried up the tunnel to the cellar. With the boat made fast, Daniel dropped agilely to the lower platform of the quay and followed to help load the cargo.

In a very short time, the boat was laden and made ready to sail.

'First I'd better send word to Catharine that we'll be missin' supper We must not cause her any more worry than we ha' to.'

Having said this, Joseph signaled to a lad who was leaning against the wall of the hotel. You, boy, will you carry a message for me'

'Aye. How much do you pay?'

'I'll give you thruppence.'

'Where's it to go?'

Thornhill, Little Ireland.'

The boy hesitated. 'Tis a stiff climb up there.'

Joseph bristled angrily. 'If you're too lazy then I'll soon find someone who will be willin' to go for the price I offer!'

The boy panicked momentarily 'Here, now, Mister, I didn' say I wouldn' go. What's the message?'

Go to Mistress Cubbin. 'Tis the third cottage in, but if you're not sure, ask someone. Tell her I'm on a bumboat run an' won't be home for supper.'

'Right Mister. I'll tell her.'

'Make sure you do, else I'll ha' your hide next time I see you.'

'I said I would!' the boy grumbled, then he boy sauntered off, obviously in no great rush to perform his task.

Daniel, simmering with excitement, cast off and the *Louisa* started slowly towards the harbour mouth.

It was a wonderful morning, he thought. But such was his excitement that, had there been a blizzard blowing, he would still have considered the day beautiful.

A slight haze hung over the sea, but the sky was a clear blue mantle. Only the merest of swells ran which, Daniel thought, was probably why the merchant had decided on a transfer at sea. Overhead a handful of seagulls circled lazily in the autumn sunshine, cawing quietly, watchfully waiting for the occasional careless fish. Then, with a sudden eye-defying dive, one would scoop a hapless, writhing creature from the water, the other gulls would attack, trying desperately and noisily to steal his catch.

Once through the harbour mouth, the *Louisa* turned sharply to larboard, to follow the coast up towards and beyond the lighthouse at Ayre, the northernmost point of the island. She was heavily laden, and low in the water, riding the swell very comfortably.

Daniel stood on the forecastle, set to keep watch because his eyes were the youngest and keenest. He stood, tall and proud, breathing in the strength-giving, briny air, his eyes peeled, fully determined not to betray Joseph's faith in him.

An occasional speck appeared on the horizon, but none that caused Joseph any concern. At last, a mile or more beyond the Point of Ayre, peering straight ahead, Daniel spotted the masts of a fairly large vessel coming into view.

'Craft dead ahead!' he called out.

Joseph hurried for'ard, staring to where Daniel pointed, hand raised to his eyebrows, shielding his eyes from the glare. For several minutes he studied the other vessel.

An odd cotton puff cloud scudded across the face of the sun, momentarily dulling the world, changing the sea from blue to grey. Then it would be gone and all would be well again.

A lone gull that had followed them from the shore, rose from the masthead to fly a lonely, searching circle in the sky.

Daniel stood, feet splayed slightly for balance, gazing anxiously from the distant vessel to Joseph.

'Aye. That looks like the collier. Good.' Joseph smiled down at the boy, clearly well pleased.

'If this is her we'll get the cargo transferred quickly an' make for home wi' all speed. With luck an' the wind on our side we shouldn't be too late in harbour.'

They closed slowly, almost casually, with the other vessel until Daniel was able to make out the name on her side.

''Tis the *Mermaid!*' he called out. Though he thought the lumbering collier was less like a mermaid than almost any other ship he had seen.

'Good!' Joseph's face cracked in a broad grin. 'That's the one we're lookin' for.'

Carefully, they maneuvered the *Louisa* alongside the *Mermaid*, edging gradually ever closer. Lines were thrown between the two ships when they were close enough, then as a swell lifted the Louisa, she rode the last few feet, to meet the Mermaid with a fairly gentle thud.

The lines were all rapidly made fast before the vessels could float apart again, then they rode the waves like conjoined twins.

With careful haste, the barrels of spirits were hefted from one craft to another. It was in this operation that Joseph, with his enormous size and strength, proved his greatest worth, for while it took two other men to lift each keg, he could easily manage one on his own.

As quickly as the transfer was made, each barrel was rolled across the deck of the collier and lowered to the hold to be secreted amongst the coal.

All was going smoothly until, when almost half of the contraband cargo had been transferred, the lookout atop the *Mermaid* main mast reported a sighting.

'Can you tell what it is?' his captain asked, peering up at him.

The man shook his head. 'Too far away yet, but it looks as though it's come up from the east o' the island.'

'Keep a watch on it then.'

The men were all well aware that in their current positon they were safe from a Customs' vessel, but if that's what it was it could bide its time then close in and search the collier the moment it moved to more than three miles beyond the Island.

The *Louisa* could not be touched in Manx waters either, but had no great wish to be involved in any arrest. So they, too, worked quickly and nervously.

The lookout kept a careful eye on the approaching vessel. Finally he identified it.

'"Tis a fishin' boat!' He called down. 'Out o' Douglas by the look o' it.'

As the boat drew nearer, all aboard the *Louisa* and the *Mermaid* stopped work, to watch curiously. A figure stood in the bows, waving frantically.

'Why 'tis Francis Clague.' Daniel was the first to recognise him, mainly because of his head, shaped strangely and made grotesque looking by a lack of ears. He had asked about this once and been told the lopping of Francis' ears had been part of his punishment for 'aiding and abetting' his sister to be married by a Nonconformist minister.

No one had ever quite understood Agnes' unseemly haste to wed, for it had been well over three years before her first child had been born. Daniel had heard quite a bit of discussion about it in Douglas.

'Francis Clague! I wonder what brings him?' Even as he asked, Joseph's voice was thick with concern.

'What ails you, Francis?' he asked as soon as the vessel was within hailing distance.

'"Tis your Missus, Joseph.' The earless man called back. 'Agnes said I should find you an' send you home.'

'Why? What's wrong?'

Francis shrugged, the corners of his lips pulling down in a grimace.

'Do you know any more?'

'Aye. She said things weren't goin' right wi' the baby. 'Tis takin' too long to come an' neither the midwife nor the doctor's there!'

'Can you take me back straight away?'

'I surely can.' Francis brought his boat within jumping distance.

'Can I come wi' you?' Daniel made to follow Joseph across.

Joseph shook his head decisively. 'No. You cannot. Philip an' William will need you to help bring the *Louisa* home. It would be too much for them to handle alone.'

Daniel wanted to plead, but knew he must not. If Catharine was in trouble he wanted to be there to lend support, for did he not love her like a mother? Yet now Joseph was treating him like a man, trusting him as a man, so he must behave like one and make Joseph proud to call him son.

Miserably he nodded his agreement and stepped back from the rail.

'Now don't you be worryin' son,' Joseph shouted as Francis heeled his ship about. 'Catharine's had four others. She'll handle this un just as well.'

Daniel watched, transfixed with fear, as the other boat moved off slowly towards the Island.

'If you come an' give us a hand wi' the rest o' the barrels we'll get off home a lot quicker, lad,' Philip said kindly.

'Aye.' Daniel turned away from the rail to help heave another keg from the hold and over onto the other ship.

At last, all the cargo was transferred, the lines let loose and the two vessels drifted apart. The *Mermaid* set sail towards Whitehaven, while the *Louisa* turned her bows towards home.

Daniel worked well, doing what the older men told him, or what he knew must be done, but his mind, for the most part, was in Douglas, or on the other boat with Joseph.

Joseph stood on the forecastle, peering ahead. What had been a light wind had faded to no more than a slight breeze and they were making very slow headway, all but becalmed. If he had thought that blowing on the sails would have made one minute's difference to their arrival in Douglas he would gladly have blown them all the way home.

He knew Catharine well enough to know by now that she did not panic easily. If she was afraid enough now to have sent for him, then there must surely be something quite frighteningly wrong. And no midwife or doctor with her, Francis had said.

The last of the dusk faded now into no more than a dull glow on the horizon, the Isle of Man showing only as a faint dark shadow rising from the sea. Straining his eyes into the darkness, Joseph saw they had passed Laxey.

A bright full moon emerged from behind a solid bank of cloud, lighting the caps of the waves with flashes of luminescence, and seeming to summon some air movement. Joseph, feeling the sudden breath on his cheek, straightened from the rail, to see the sails fill and swell.

'Soon, my Catharine. Soon I'll be with you!' he said aloud as they cleared the headland and he saw the lights of Douglas in the distance. 'Won't be long now,' Francis said quietly, moving up beside him. with luck, it will be over by the time you get there an' all will be well.'

'Aye.' Joseph nodded. 'Catharine will be fine. She's brought plenty other healthy babes into the world wi' no real problem. 'Tis jus' I don't like to think o' her sufferin' an' maybe frightened with havin' no medical person with her.'

'She has Agnes an' your urchin, Isabella. That girl's a good 'un. An' so's our Agnes.'

'Aye. But they's got no trainin' for this sort o' thing. Mind you Isabella was there an' helped when Sarah was born. Catharine said she did a real good job too. But she's only a girl, just fourteen years old. Not ready to be bringin' a baby into the world.'

'From what I've heard o' that midwife, she's not so great anyway. Too interested in the money. Anyway, 'tis likely she an' the doctor both got there before the young un arrived,' Francis said quietly.

'Aye. Likely.'

It seemed a lifetime later that they finally sailed in through the harbour mouth, making as good speed as they safely could.

Francis edged his boat in, leaping ashore with a line as it swooped the last few feet, to burp against the quay side.

'Many thanks, Francis,' Joseph called as he jumped alongside him to the wharf. 'I'll catch up wi' you later. Buy you an ale for your trouble.'

'No trouble. Hope you find all is well up there.' He lifted his eyes towards Thornhill.

With a quick wave of his hand, Joseph took to his heels, running along the quay as fast as he could make his legs work. He almost bowled over a finely dressed gentleman who was stepping out of one of the large houses, and he remembered how often he had promised Catharine he would buy her a nice house. Well, he would! Very soon now, he would! Already he had made her wait too long.

Then he was dashing along the maze of twisting, narrow alleys that led towards the steps. Rushing up those steps two at a time, his heart pounded and every breath burned its way into his lungs.

At the corner, Joseph paused to take a deep breath, then strode toward his door. He stopped abruptly, his heart sick, on seeing James huddled on the doorstep with his shoulders heaving.

Tears flowed down the boy's face to drip, unchecked onto his jersey. Joseph put out his hand to the doorknob, but hearing the sound of sobbing from indoors, stopped, unable immediately to open the door and face what he might find there.

Chapter 15

Isabella closed her eyes and took a deep breath. Now what? She had heard of babies being born wrong way round. Knew it could be dangerous for them. But what to do about it? She let her breath out slowly. What did one do? On farms — with animals — they pushed the baby back in and turned it around, didn't they? Or did they? Isabella wasn't sure. Did they do the same with humans? She didn't know. Anyway, even if they did, she couldn't. Could she? No, you would have to know what you were doing. If she tried she would certainly kill the baby.

'Oh if only that dreadful woman would come!' she cried aloud. She can't have been needed down at the big house all this time. Doesn't she care?'

'Something's wrong isn't it?'

Isabella hesitated, preparing herself to offer reassurance.

'I know it is, Isabella. This isn't like the others. I know there is something wrong. An' I could see it in your face when you checked.'

The girl nodded miserably, and had to wait while Catharine screamed and writhed through another bout of agony before she could answer.

'I — I think the baby is wrong way round. I think it is its bottom I can see. What shall 1 do?'

Catharine was silent for a moment, wracked with pain and fear 'A breech birth!' she said quietly, 'Then there is nothin' you can do except pray.'

Agnes arrived back soon after. 'The childher are all safely wi' my mother, except James, an' he's outside. Has the midwife an the doctor not come yet?' she looked around fearfully.

Isabella shook her head, tensely explaining the situation.

'Well, that woman will ha' to come now!' Agnes spat out indignantly. 'I'll run down an' get her!'

'No! 'Tis too late. Don't leave me now!' Isabella begged, and at that moment Catharine screamed.

The baby had slipped partway out, with only its head and feet left undelivered, seeming to be jammed there by its chin.

Without hesitation Isabella knelt beside the bed, fumbling to get her fingers around the baby's chin and ease the rest of its journey. Moments later it slid onto the bed to lie, blue and unmoving. Isabella stared, horrified, at the boy child for a moment, then she snatched him up, suspending him by his feet, and smacked his buttocks gently. When there was no response she slapped again, but harder.

Still, he hung, limp and lifeless. Isabella looked up at Agnes, tears and pleading in her blue eyes.

'Put your mouth over his and blow gently. Make him breathe.' Catharine ordered breathlessly, in gentle desperation.

Isabella did as she was bade. Watching the tiny chest rise with her breaths, then fall again when she stopped. But it would not move of its own accord.

Suddenly Catharine cried out, arching again in pain. Isabella, looking to see what caused such pain, found to her shock, the head of another baby waiting to be born.

'Tis to be twins!' she gasped. Thrusting the still form of the little boy into Agnes' arms, she begged her to keep trying to make him breathe, then turned her attention to Catharine and the delivery of the second twin.

The baby, a girl, slipped into the world very easily, with no complication and very little pain. Though very tiny, she was yelling strongly even before she was fully delivered, and there was never a moment's concern about her breathing ability.

Agnes worked like a demon to try to force life into the little boy, but it was not to be. His lungs steadfastly refused to work and he never for a moment gave them hope he might live. In the end, her face and bodice drenched with sweat and tears, Agnes laid the fragile little scrap at the foot of the bed.

Catharine smiled and, in a whisper, weakly thanked Agnes for her effort.

'Well, at least we have one healthy baby.' she comforted. 'That was all we expected, so we should thank God for her.'

'Aye, that we should.' Isabella and Agnes agreed in unison.

'I'd best get you cleaned up an' get rid o' all the rubbish an' put clean sheets on the bed,' Isabella said after she had the baby girl washed and warmly wrapped.

When she pulled back the sheet, she stopped, horrified and had to turn quickly away so that Catharine would not see her face.

'Oh — Agnes!' she whispered, her mouth dry, tongue cleaving to the roof of her mouth. 'What are we to do?'

Agnes looked towards the bed, then closed her eyes, swaying. For a moment Isabella thought she was going to swoon clean away.

'We must stop the bleeding. Do you know how?'

Agnes shook her head. 'I think we had best send James to try again to get the doctor. Only he will know what must be done.' Isabella nodded, moving quickly to the door.

James was sitting anxiously on the doorstep. He looked so small and young, it hurt Isabella to concern him further. But then, she realised, he was older than she had been when she had been released from Castletown gaol.

'James, I want you to run down to the doctor's house as quickly as possible. Tell 'im the baby's bin born, but your Mammy's bleedin' real bad. Tell 'im he's got to get here fast. An' if he's out, leave a message wi' his wife an' run aroun' to the midwife's house. If she's not at home she'll likely be at *The Brig*' An' tell 'em both 'tis a matter o' life an' death!'

James, blanching, leapt to his feet and raced off towards the steps.

Isabella returned to the bed and, knowing there was nothing she could do to staunch the flow of blood, pulled the sheet over Catharine. Sitting beside her, she gently sponged the perspiration from her brow.

'James has gone for the doctor,' she said quietly.

Catharine nodded weakly. 'We must pray to God he comes quickly for I'll not live much longer,' she whispered.

Isabella, feeling her lips trembling, bit into them to still them.

'It's not so bad really. Likely it feels worse to you than it is, 'cos you're so weak after the ordeal you've been through.'

It seemed a lifetime they waited, hand in hand, while Catharine's life's blood flowed from her womb.

'Isabella.' So weak was Catharine, that Isabella hardly heard her. Leaning down, the girl put her ear close to Catharine's mouth. 'Look after my babies for me, Isabella. An' Joseph too, for in many ways he's just a child too.' Her voice was little more than a breath now.

Isabella shuddered at the implication. 'I'll take care of you all until you are well again.'

Catharine shook her head tiredly 'No, Isabella. I won't get well. You know it. You must accept it. Now, please promise me you'll keep my family together. Don't let my babies end up the way you an' Daniel were when Joseph found you.'

'Oh, I promise!' Isabella bit on her trembling lips. 'I love them all. I won't ever let any harm come to them. Your babies will always know what it is to have a loving home.'

Catharine smiled peacefully. 'Thank you, Isabella, now I can die in peace.'

'No!' Isabella almost shouted. 'Don't give in. Keep fighting. The doctor will be here soon. God won't let you die! I won't let you die! We need you! If you die I won't ever believe in God again. I shall hate him for ever more!'

'No, Isabella. When I die — and I will very soon — it will be because God has a special task for me. He must know my little boy will have need of me to care for him in heaven. Don't ever hate Him for anything. He brought you to me. It is all a part of His great plan.'

Isabella nodded, suppressed tears aching her eyes.

'Where are my babies, Isabella?' The words were only mouthed now, Catharine's voice gone completely. 'Bring me my daughter, so I may see her and know her before I am called to leave her.'

Isabella lifted the girl baby from her wooden crib, placing her carefully in her mother's arms.

Catharine took the tiny baby, cuddling it gently, pressing the tiny, soft, sleeping pink face against her own, her eyes closed in the joy of new motherhood.

They were in this pose when there came a sudden loud banging on the door. Agnes, who had been huddled, quietly in a corner for quite some time, rushed to open it.

Oh, Doctor,' Isabella heard her say, 'Thank God you're here at last. I hope you're not too late.'

'I trust this is as great an emergency as the boy told me, for I was called away from another patient to come here. Never have I seen such a hysterical child.'

The man stormed into the room, his expression changing suddenly from anger to concern when he saw the still, pale figure on the bed.

'The baby is born, the boy said?'

'Aye.' Isabella noticed James peeping round the door, his face tearstained, and motioned to Agnes. As in a dream she saw the other woman gently push the boy out, closing the door softly behind him.

The doctor leaned down to examine Catharine, then straightened again, looking grave, shaking his head. 'I'm sorry.' was all he said.

'Can't you take her to the infirmary?' Isabella asked desperately. 'They could save her there.'

The doctor shook his head. 'She would be dead long we could get her there. Better to leave her here an' let her go in peace.'

Returning to the bed, he took the baby from Catharine's arms. When she tried feebly to resist, he said gently, 'Only for a moment, till I check it.

'There was another one,' Isabella said quietly. 'A boy. Born breech an' dead. We tried to breathe life into him for a long time, but he wouldn't take up.'

The doctor nodded solemnly. 'Let me see the body.'

Without a word, Isabella fetched the little bundle from the corner and handed it to the doctor. She had wrapped the tiny, limp body in a clean cotton rag and placed it safely out of the way. The man took it from her and, laying it on the table, unwrapped it carefully.

'He would have been a perfect little boy,' he said quietly.

Isabella, looking at the babe properly for the first time, saw the well-formed little body, sturdy little limbs. The tiny fingers and toes were perfect in every detail, the nails complete and beautiful on the ends of long, slender fingers. The blueness had gone from his complexion now, as had the worried frown he had worn when first born. Now he looked at peace, his skin perfect, unflawed, like a pretty wax doll.

Isabella gazed in awe. 'He just looks as if he's sleepin'.' She spoke quietly, as though not to awaken him.

'Aye.' The doctor agreed, then moved as though to wrap him again. Catharine held weak, wavering arms towards them. 'Let me hold him,' she whispered, 'Then we can go to Heaven together an' be sure o' not bein' separated. We must be buried together too. Promise me we'll go in the same box.'

Unable to trust her voice, Isabella nodded. Finally, she managed to mumble, 'I promise. I'll tell Joseph it's what you want.'

Her mouth was dry and she just wanted to scream at Catharine not to go. To tell her that those still alive needed her more than the unnamed dead baby. But she could not. It was God's will, not Catharine's that she should die.

Without a word, Isabella took the little boy from the doctor's large hands to place him gently, as though he still lived, in the crook of his mother's arm.

Catharine mouthed her thanks, smiled down on her little son, tightened her arm around him, then closed her eyes and slipped quietly away.

The doctor lifted her hand to feel for the pulse in her wrist then, placing it gently back on the bed, put his ear to her breast. Standing, he shook his head.

Isabella stood, for she knew not how long, staring in disbelief at the pair on the bed. They just looked to be sleeping. So quietly. So at peace with the world — both of them. Both so pale and so perfect looking with all the agony of the last hours gone from their faces. They were smiling even, Catharine looking like an angel and the little boy like a plump cherub.

'They just look as if they'll wake up any moment. As though they're not really gone.' Isabella said quietly.

The doctor looked at her, frowning slightly, then moving to the bed, he pulled the sheet over the two bodies. After that he took his leave, explaining he had to return to his other patient.

Isabella slumped into the chair, trying hard not to look at the bed, and the shape under the sheet, but her eyes kept wandering back. All the time she was willing the sheet to move, to be thrown back, for Catharine to be smiling up at her, the boy baby wriggling in her arms. But nothing happened.

There was a terrible pain in the girl now, growing, tearing. Her heart pounded, hard but slowly, as reality hit her agonisingly, like the aftershock of a deep wound. At first, there was no feeling at all. Just numbness. The mind protecting itself, her consciousness narrowing as she struggled against it. But then the limit was reached and unbearable pain flooded in as the realisation came. The person she loved most in the world, gone in the wink of an eye. Just a flutter of time, in the space it took to draw a breath, it seemed, two lives had been snuffed out. Like a candle flame.

Agnes had been too dumbfounded to speak for a while, but at last she arose. 'Will you be all right if I leave you now?'

Isabella looked up, her eyes empty and dazed. 'Leave?' she repeated, not comprehending.

'Aye. I'll fetch all the childher from my mother's an' keep them at my cottage for tonight — or a few days if you think that would be best.'

'Aye. Aye, thank you, Agnes. I'll let you know. I'll see what Joseph thinks when he comes.'

Agnes paused with her hand on the latch. 'There's James outside,' she said quietly. 'He'll ha' to be told somethin'.'

Isabella nodded. 'Truth's best. He's got to know it. I'll tell him.'

James looked up, half rising when they went out. Isabella sat on the step, gripping the boy's arm to pull him back down beside her. Drawing a deep breath, she took hold of his hands and said, 'You must be brave, James, I have some bad news for you.'

James looked deeply into her eyes, seeing the pain reflected there.

'My Mammy's died, hasn't she!' It was a statement, not a question.

Isabella nodded, choking on the lump in her throat. 'Aye.'

'The baby too?"

'There were two babies, A boy who died an' a girl who has lived.'

James nodded. He was taking it too calmly, Isabella thought. 'Cry if you want to,' she said quietly. 'Twill do you good. You're not too old yet.'

James shook his head. 'I think I'd like to be alone.' He wriggled his hands free of hers, wringing them in his lap.

Isabella felt tears stinging, and the anger of impotent frustration.

She looked at James and saw also four other, motherless children — and herself and Daniel of course. The focus of reality, at last, forced itself upon her and all the raw hurt and rage she had held in abeyance these long hours flooded in on an inexorable tide.

There was an almost overpowering fury with the midwife who would not come. The doctor who came too late. Joseph who had made his wife pregnant then was too busy smuggling to be at her deathbed. And that of his son! The third son that he had wanted so badly They all had left her, just a fourteen-year-old girl, to face this horror alone.

Suddenly there came a feeble cry from inside the cottage, reminding Isabella of the girl baby. Shaking herself, as though the movement would somehow cleanse her thoughts of their anger, she rose and went inside.

Glancing briefly at the shroud on the bed, she lowered her eyes and moved to the goat in the corner. The living child had need of her and must be fed if she were not to join her mother.

The little girl was tiny and fragile; the smallest Isabella had ever seen; and felt like a 'Will o' the Wisp' in her hands. To Isabella's relief, her appetite did not match her size and she sucked greedily on the cloth that Isabella dipped in goat's milk.

While the baby was feeding, her tiny fingers trustingly gripped Isabella's. The little eyes were closed tight with contentment as she sucked. Isabella stroked the gossamer hair, feeling her heart swell with overwhelming love.

Outside she could hear James sobbing in lonesome misery. When she had finished with the baby, she placed her, asleep once more, in her crib. There seemed an unnatural hush then, interrupted only by the quiet sounds of James' heartbreak.

Slumping at the table, Isabella buried her face in her arms and wept, her whole body lurching with the power of her sorrow.

The door swung open slowly. Raising her head, Isabella saw Joseph framed there. His eyes went straight to the bed, taking in the shape beneath the sheet and for a moment he stood, transfixed. Slowly he crossed the room, then, taking a deep breath, slowly drew back the shroud. He stood, gazing in stunned disbelief at the two beautiful, waxen faces, smiling as they enjoyed their journey together. His eyes clouded with tears and suddenly he seemed to shrink before Isabella's eyes, sinking to his knees, he lay across Catharine, embracing her and the baby boy, his body shaking.

'Not you too, Catharine!' he cried in an agony of remorse. 'I could bear to lose our baby, but not you too.'

After a few moments, he raised his head, looking toward the roof. 'God in Heaven, be kind to them,' he pleaded.

He rose from the bed then, moving to sit at the table with Isabella.

Taking both her hands in his he asked, 'What're we goin' to do now, girl, wi' your mother gone? An' the baby too.'

'There's another baby.'

Joseph frowned at her, uncomprehending. Isabella nodded towards the crib.

Following her look, Joseph saw the tiny bundle sleeping there. He rose and, crossing to the corner, stood looking down in wonder. Shaking his head in awe he mumbled, 'In the midst of death we are in life.' He turned slowly back towards Isabella, as though in a dream.

It crossed Isabella's mind, absently, that he had it wrong way round, but she said nothing.

'What is it — boy or girl?'

'A girl.'

'And the one that died?'

'Boy.'

Isabella watched Joseph's face for a sign he thought the wrong child had died, but none came.

'We must thank God, then, that it was not all in vain and we must treasure our little girl.' Returning to the table, he asked again, 'What are we goin' to do now, girl?'

'I made a promise to Catharine that I would look after all her babies. That we would all stay together as a family. She was feared her children might finish up on the streets as me an' Daniel did.'

'Do you think you'll be able to manage?' Joseph asked. 'Bein' mother to this lot would be no easy task for a grown-up. An' you're only fourteen.'

Isabella nodded solemnly. 'They're my brothers an' sisters. I love them all like my own. An' I love you like you was my real father. We're family, an' family look after each other don't they? Look at the mess me an' Daniel was gettin' in before we had you.'

Raising her head, she looked Joseph straight in the eye and said strongly, 'Yes, I can manage. I promised Catharine I would. An' I will!'

Chapter 16

JOSEPH made the box himself, refusing any offers of help. He worked day and night, determined it would be worthy of his loved ones. For lining, he used a bolt of silk Charles Drinkwater gave him that had been spoiled with sea-water.

When the box was to his liking, he gently lifted Catharine into it arranging the boy baby in her arms as she had wished. Then he covered them with the silk, except for their faces, and they were buried together like that.

Isabella watched Joseph worriedly, for all the fire and life seemed to have gone out of him. His desolation and emptiness appeared limitless; awesome.

Joseph insisted on pulling the sled with the box all the long journey to the church at Braddan by himself. Only occasionally would he allow Daniel to lend a hand if the runners caught on a large rock.

Isabella had watched a guilt grow in him, knowing he blamed himself for Catharine's death. So many times she had tried to talk and to point out that his presence would not have saved his wife's life. But each time he would just shake his head angrily, the pain in his heart ever increasing.

'If only I had been here,' he said repeatedly. 'If I had stayed instead of goin' on that run. I should have been here for her.'

'There's nothin' you could ha' done,' Isabella reassured him quietly but in vain.

'Aye, there is,' he replied angrily. 'I'd have got the doctor an' the midwife here. If I'd had to pick 'em up an' bring 'em by the scruff o' their necks an' the seat o' their pants they would have been here! If I ever see that woman again I'll get her by her scrawny throat an' strangle her!'

Walking to the church on the morning of the funeral, Isabella followed behind Joseph and the rest of the family, with the new baby warmly bound to her. She watched Joseph, and worried about the new, defeated sag to his shoulders and the sorrow and anger burning in his depths, which gave him the hideous strength to drag the sled, unaided.

During the service, Joseph stood like a statue, showing no emotion, but as the box was lowered into the grave his resolve crumbled and he collapsed to his knees in tears.

With a sigh of relief, Isabella moved to his side, placing a comforting hand on his shoulder. For a long time afterward they all knelt in prayer beside the grave, Joseph huddled and shrunken looking.

'Can we go home now?' Sarah had been alternating between picking daisies and rolling, giggling, down the steeply sloping churchyard.

Once or twice Joseph had glanced at her, registering slight irritation, then he had bowed his head again.

Now she was starting to feel the autumn chill creep through her clothing and was growing impatient to leave.

Isabella looked up, smiling tremulously. 'Yes, love. We will.'

'Come, Joseph, we must go home,' she said gently. ''Tis getting' cold for the childher, an' it looks as if it might soon rain.'

Slowly, it seemed, he became aware of her plucking at his sleeve. He moved his head to look down at her, his eyes empty of recognition.

'We must go home. Look at the rain clouds gatherin'. There's the childher to think o'. No sense in havin' them soaked. An' this new one will need feeding soon.' She looked down at the tiny scrap nestled closely against her and starting to stir.

The meaning of her words seemed to suddenly penetrate and Joseph started, as if waking from a deep slumber.

'Oh, yes. Yes. Of course. The childher.' He scrambled to his feet and, putting an arm around Isabella's shoulder, started to move away. Several times he looked back, even after they were well along the road, walking almost sideways, reluctant to leave his Catharine.

Almost, thought Isabella, as though he felt that if he stayed long enough, she would come back to life. She sighed sadly.

'I'm tired. Carry me, Daddy?' Sarah looked hopefully up at Joseph, adding 'Please?' when he seemed to pay no attention.

Lost in his own world of misery, he did not hear her. All words seemed to come from a long distance off now and took a long time to penetrate his consciousness.

'Here I'll carry you.' Daniel swung the grass-stained toddler to his shoulders, glad to be of some use at last.

Ever since that awful night when he had come home and learned of the tragedy, he had felt helpless. Desperately he had wanted to help Joseph, first to make the box, then to assist in pulling it to the church. But Joseph had pushed him gently aside, determined to manage everything alone. It seemed to Daniel that his friend regarded it, almost, as some sort of penance he had to pay for not being there when he was needed. As though he felt, somehow, that he alone was responsible for Catharine's death.

Many times Daniel tried to show his friendship, to let Joseph know that he cared, but Joseph looked at him, as if at a stranger. He could not think what he might have done wrong, only knowing that Joseph had brushed him out of his life as though he did not belong there. Now, carrying Sarah made him feel he was pulling his weight in some small way.

Agnes had a pot of broth boiling and ready to serve. When she saw them all straggling up the steps, shivering with a combination of cold and shocked nerves, she called them in.

'You won't want to be makin' a meal now, Isabella,' she said kindly. Would you all care to come in an' eat wi' us? 'Tis only broth,' she added almost apologetically.

Isabella looked at Joseph. It was his decision. After a long moment, he nodded and they all trooped into the warmth of Agnes' home and embrace.

Afterward they went home, Joseph slumping immediately into the chair by the fire, staring unblinkingly into the flames.

Isabella bustled to prepare Sarah for bed and to feed the new baby, yet again, and get her settled.

Daniel sat in the corner, absently scratching behind the goat's ear wondering where he fitted in now. Finally, he stood up.

'I think I'll take a walk up to the Brow,' he said, heading for the door.

Isabella looked up questioningly. She had sensed a change in Daniel since Catharine's passing. Not just the sadness they were all feeling. Yes, that too. But more. She knew him almost as well as she did herself and she could sense another feeling in him, running deeper than just the general distress.

'I'll come wi' you.' She stood up, reaching for her cloak

Daniel stopped with his hand on the latch, turning. His face lit in a smile. The first smile she had seen from him since Catharine's passing.

'That would be nice.' He held out his hand to her.

They stepped from the candlelit room into the early autumn evening. The street was still dusky with the lingering dregs of afternoon, so they did not have to pause in the gloom of the alley for night vision to adjust.

They strolled in silence to the end of the street, then turned up a narrow stairway. The stone steps were damp and from somewhere nearby came the steady slap of dripping water.

'There must've been a shower,' Isabella said quietly, and Daniel absently nodded his agreement.

They toiled on upwards without speaking again, wading through the wet grass of Shaw's Brow, the tangle of gorse catching at their clothes. Then on up to the top of the hill, from where they could watch out over Douglas Bay and all the sea to the east.

Many long minutes they stood, with their fingers strongly entwined, gazing down on the mist that was forming over the water, dimming the sparkle of the moonlight on the wave-caps.

A nearby stand of trees rustled in the wind, flinging moisture, slapping it noisily to the ground.

Birds sang sweetly, safely folded within brown branches and autumn leaves. Apart from that, there was no sound to be heard, save the rustle and drip of the soaked foliage.

'What is it that's troublin' you?' Isabella asked, at last, her voice quiet, concerned.

Daniel looked down at her, puzzled. 'Troublin' me?'

'Aye. An' don't tell me it's nothin'. I know you well enough by now.' She looked up at him, but with what little light there was at his back, his face was in deep shadow and she was unable to see his expression.

'I'm upset over Catharine. We all are.'

Isabella shook her head. 'No 'tis more than jus' that. I'd like it if you would tell me. Maybe I could help. Is there trouble wi' a girl perhaps?'

Daniel looked down, laughing a little harshly. 'A girl? No! No girl. I wish that's all it was.'

Isabella felt a rush of relief sweep over her. Unreasonable relief, she thought but did not know why she should feel it.

'Well, what then? What is it that's making you so unhappy?'

Daniel heaved a sudden great sigh. 'I don't know what to do,' he confided. 'I feel Joseph no longer wants me here. Do you think I should leave?' He stopped then, his breathing hard and irregular.

Isabella looked up, shaken. 'Leave? No, you can't leave. You mustn't! We need you.'

Daniel sighed and shrugged.

'What makes you feel this way?'

'Well, we no longer go to sea. We don't even work on the boat. When I asked Joseph if I could go down to check and clean the *Louisa* he became quite angry an' forbade me to go near her. I wonder if perhaps he blames me because I persuaded him to go on the run the day Catharine died. I think he only went because I was so keen. This is Joseph's house, Isabella. If he doesn't want me here then I cannot stay.' His voice carried a peculiar note — of fear, perhaps — as abruptly the realisation came that he had no idea of where he might be headed.

Isabella squeezed his hand. 'He wants you. Of course he does. He loves you like a son. But he is hurtin' jus' now, an' grievin' an' in shock. He isn't really thinkin' right jus' yet, but now Catharine's bin put to rest he'll start to get his mind sorted out. 'Tis not you he blames, but himself for leavin' her at such a time. He has been sufferin' greatly from remorse an' shame. I'll talk to him later, when I think the time is right. But don't leave, I know he wouldn't want you to. *I* don't want you to!'

With a shudder, Isabella realised how empty her life would be without Daniel. There were the children, an' Joseph, of course. She loved them all dearly. But Daniel was special, He was half of a rare partnership, a real part of herself. If he were to leave, it would be like having her body torn in two, leaving a gap in her life that she knew, could never be filled. Not even by all the rest of them put together.

'I could not stay here without you,' she said shakily. 'An' I cannot leave, because I promised Catharine.'

Daniel, a man now, and grown tall, looked down on this girl he had long thought he regarded as a sister, and knew he could never leave her. Suddenly he saw her in a new light altogether. As she looked up at him, her blue eyes wide with fear, eyes which were clouded now like the sky on the dawn of a stormy day, he realised she was no longer a child. He became aware, for the first time, that she had changed, without him ever noticing, into a woman.

It started to rain, but standing thoughtfully in companionable silence, neither seemed to notice.

Daniel stood facing southward, watching the shredded clouds, silhouetted against the moonlight, tumbling, billowing, blown across the sky by the high winds aloft. He felt the strong gusts, chill and damp, plucking at their cloaks, shivering the lines of tall trees.

'I think we should go home.' Isabella said quietly. 'It will help no one if we both catch pneumonia. I'll talk with Joseph, if it will help set your mind at rest. Though I'm sure you ha' nothin' to fear.' The face she turned up towards him had little rivulets of water running down it from her hair.

'Aye.' He nodded, realising, for the first time, how heavy the rain had become.

They started down the hill, sliding unsteadily on the wet grass, Isabella a few paces ahead. Watching her move, Daniel became aware that she was now developed where a lass ought to, her buttocks rounded under her skirts and her breasts already straining at the bodice of her frock. He had sudden thoughts and feelings towards her that were not brotherly, and he knew with a shock he would never regard her in quite the same way again.

When they arrived home Joseph was still as they had left him, in his chair, staring absently into the flames. The other children had put themselves to bed and all appeared to be sleeping.

Isabella watched thoughtfully for a while, then crossing to Joseph, she knelt on the floor at his feet, taking his hands in hers.

'There is something we have to discuss. A decision we have to make.' She looked searchingly into his dead eyes,

'A decision?'

'Aye? I was talkin' to the minister today, an' he asked me the name of the new baby girl.'

'The new baby? Oh, yes. Her. I hadn't thought about a name.' He looked towards the crib.

'Aye. We must give her a name.'

Joseph looked lost. For a while he just stared at the tiny bundle, then he shrugged helplessly, 'I dunno,' he said finally. 'What do you call her?'

Isabella smiled. 'Baby. But we can't go on calling her that forever. We certainly can't christen her Baby.'

'No. That we can't,' Joseph agreed, then he shrugged again and returned to staring into the fire.

'I — I thought . . .' Isabella started tentatively. 'Well, I wondered if might call her Catharine?'

Joseph was still for a moment, and at first Isabella thought he hadn't heard her. Then slowly his face took on a different expression, he did not answer immediately, but walked away from her, and from the light. At first she thought he was angry with her, but then he turned to look at her and, for the first time in days, she thought she saw a flicker of life in his eyes.

'Catharine? Yes! Catharine. She would have liked that. We'll christen her that, but we'll call her Cathy — so there'll be a difference.'

'Cathy'. Isabella's heart leapt. Joseph was coming back. She was sure of it. His mind was working again. 'Yes, Cathy,' she said. 'That would be nice.'

Joseph studied her cautiously for a while. 'Are you goin' to manage all right? Wi' all these childher, I mean?'

Isabella gasped with a sudden thrill of excitement that ran through her. Joseph was thinking again. Coming alive. Taking an interest.

'Oh yes. Easily. There's only really Sarah an' Cathy who need a lot o' lookin' after. The others will all be able to help me a bit. Please don't worry about me Joseph. But there is something else worryin' me a bit I would like to talk to you about.'

'Aye lass?'

'Tis' Daniel. He's concerned what his future will be.'

Joseph frowned blankly. 'I don't understand.'

'Tis jus' that you haven't been near the *Louisa* for a while an' get angry wi' Daniel when he wants to. He needs to work, I think, an' to keep his mind busy. He seems to feel you're against him for some reason, an' I think he's scared you won't want him aroun' now.'

'Not want him around?' Joseph looked incredulous. 'Not want him around?' He repeated. Shaking his head, he looked over to the corner, where Daniel sat uncomfortably trying to look as though he wasn't listening.

Joseph silently studied him for a few moments, then suddenly he roared, 'Come here boy!'

Daniel started, his head shooting up, turning to meet Joseph's eye.

Straightening, he strode across the room to stand before the other man.

'Not want you, boy!? Did you really think that?'

Daniel shifted uncomfortably. 'I…I didn't know.'

'You could've asked. Did you not think o' askin'?' Joseph looked hurt.

'Well — I…It's jus' you always seemed so angry wi' me whenever I tried to talk to you. I thought maybe you blamed me for you not bein' here when . . . Well, it was me what talked you into goin' on that run out to the *Mermaid*. So I thought maybe you felt me responsible for — for Catharine. Thought my bein' here brought unhappy memories.'

Joseph was speechless, he stood looking into Daniel's odd, scared eyes, saw the boy was trembling. Shaking his head, he sighed.

'Oh — lad — you're my son. I've all'us looked on you as a son. An' I allus will. I'm sorry I pushed you aside, lad, I didn't mean to. I've been so wrapped up in my own misery an' gloom I've had no time to spare a thought for anyone else. I know I've been harsh wi' you, but it's not because I don't care for you.'

Daniel heaved a sigh of relief and managed a tentative smile.

'You're a good lad. I should have let you help more wi' — well, wi' everythin'. I realise that now. This will always be your home, Daniel at least for as long as you want it to be. Don't ever be in any doubt about that again.' Abruptly he threw his arms around Daniel, gave him a huge bear hug, then held him at arms length again.

Daniel's face glowed with pleasure and relief. 'When will we start work again?' he asked tentatively.

Joseph laughed suddenly — a welcome sound the children had begun to think they would never hear again.

'Tomorrow, boy, since you seem so keen, we'll go an' scrub the ship out an' check all the tack. Then we'll see if we can get hold o' Charles Drinkwater an' see if there's any work he can put our way.'

Isabella smiled up at them both, relieved they had worked out whatever differences they may have had, however imaginary. Already she could see how Joseph had come alive again with the thought of getting back to sea.

Just the same, she felt a niggling doubt, and could understand the fear Catharine had always held of this smuggling game!

Chapter 17

Daniel was in a fever of excitement the following morning. Back, at last to his beloved *Louisa*. To the harbour, the bustle of activity and excitement and, most of all, to the thrill of just being busy again.

Joseph too, Isabella noticed, had a spring in his step again and there was an undercurrent of excitement in the home that had been absent for a long time and seemed, now, to lift the whole family.

For the first time they were talking normally, instead of in the muted tones they had all seemed to instinctively adopt. There was animation in the faces again and even one or two muffled laughs during breakfast.

It was true, she thought suddenly, the saying about time healing. The wound in her family had seemed so deep and so painful, she had been afraid it would never heal. Yet here they were, only a week after Catharine's death, starting to put their pain behind them and behave like ordinary people again. Isabella knew they would never forget; could never forget; nor would they want to. Catharine had been too good a person, too well-loved and would have an important part in their thoughts and hearts forever.

Still, though, it pleased her to see them putting their lives back together as quickly and as well as they seemed to be. It would have pleased Catharine to see it, Isabella thought. She would have been proud of their strength. Catherine would have wanted her family to be happy, not to be forever mourning.

When the family had all been fed, the three older children packed off to school and the menfolk off to the harbour, Isabella settled down to feed Cathy. Looking towards heaven she said, 'I promise, Catharine, I'll always keep Sarah's memory of you alive. An' someday, when Cathy is old enough, I'll tell her about you an' her brother who died. She'll grow up knowing you both as if you were here.'

The *Louisa* lay exactly as she had been left after the trip out to the *Mermaid*. Seeing her at first, Daniel's heart gave a lurch of dismay and his stomach turned somersaults as the memory of that dreadful day returned. He remembered what a painfully long time it had taken to sail back to Douglas, there being almost no wind for the best part of the journey.

Then when they did dock, he had wanted to jump ashore and race straight home, but he had felt the *Louisa* to be his responsibility, so he had stayed to help secure her. That activity, that day had seemed to take forever, for all the while he worked he had held this terrible premonition of doom.

As soon as he had seen the *Louisa* securely tied up and the hatches battened down, he had raced home, bounding up all the steep steps two at a time. Then he had rounded the corner at the top and, seeing James sitting, weeping, on the doorstep had known the worst straight away.

'Are you all right, Daniel?'

Suddenly he became aware that Joseph was speaking to him.

He looked up, startled. 'Sorry. I was thinkin' o' somethin'. Off in a world o' my own.'

Joseph's face softened and he laid a hand on the boys shoulder. 'Aye. I know. But it doesn't do to dwell on things. It only makes a man bitter an' twisted. This world is for the livin' an' we've got to get on wi' our lives an' make the most o' them. Like Isabella's doin'.

Like she has been doin' ever since Catharine . . . ever since she died. The girl's taken over an' coped wi' it all better than most grown-ups could ha' done.'

'Aye. She's a grand lass!' Daniel said feelingly.

'Aye.' Joseph agreed. 'More than just grand. Next to me, she was closer to Catharine than any, yet she handled it the best o' the lot o' us. An' she was the one what had to sit there watchin' her mother die. Now look at her, fourteen years old an' mother to all these childher. An' she hasn't said one word o' complaint.'

'We must all do the best we can to make her lot as easy as possible,' Daniel suggested, and Joseph nodded his agreement.

'I think what Catharine would like most of all would for me to buy Isabella that big house by the harbour I was always promisin'.'

'Aye.' Daniel said, smiling, 'The cottage is gettin' a mite crowded' wi' eight o' us an' a goat in only one room.'

'Soon then, Daniel. That's what we must work for. We must take on as much work as we can to get the money to buy the big house as soon as it can be managed.'

A week of neglect had done the *Louisa* no good at all. Some of the rigging, made fast in too much of a hurry, had come loose in the wind there had since been. Flapping unrestricted, it was in a terrible tangle which took Daniel a long time to sort out.

A flock of seagulls, obviously taking the boat to be abandoned, had moved in, perching on every available strut, covering the boat, in white, grey and yellow lime.

Daniel groaned when he saw it. 'It will take forever to clean this lot.'

Joseph looked around, shaking his head resignedly. 'Well, it has to be done, so I guess the sooner we start, the sooner it will be finished. Find two brushes, lad, an' I'll gi' you a hand wi' it.'

It was well on towards supper-time before they stood, side by side, man and man, at the bows, surveying their handiwork.

'Well, doesn't she look good,' Joseph said proudly. 'Almost like a new boat. Now I think we'd best get up the hill afore Isabella starts to fear we've gone out on a mission.'

The following morning Charles Drinkwater came hurrying towards them when they arrived at the harbour.

'I've been watching for you from the hotel, Joseph.' He started abruptly, as soon as he was close enough.

'Oh, Aye? What's up?'

'Nothing. Nothing at all wrong. It's just that I heard from Francis Clague that he'd seen you cleaning the boat yesterday. Said he thought you might be readying it for sea.'

'Aye. That's exactly right. Indeed I am.'

'So you're back in business then?'

Joseph nodded.

'Good! Good!' Charles sighed heartily. 'Richard Curphey has been making my runs while you've been resting. Glad to have the work too, I shouldn't wonder, but I don't like using him. I really don't.'

'Why? What's he been up to?' Joseph frowned.

'Nothing I can prove, but I just don't trust him. He's too greedy for my liking, an' I'm quite certain he pilfers from his cargoes.'

Joseph raised his eyebrows. He'd heard this sort of claim before, but the man seemed too clever to be caught.

'Are you sure?'

'Sure as I can be without actually catching him at it. It's my reckoning, he runs some spirits off each keg and fills it up with water. And I've had complaints about tobacco he's delivered for me too. More weed in it than tobacco! I've never had complaints like that when you've been shipping for me.'

Joseph shook his head, pulling a face. 'Well, we'll be glad o' all the work you can give us, for we're savin' hard. Catharine wanted her children to grow up in a nice house, an' so they shall.'

'Good!' Charles thumped Joseph's back heartily, his face covered in a smug smile. 'I'll put as much work your way as I can, an' put the word around there's a good honest man looking for cargoes.'

Daniel allowed himself a quiet smile, behind the men's backs, at the thought of an honest smuggler. He doubted if the British Crown would agree too strongly with that description.

'I've got a run for you tonight, if you can take it,' Charles said hopefully.

'Aye.' Joseph nodded enthusiastically. 'Tonight will be fine. Where's it bound for?'

'Whitehaven. Tea an' silks mostly, but a few barrels of brandy too.'

'Fine. We'll see you this evenin' then.'

To Daniel, the rest of the day, spent checking sails and rigging, preparing the boat for its night-time sojourn, seemed interminably long.

After dinner, Isabella dressed Sarah up warmly, bound Cathy to her chest and took them for a walk up to Shaw's Brow and beyond. It was one of her favourite spots, the little copse of tall beech trees. From there, it seemed, the whole world was visible.

The day was clear and as she stood, drinking in the autumn sun, she looked out over the bay, with the sinister shape of Conister Rock all too close to the harbour mouth.

The sun was high, well advanced in its quotidian trek across the sky. Screwing up her eyes she peered out beyond the bay. So perfect was the day that she could see the English coast so clearly that she felt as if she could almost reach out and touch it.

Cathy snuggled cosily against her, sleeping soundly, while Sarah ran around, chasing birds and rabbits, giggling high-spiritedly. It was strange, Isabella thought, how resilient children were. Sarah had shown almost no sign of being upset about her mother's death — had hardly seemed to grieve at all. But then, she supposed, the toddler was likely too young to understand the meaning of death.

The trees behind her on the hill had shed their leaves, spreading a golden carpet across the countryside. High in their bare branches, small birds sang happy songs, to tell that all was well in their world.

Sarah ran around giggling, rolling amongst the damp leaves, picking up armfuls and throwing them in the air, laughing and hugging herself with joy as they fell to earth again.

Watching, Isabella found herself laughing with and at her. The baby stirred against her, smiling contentedly.

In the harbour, she could make out the *Louisa* and the two figures moving about, busy at something. Joseph was easy to recognise because of his size, and she could only guess that the other one must be Daniel. After a while, she saw them move together on the deck, as though holding a conversation, then they left the boat and started to walk along the harbour towards the foot of the hill.

'Sarah. 'Tis time to go home,' she called.

Sarah, trying to creep up on a rabbit, turned, pouting. 'No, Ishbel, I wanna to stay here.'

'Not now. Daddy an' Daniel are comin' home, so we must go an' get supper for them.'

Sarah glared stubbornly for a moment, then stamped her foot and did as she was bade.

'Can we come back an' play here again tomorrow?' she asked, her large grey eyes pleading.

'We'll have to wait an see what the weather's like. If it's dry I promise we'll come.'

Sarah nodded her acceptance and ran down the slope ahead of Isabella.

They had a strange sort of meal, with Sarah excited and squealing about the lovely play she'd had; Daniel and Joseph simmering with excitement of a different kind, heads together, talking and planning the night ahead.

'You'll have to keep your wits about you every moment!' Joseph said emphatically. "Tis not at all like the bumboat run out to the Point of Ayre. This time we're goin' out o' Manx waters an' into the jurisdiction of the English Customs. They can chase us, catch us, sink us, whatever they like, for we'll be in their waters. If they were to capture us, we'd be tried in their courts, answer to their laws an' ha' to take whatever punishment they cared to inflict on us. If we were imprisoned it would be in England, not on the island.'

Daniel nodded his head at every point Joseph made. 'We won't be caught,' he said confidently.

'Our biggest advantage,' Joseph continued, 'Is that *Louisa* has a much shallower draught than the Customs' cutters. So if they spot us, an' give chase, we can run into shallow water an' hope to lose them that way, then wait for some clouds an' slip away under cover o' darkness.'

'Will it be cloudy tonight, do you think?'

Joseph looked out of the small square of window, peering up at the early evening sky. There was very little blue to be seen, just an occasional slash peeping out from between the clouds.

'Aye. More cloudy than anythin'. It should be a good night for it if the wind doesn't strengthen too much more. The most important thing, tonight, will be for you to keep your eyes well peeled — an' your ears. You're the youngest amongst us an' wi' the best sight an' hearin', so we'll leave that up to you. Look an listen — them's your keywords. Anythin' that don't look or sound quite right, you let me know.'

Isabella listened in growing horror. Never before had she realised what a lot was involved, what a dangerous game they were playing, because the discussion the men were having now was not one that had been held in the cottage in the past. Now she was becoming aware of the full implications, she could better understand Catharine's fears when Joseph was away. And why she had been so much against Daniel joining him in his escapades.

When they donned their coats at dusk, she watched from the

door until they were lost from sight around the corner, then she went indoors and asked the three older children to pray with her for their safe return.

Joseph had sent word to Phillip and William in the afternoon and both were there waiting at the boat.

'We've to pick the cargo up below the hotel,' Joseph told them quietly, and the men nodded.

The *Louisa* was untied and slipped quietly along the quay, to tie up again by the tunnel to the cellars of the hotel. Charles Drinkwater was waiting in the vault, the cargo they were to carry carefully separated from the rest of the contraband hidden there.

'Good to have you back workin' for me, Joseph,' he said enthusiastically when he saw them coming.

'Nice to be back,' Joseph agreed. ''Tis good to be gettin' my life back in order.'

'Yes. Yes, quite. I don't mind telling you it will be a relief to send off a cargo and know it won't be tampered with.'

Joseph nodded. 'Aye, well, Richard is only cuttin' his own throat in the long run, 'cos it'll get that no one will gi' him any work. Where's this for? Usual place is it?'

'No. We had to change the drop-off point, for the Customs were onto the other. Last time we tried to deliver there, there was a cutter waiting as close to shore as it could get, and there were soldiers on the shore. My customer's men were nearly captured and the cargo had to be dumped overboard.'

'That's poor. So where do we drop it now, an' what's the drill?'

'Stay well out past St Bees Head and go on round towards Whitehaven. Be there in plenty of time and drop anchor about a mile short of Whitehaven. At two of the clock, there will be a beacon lit on the hillside. If you head straight to it my customer's men will be on beach to meet you.'

'An' the Customs? What chance o' them showin' up?

'Tis too shallow there. They can't get near. So as long as they don't catch you before you unload you'll be safe.'

Joseph nodded approvingly. 'Sounds well organised.'

It took only half an hour to load the *Louisa*, and not many more to make sure the cargo was made fast and the hatches battened down.

Daniel felt his stomach churning in a mixture of excitement and apprehension. It was with a sigh of relief that he cast off the lines, jumped aboard and felt the boat moving under him. The anchor chains rattled as William painstakingly turned the capstan, dripping water on the deck. The first sail unfurled to capture the light September breeze in its flapping canvas.

'Safe journey,' Charles Drinkwater called from the shore. 'And if you run into trouble on the way there, jettison the cargo. 'Tis not worth being arrested for.'

Joseph raised his right hand in recognition, then turned to the task before him.

Daniel felt a nervousness new to him, but as he stood at the bows, the familiar tilt of the deck under his feet, he thrilled to the adventure ahead. As they made their way through the harbour mouth, he looked back towards Douglas, looking for the scattering of tiny cottages high on the hill. But a sea mist had crept in with the evening, shrouding the town in a veil of grey.

It was eerily silent, the mist muffling the sounds of the sea. Conister Rock came at them like a huge grey ghost, then they had slipped safely past and were heading out to sea. Away from shore the mist cleared and the moon shone through an occasional break in the clouds.

Turning his face, and then his body until he was facing north-east, Daniel's spine tingled to the enormous, glowing expanse of the sea. It was almost as though they were the only ones alive in a shimmering wet world.

William unfurled the mainsail and there came a powerful lurch as it caught the wind and the vessel leapt into the waves.

Daniel turned slowly to gaze lovingly at the Louisa, his eyes exploring the high prow and the sweep of her beam, all the way to where William stood, ever watchful and alert at the helm. He strode along the smooth deck, running cold fingers along the top of the low cabin, to stand by the main mast. In his eyes she was the most beautiful boat ever built.

Joseph came to stand beside him, a huge hand laid gently on his shoulder. 'This is the life, is it not, boy?'

Daniel nodded, his eyes misty. 'Aye, indeed it is.'

His eyes roved constantly, alert for any shadow of movement that could herald the presence of another vessel. For this moment in time, the events of the recent past dimmed mercifully. The man was at one with his boat.

'This is a cold, thankless job, boy. I'll take over from you for a while. Go below for a few minutes. Give your eyes a break an get warmed up a bit.' Joseph gave him a gentle shove towards the cabin.

Daniel nodded, thankful for a respite. Tucking his hands under his arms, he turned away. With a final glance at the fastness of the rigging he went below.

Philip was sitting on the bunk and looked up, smiling, as he entered. A dim lamp, hanging from a beam in the cabin's low ceiling, had been lit. Swinging with the ship's motion, it sent grotesque shadows fleeing across the bulkheads.

'How're you, feelin' boy?' Philip asked, the flame of the swinging lamp reflecting in his eyes, making them colourless, glittering like frosted glass.

Daniel shrugged, grimacing. 'If I'm to be right honest, I'm a little scared. But excited, too. I'm enjoyin' the thrill o' it.'

'Good. I'm glad you're honest. You know you've got to be a bit scared. If you're not you get careless. 'Tis the fearless, cocky ones what gets caught.'

'Are you scared?'

'Aye. Every time — excited, too. You don't never get used to it. Now I'd better get back on deck.' Philip rose to leave. On the threshold, he stopped and turned. ''Tis good to have you aboard, boy. You'll make a worthwhile addition to the crew I'm sure.' He touched a finger to his hand-knitted cap, then was gone.

Outside, the wind was rising, plucking at the rigging in mournful melody. Daniel stayed below only until the cold stiffness had gone from his fingers, then he went back to resume his post as lookout.

'We've rounded Bees' Head an' gettin' closer inshore, so keep a keener eye than ever now.' Joseph came close behind him to speak quietly in his ear.

The *Louisa* rolled as they rounded the headland, sailing into a different current, then soon settled.

Daniel stood at the bows, staring into the blackness. The night, he thought, was an expert shroud, shutting out everything. He saw nothing, nor heard anything bar the shushing of the sea sweeping past the hull.

Joseph turned the *Louisa* towards shore and William lowered the sail. The anchor was a-cockbill at the cathead, just ready for when they hove to. Philip stood ready to raise the drogue to keep the bows into the wind.

Suddenly the moon broke from its cloud cover for a moment and, peering uneasily to seaward, Daniel had a fleeting impression of another vessel, far in the distance. Catching Philip's arm, he pointed.

'I'm not sure, but 1 think I saw something — just for a second. Over there.'

Philip froze, following Daniel's gaze. 'Did you see what it was?'

Daniel shook his head, 'I'm not even certain I saw anything.'

Joseph and William, sensing something amiss, had stopped work and now all four men stared into the velvety blackness

195

Chapter 18

The four men stood like statues, motionless, save for the swaying movements their bodies made to counter the heaving of the deck. Patiently, tensely, they waited for the next rent in the clouds to light the sea. Not one of them held any doubt there was a vessel of some sort out there.

At last, the moon broke free, beaming down upon the world to light the sea with luminescent jewels. Peering past this beauty the four men, as one, saw the other vessel and four arms rose simultaneously to point.

There was total silence for a moment, then Philip let his breath out in a long hiss, saying thankfully, "Tis nothin' lad. Jus' a small schooner. A merchantman — out o' Whitehaven most likely'

Everyone relaxed and the atmosphere on board became almost jovial, though not one set of eyes ceased its vigilant roving. The moon stayed free for quite some time and they were able to watch the schooner until it sank from view beyond the horizon.

'There 'tis!' William's voice came in a sibilant whisper now, controlled, but excited. He was standing by the starboard rail peering eagerly towards the shore.

The others turned and saw the beacon, burning brightly, apparently hovering in the sky; like a warning bolt from the Gods.

'Good!' Joseph's voice pitched higher with the release of tension. 'Let's get in there an' get the job done as quickly as possible.'

The *Louisa* immediately bustled with activity. The anchor weighed, sails raised and she set course, cautiously, in a direct line towards the beacon.

In no time, it seemed, there was a boat alongside, a small lighter securely tied and scraping up and down the side of the *Louisa* with a sound like the low rumble of distant thunder.

There followed about half an hour of feverish bustle, during which the cargo was expertly transferred to the lighter.

'Are we near finished?' asked one of the Englishmen after a while.

Joseph glanced back towards the hatch. 'Not much more to go,' he called, raising his voice over the crying of the wind.

Finally the last of the contraband was safely stowed in the lighter, the crew took to their oars and with a quick wave of their hands they were bending their backs, digging water. Then breaking a rip, they rode atop a swell and vanished into the night from whence they had come.

Joseph stood for a few moments, watching until they were gone from sight then, turning, he placed a hand on Daniel's shoulder.

'That's a good job well done,' he said smugly. 'Now 'tis time for home.'

'Aye. It's bin a good night,' Daniel agreed enthusiastically. 'I never thought it would be this easy.'

Joseph laughed. 'Tisn't over yet. We've still to get home.' The clouds had broken up well now, and the moon had taken over the sky.

Daniel stood for a few moments, the invigorating, briny breeze, mixed with spray from the sea, fanning his cheeks while he studied the heavens. In one place he noticed, with awe, a bridge of light which was formed by the vast number of stars within its width. The milky way, he thought Joseph had said was its name.

The anchor chain rattled up through the hawsehole, the capstan groaning all the way, the mainsail was hauled aloft and the bows set towards the west.

The feeling on board was of relief and exaltation. Joseph began to sing a bawdy sea-shanty and quickly the rest joined in, Philip giving Daniel a knowing wink.

Before long the moon set behind jagged clouds, the sky in the east began to lighten. Soon the grey cumulus took on a shade of pale saffron as the sun lifted itself from the sea and began to march up the sky, driving out the night and trumpeting a new day.

Daniel heaved a deep sigh of satisfaction, then shrugged and busied himself with the rigging, tightening knots which had loosened during the night, and checking sails. In the pale wash of first light, the sky appeared as a feathered shell of mother-of-pearl.

Above them a flock of gulls, flying high, moved swiftly southward before the oncoming winds.

With the morning growing older, the Louisa and her crew sped through the new day, the light quickening about them like molten metal, the winds of autumn whipping at their faces.

Suddenly Daniel saw a mast — no more — but clearly visible, standing above the horizon.

'Look!' he yelled jumping to his feet, pointing.

'Check the boat quickly, Philip. Make sure there are no signs o' any contraband.' Joseph's voice was tight.

By the time this task was carried out, the other vessel had come fully into view and was clearly a Customs' cruiser.

Daniel felt a crawling in his scalp and his spine tingled.

'Are we within the three miles o' the Island?' he asked dryly.

William looked solemn. 'No, lad, but there's nothin' to fear. They can't arrest us for havin' an empty boat. They dare not make one wrong move towards us after the fate met by George Dow.'

Daniel nodded and sighed, wishing he could feel as confident as his friend sounded. It was fourteen years, almost, since Captain Dow's clash with Manx law, but still, it was talked and laughed about amongst the smuggling fraternity.

The Customs' vessel closed with terrifying swiftness, leaving Daniel weak in the knees, holding the main mast for support. He felt it tremble with every gust that touched it.

'Mornin',' Joseph said conversationally, catching the line the Englishmen threw as they came abreast.

'What cargo are you carryin?' the cruiser's master called over.

'None.' Joseph replied honestly. 'We've jus' bin to Whitehaven wi' a catch o' fish.'

'Hold fast. We're coming aboard!'

Eight of the King's best men, all well armed, leapt aboard the *Louisa*.

Daniel watched, wide eyed and trembling, from his position by the mast.

'I want you all together on the stern. How many are there below.' The Master looked to Joseph, obviously picking him to be captain of the *Louisa*.

'None below. There are only the four o' us,' Joseph replied gruffly.

The man glared suspiciously at him, then set two men, pistols armed and cocked, to guard the Manxmen, while five more were sent to search the hold and cabin.

Daniel stood, spellbound, watching, fear haunting his eyes, making them glassy and bulging, until the last man vanished below, the hatch slamming shut behind him. Then, his eyes glued to the deck, he listened to the creaking and moaning of joints under stress. He heard the incredible singing of the rigging in the wind as its trembling matched his.

Joseph's hand was firmly on Daniel's elbow and he leaned behind the boy to whisper, 'Don't be frightened, lad. There's nothin' they can find.'

Daniel smiled nervously, turning his head slightly, and an exciseman twitched his pistol towards him.

After an interminable period, a lifetime it seemed, the hatch swung open again and the searchers returned from below, blinking in the sudden, blinding sunshine. The last on deck looked to his Master, dejected acceptance on his face, and shook his head.

In answer to a quick jerk of their Master's head, they all scrambled back on board their own vessel.

I'll remember you!' was all the Master said before he followed them.

'Aye. An' I you!' Joseph muttered as he watched the cruiser swing away to search for other prey.

Daniel drew a deep, trembling breath, releasing it slowly as a surge of relief spread through him. Like the first pull of wine, he thought, when an overwhelming sense of exhilaration warmed his chest and a new strength flowed into his rigid arms and neck.

After that, the rest of their journey was pleasant and uneventful. The sea remained peaceful, rolling the *Louisa* gently, for the most part, with only an occasional sudden gust of wind to disturb her complacency.

At the head of a gentle breeze, they sailed quietly down the east coast of the Isle of Man, the day so clear they could almost see the people on the shore well enough to wave to them.

The pier at Ramsey straggled out across the water to meet them, but they passed on by. Past Laxey with its scattering of cottages on the shore and fishing boats in the bay. On, southward under the threatening, lowering magnificence of the grey, eastern coast cliffs.

Daniel watched, in breathless delight, the sea wash against the cliffs, roll up then break in a flurry of foam, splintering the sun into a million shards of light.

Then suddenly they were rounding the headland at Onchan and there was a thrill and a quickening of his heart as Douglas hove into view.

The scare of their encounter with the Customs' men was quickly put to the back of Daniel's mind. But at the same time, he had become well aware that his new way of life, with its better prospects for the future, was also fraught with danger.

Douglas, when they arrived, in spite of its fishy smell and hordes of grubby, starving beggars, had never looked so sweet.

Charles Drinkwater, looking impatient, was waiting at the end of the wharf and followed the *Louisa* along as she moved to her berth. Then he stood watching for several minutes while the boat was secured. This done, Philip and William went off home, while Joseph and Daniel joined the merchant on the wharf.

'You're a fair while late. Did you have problems?' he asked anxiously.

'Nothin' too bad,' Joseph replied jovially. 'It all went well an' wi'out a worry until after we left Whitehaven. The cargo was delivered safely. But we ran into an excise vessel on the way home. They boarded us searched, tried to look tough, but of course they found nothin'.'

'Good. Good. One or two of the others who came in this morning said they'd seen a Customs' cruiser around, so I was a little concerned when you were late.'

'The men you have over in Whitehaven are good. Very efficient. They were on us almost before we saw them this mornin', an' had cargo transferred almost before we could blink.'

'Aye,' Charles agreed. 'They're a good lot. Of course, my son's the man in charge of that operation and he's very careful who he picks. Now, if you feel you can handle another run tonight, I've a cargo to go.'

Joseph looked searchingly at Daniel. 'What do you think, boy? you up to takin' another chance so soon?'

Daniel had the bit between his teeth, intoxicated by the thrill of chase, and could think of nothing he would rather do. He grinned, nodding enthusiastically.

'Oh, aye.' he said excitedly. 'An' it'll help get that house all the sooner.'

Joseph looked over Daniel's shoulder, nodding knowingly, winking at Charles. 'We'll take the job.'

'Good. Good.' Charles beamed.

'Same time, same place?'

'Aye. Similar cargo too. Same arrangements at the other end.'

'Fine. We'll see you this evenin' then.'

* * *

Isabella took Sarah up on the Brow again, as she had promised the previous day, to play in the sunshine. Whilst she frolicked amongst trees, stalking rabbits and kicking the fallen leaves, Isabella sat on a smooth rock, gazing out to sea and Cathy slept snuggled against her. Now and again the baby wriggled a little, screwing her face up as wind shifted inside her, then she relaxed and settled again. From time to time Isabella would see a vessel approaching and, straightening her shoulders, would peer for a better view. Then when it proved to be a false alarm she would relax, slumping over the baby again.

Looking down lovingly at the angelic, oval face Isabella felt her heart swell to overflowing with love for the tiny mite. What a dreadful injustice, she thought that Catharine had not been allowed to live long enough to know this child. There was something about her, Isabella fancied, something that made her special. But then, she thought, that was probably the way all mothers felt about their babies. The way Catharine must have felt about her older children.

The warm autumn sun had a euphoric effect, and Isabella had a sleepily amused sensation as she watched Sarah's happy play. It struck her suddenly that although she still felt, deeply, the loss of the only real mother she'd ever had, the pain was duller now, the sharp razor edged cut gone from her heart.

Sarah came towards her, walking carefully, her hands cupped. Every few steps she stopped to lift a couple of fingers and peep inside.

'Look, Ishbel. Look what I got.' She pressed close, holding her hands right under Isabella's nose.

'What is it? what have you got there?' Isabella looked down a trifle apprehensively at the tiny, slender fingers.

Two round little grey eyes gazed solemnly up into hers. Eyes so like Catharine's it made Isabella's heart lurch.

Sarah opened her hands and Isabella saw, clinging to one, a butterfly. It was a beautiful, brightly splashed creature, like a mad artist's palette. And it stayed on the tiny hand, making no effort to fly away, sensing the child would never harm it.

Such trust. Such love. Such gentleness. Isabella gazed down at the fragile, beautiful child, tears pressing, bulging, aching the back of her eyes.

Sarah held her hand aloft, seeing the sunshine through the fine wings, the breeze making them tremble. Then she blew gently and the creature leaned, clinging to her for a moment before it let go and fluttered away, brushing fearlessly against her cheek as it passed. Giggling the child put her hand to where the butterfly had touched her, and Isabella impulsively tightened her arm around her flimsy body.

Cathy, gently crushed, wriggled, screwed her face up, grumbled quietly for a moment, then went back to sleep.

Looking over Sarah's shoulder, Isabella's heart leapt joyfully. In the distance, at the north end of Douglas bay, she felt sure, was the sight she had been watching for all afternoon. It was too far away to be certain, but some inner sense left her in little doubt that the craft she saw was the *Louisa*.

Standing to gain a better view, she remained motionless, watching the boat's leisurely progress across the bay. The sparkling of the sun reflecting from the sea hurt Isabella's eyes, making them water and blurring her vision. The vessel was nearing Conister Rock before she could thrill to the certain knowledge it was the Louisa. To her relief, as the boat edged through the harbour-mouth, she could see four figures moving around.

A man waved from the end of the quay, then walked alongside as she moved to her berth. After a few minutes hustle on board, two of the men walked away and the other two, one definitely Joseph, stopped to talk on the wharf.

Collecting Sarah from her play, Isabella started down the hill at the same time as Joseph and Daniel were leaving Charles Drinkwater, arriving home only moments before them.

'Joseph.' Daniel clutched at his arm just before they reached the cottage.

'Yes?' Joseph turned to face him, eyebrows raised.

'I think it would be best if we didn't tell Isabella we had that bit o' trouble today.'

Joseph nodded. 'Quite right, boy. I didn't intend to. No need to give her any more worry than we ha' to. There's been a lot happened on past journeys that Catharine knew nothing about.'

So saying, he lifted the latch, swung open the door and was met by a human hurricane.

'Daddy, I had a butterfly!' Sarah squealed, exploding into Joseph's arms as he ducked through the doorway.

Catching her hurtling body, he swung her so high her heels almost scraped the roof.

'A butterfly?' he questioned.

'Yes. A real one. It came on my hand.'

'Where is it now, then?'

Sarah screwed her nose up. 'Oh! I blewed it an' it flied away. Swing me up again, Daddy, then I can feel like a butterfly.'

Joseph obliged and they all dissolved into fits of childish laughter

'Did all go well for the trip Across?' Isabella asked when everyone had settled down again and she was tending the supper.

'Aye.' Joseph and Daniel said together, exchanging conspiratorial looks behind her back.

'You found no difficulties?'

'No! None!' Daniel said, a little too quickly.

Isabella turned sharply, frowning, holding his eyes, her look penetrating.

Joseph laughed. 'Except that he saw a schooner a merchantman — and almost threw a scare into us all. I'm goin' to have to teach him one boat from another.'

'I thought you already knew the difference? You've bin aroun' boats all your life.' She was still looking doubtful.

'Well, it was dark,' Daniel excused himself, his face red. 'I only caught a quick glimpse o' it in a flash o' moonlight.'

Isabella returned to her cooking pot and the man and boy exchanged relieved glances.

After supper Elizabeth sat on her father's bed, her nose buried in a book that Agnes had lent her. Isabella found it delightful that she had turned out to be such an avid reader, something she, herself, longed to be able to do.

James and Thomas were wrestling in a corner and Isabella remembered, with a smile, that that was what they had been doing the first time she had set eyes on them.

Sending Sarah away from where she played on the dirt floor at her feet, Isabella swung the heavy kettle from over the fire. Half filling a battered tin basin on the ledge with boiling water, she added some cool from the pail. After washing the remains of the potatoes and herring from the bowls, she returned them to their place on the shelf. This done, she warmed Cathy's milk and sat at the table to feed her. How glad she was now that Catharine had always insisted they keep a goat in the house. Joseph and Daniel sat before the fire, each leaning forward in eager, companionable conversation, their heads so close they almost touched. Isabella watched, enjoying the warmth of the family closeness.

Finally, the pair at the table nodded, then turned towards her, looking, she thought, a little guilty.

'We have to go out again tonight. You wont mind bein' alone wi' the childher again will you?' Joseph asked.

'Out? There?' Her stomach knotted.

'We ha' to take another cargo 'Across'.'

'Again? So soon?'

'Aye. Charles Drinkwater has a lot what needs deliverin'. An' we have need o' the work.'

Isabella nodded dumbly. When they left she watched them to the corner, then stepped back into the cottage, shaking her head sadly. Another night of worrying. Another day tomorrow. Drawing in her breath for a deep sigh, she thought, well I suppose this is what Catharine had to live with. This is the price I'll have to pay for being a smuggler's woman.

Chapter 19

While autumn and winter dragged wearily through, the family slowly recovered from the loss of Catharine. James and Thomas, though subdued and troublesome for a while, soon rallied and were as boisterous as ever.

Elizabeth, as always, kept her nose firmly buried in a book. Not so much so, though, that she didn't notice when Isabella was overtired and needed help with the two younger girls, or some of the more tedious household chores.

Indeed, as well as helping out herself, she often delegated to her two elder brothers. In fact, Isabella noticed, Elizabeth seemed to have easier success at getting work out of the boys than she did herself. Perhaps, she reflected sadly, because Elizabeth was *real* family and she, just a pretender.

Isabella herself soon adjusted to being in charge of the household. At first, it was trying and she felt herself overworked, especially while Cathy, so tiny at birth, and greedy, always hungry, was waking her every two hours for a feed. But as she grew, and demanded less frequent feeding, it became easier for Isabella to cope.

Joseph and Daniel, to her great concern, appeared to be taking on an awful lot of work. They seemed to be out almost every night, rarely sleeping for more than two or three hours at a stretch and

Isabella worried that tiredness would make them less observant of enemy craft at sea.

The boys, she felt, missed their father, for when he was home they were at school and almost never saw him.

For the first few weeks after Catharine's death, they were reasonably well behaved, but then resentment seemed to start and rapidly build. First James, then Thomas, decided he did not want to go to school and Isabella had the most awful battle every morning. Had it not been for Elizabeth scolding and hustling, often she felt she would not have moved them.

On the occasions Joseph was home, however, they behaved perfectly and scuttled off to school quite cheerfully.

'Please, can't you do less work?' she pleaded with Joseph often. 'The childher see nothin' o' you since they lost their mother. They need you here. Especially the boys, I think.'

'This won't go on much longer,' Joseph sighed every time. 'But we must keep at it for a while yet. We need the money.'

Isabella had no choice but to accept it, though not easily, and she would shake her head and turn away with a tear in her eye. Often she wondered what happened to all this extra money they made. Certainly the family's lifestyle did not seem to improve.

At first, Agnes came often to help and in spite of their age difference they soon became firm friends. Isabella was able to spill out her worries to her, because more and more, the boys became harder to control. James absolutely refused to do anything she bade and Thomas, following his lead, did likewise.

'I truly fear for them, Agnes,' she wept after a particularly unpleasant scene one morning. 'They seem so rebellious and resent me so much. Everythin' I do is wrong. Had it not been for Elizabeth, this mornin', threatenin' to tell their father, they would not have gone to school at all. They were refusin' absolutely to obey me.'

Agnes frowned crossly. She had always felt it too great a burden to be put on fourteen-year-old shoulders. Then for Joseph to be away so much! Really!

'This really is bad of Joseph,' she said angrily. '*His* children should be *his* responsibility. He has no right to stay out so much an' leave it all to you to deal with.'

'He says he has to. That we need the money.' Isabella said miserably 'But surely he has the sense to see his children need him. More now than ever. It is only months since they lost their mother. He should ha' been there for them then. They needed him here, with them, but instead he got this obsession about money an' went out chasin' it all the time.

'Are you livin' any better for all his work?'

Isabella shook her head, sobbing back a tear.

Then maybe Elizabeth is right an' their father should be told o' their behaviour.'

'Oh no! No! I don't want to make trouble for them with him. That would only serve to make them resent me more.'

'Not with the idea of making trouble. No, I didn't mean that. They are certainly unhappy about something, and unless Joseph knows what is going on it will never be dealt with.'

Isabella gnawed her bottom lip. 'I suppose you're right. But they would only think I was telling tales.'

'If you like, I'll have a talk with them, especially James as he seems to be the one at the back o' it. Sometimes 'tis easier to talk wi' someone from outside o' the family.'

'Oh, thank you, Agnes. You don't know how much it helps to have a shoulder to lean on. Someone to help me bear the burden. I know I cannot stand up to much more o' this.'

When Agnes left, Isabella felt much lighter of heart and when she saw her friend, that evening, waylay the boys on their way home from school, she was swept with a wave of relief.

'What does Agnes want wi' the boys?' Elizabeth stood in the doorway, frowning back along the road.

'She's goin' to see if she can find out what's troublin' them an' makin' them behave the way they do to me.'

'Good.' Elizabeth nodded approvingly, but said no more.

When the boys slunk in about half an hour later, they were both subdued, but polite and co-operative. After supper James even offered to wash the dishes and ordered Thomas to wipe them.

Isabella felt her jaw drop, but merely said, 'Thank you,' and left them to it. Turning, she saw Elizabeth watching and raised her eyebrows questioningly. The youngster smiled in surprise, turned her hands palm upwards and shrugged.

In the morning they readied themselves for school, breakfasted and left without a quarrel. Isabella, waiting for a sudden explosion of argument, was left instead with a sensation of happy anticlimax.

'What happened?' she asked, letting herself into Agnes' cottage later in the morning. 'What did you do to that pair. They've been like little angels ever since last night.'

'I didn't really do much, apart from listen. They seemed to need to talk. At least James did. Thomas was really just followin' his brother's lead. Then when they'd finished I just put a few facts to them an' made them see things a bit straighter. Mostly it was all in James' mind. He was feelin' neglected, because his mother went off an' left him.'

'His mother died! She didn't leave him by choice!' Horror clenched Isabella's stomach.

'Aye. But he seemed to have it in his head that she didn't need to go. That she *had* gone by choice because she preferred to be wi' the new baby. An' he was behavin' so bad wi' you because he felt you had killed her. Then, 'cos you was the one in here deliverin' the babies he thought you could ha' saved her, but didn't so that you could step into her place where he felt you'd no right to be.'

'Oh, poor James!' Tears stung Isabella's eyes, 'Why didn't he tell me?'

'How could he?' Agnes asked gently. 'When he regarded you, almost. as his mother's murderer.'

Isabella hung her head, shuddering. 'I must find a way to make him see the truth.'

'I think I have already, an' probably more successfully than you could. From you he might ha' taken it as an untruthful attempt at self-defense. An' to make it all worse, he feels his father's deserted him, because he's been away more'n he's been home ever since Catharine died. James was blamin' you for that too, 'cos Joseph jus' kept saying he needed more an' more money an the boy thought he was givin' it to you. What *is* he doin' wi' it all anyway?' Agnes finished curiously.

Isabella shrugged, shaking her head. 'I really don't know. I wish I did. All he will say to me is that we need the money. Anyway, what was it you said to James to bring about this change?'

'I told 'im, in no uncertain terms that you had in no way wished his mother dead. Pointed out to him that she'd been just as much *your* mother as his. An' I told him that no one in her right mind would want to take on all the work and worry o' all 'em childher. Then I told him what a desperate fight you'd put up to save his Mammy an' his brother. I tried to make it very clear that if you hadn't taken over his Mammy's work, then they'd all likely have finished up on the streets, 'cos a man could never do for them what you do.'

'What did he say to that?'

'Well, he cried for a while, an' said how sorry he was. Said he wouldn't treat you so bad again. But you know, Isabella, he's still not happy, 'cos he still doesn't understand why his Daddy is neglectin' him so. A boy his age needs his Daddy. His Mammy can't never come back, an' no matter how well you do for him, you can never take her place.'

'Nor would I want to!' Isabella said feelingly 'I don't want any o' them ever to forget their Mammy even the slightest bit.'

'No. I do know that. But he does need his Daddy to spend some time wi' 'im an' show that he cares.'

'I'll ha' a word wi' him tonight,' Isabella said thoughtfully.

'I thought maybe it would be best if I asked Henry or Francis to talk to him. It might come better from a man, then he won't jus' think 'tis women naggin'.'

'Aye. Happen you're right. I'll leave it up to you then.'

It was a few nights later Joseph wandered in looking more thoughtful than usual. His bemused expression lasted through supper, then when the boys had gone from the cottage to meet some friends, he called Isabella to sit beside him.

'May I wash the bowls first?' she asked a little hesitantly,

Joseph frowned momentarily. 'No. Leave them. Elizabeth will do them.'

With no further bidding, Elizabeth rose to collect the bowls from the table. Nervous of the youngster handling the heavy kettle of boiling water, Isabella took time to fill the tin basin for her. Then she obediently went to sit on the floor at Joseph's knee. He might be the father of 'her' children, but to Isabella he was still her own father and, as such, to be obeyed.

'I believe you've been havin' trouble wi' the boys?'

Isabella felt the hot blush sweep her face. 'Not really trouble,' she stammered.

'What name would you give their behaviour, then?'

Isabella thought for a moment. 'They've been unhappy. Confused. Frightened. Especially James, for he was the one who sat on the doorstep while his mother's life's blood drained away. He was the one who ran around the town trying to get the midwife and the doctor to come. An' he was the one who finally got the doctor back here — but too late.'

'Aye. Henry Quirk told me. He said a lot o' it was my fault, too, for neglectin' the lad.' Joseph was silent for a few moments, then he asked, 'Do you think I have?'

Isabella shifted uncomfortably, gazing wordlessly into the fire.

'Be honest now, girl.'

Isabella heaved a huge sigh and nodded her head thoughtfully

'Yes,' she whispered dryly. 'But not only the boys. All of us. They were just the ones who showed it most.'

Joseph's eyes misted. 'Aye. Henry said that too. I didn't mean to hurt any o' you, I thought I was doin' it all for your own good. I allus promised Catharine a big house down by the harbour, an' I've been trying to get the money for one. I thought it was what she would ha' wanted for you all.'

Daniel was in a shadow in the far corner, carving a doll for Sarah, but Isabella could sense him watching the scene by the fireplace listening to every word.

'Aye. She might like to see us in a fine house, one day,' Isabella, agreed, 'But most of all she would want to see us all happy An' none of us, the boys in particular, will be happy unless we see more o' you. An' Daniel!' she added as an afterthought, turning to smile at him.

Suddenly it occurred to her that it was Daniel she had missed most of all. For she had seen no more of him than of Joseph in the past months, and he was the one with whom she felt the closest bond.

'Well then,' Joseph said cheerfully, 'I shall have to tell the merchants I must spend more time wi' my childher, an' they will have to find themselves new Captains to carry their contraband.'

'You don't mind?'

'Not if you don't mind waiting longer for your fine house.'

'The house doesn't matter. I just want us all to be happy again.'

'We will be,' Joseph promised.

Heart singing, Isabella leapt to her feet and throwing, her arms around him, held him in a tight hug.

'An' I won't ha' to worry so much about you gettin' caught.'

Joseph laughed. 'There's no need to worry any time. We're never in any real danger. Are we, lad?' he looked to Daniel for confirmation.

Daniel shook his head, then standing, he laid his carving on the table. ''Tis a nice evenin' for a walk. Would you care to come wi' me, Isabella?'

The girl nodded. 'Aye, that would be nice.' Picking up her cape, she moved towards the door.

'Me come too?' Sarah ran to Isabella, clinging tightly to her legs. Isabella looked questioningly at Daniel, knowing he might not want the toddler with them.

'Oh, no you don't, miss.' Before Daniel had time to give a reply, Joseph had scooped the youngster up, swinging her in the air. 'Isabella has your company all day, I think we should let her get away from you for a while.'

Isabella hesitated, but Joseph jerked his head towards the door.

'Go on. Have an hour or two away from bein' a mother. I've been thoughtless an' left far too much on your shoulders these last months. 'Tis time you got out away from the childher for a while. 'Tis a lovely mild evenin', so enjoy it.'

Isabella looked doubtfully towards the crib in the corner. Following her gaze, Joseph laughed again. 'Aye. An' leave her too. Between us Elizabeth an' me'll manage Cathy if she wakens.'

Daniel opened the door and they strolled out into the early evening sunshine. Off on a rocky outcrop to seaward somewhere, came the strange, unmistakable alarm call of an oyster-catcher.

'Something must be after his nest,' Isabella said quietly, listening intently.

'Aye,' Daniel agreed, giving her his hand to assist her over a steep hump of rock. 'Most likely a gull or a cat.'

After a while the calls ceased and they knew that either the danger had passed or the chicks were eaten.

The spring flowers had seen their glory and wilted, while the gorse, as ever, kept blooming, the bracken ferns had poked well through and the heather buds were starting to swell and colour.

Isabella and Daniel stood in the corner, near the stand of beeches, green now, and thick with leaves.

'Let's sit here,' Isabella suggested, lowering herself gracefully to the grass, tugging Daniel's hand. 'I think this is my favourite place in all the world.'

'Aye. 'Tis peaceful.' Daniel agreed, dumping himself unceremoniously beside her.

'Listen,' she said, still holding his hand.

'To what?' Daniel could hear nothing.

'If you stay silent for a while, you'll hear.'

For several minutes they sat motionless, listening to the silence. Then gradually the creatures around grew accustomed to their presence. Bird noises started, sparrows, chaffinches, wrens and blackbirds sang and twittered amongst the trees. The harsh cries of distant crows and rooks blew to them on the breeze, while from somewhere just below them came the strange, penetrating cry of the curlew.'

'Bird song has such a peaceful sound,' Daniel said reverently.

'Aye,' Isabella agreed. 'An' look at the view. How blue the sea is on such a day.'

"Tis nice to see it from here, Daniel said feelingly. 'I'm well pleased Joseph is goin' to do less smugglin'.'

'Does it frighten you?'

Daniel thought for a moment, wondering if he should lie, but decided she would know if he did. 'Aye,' was all he said.

'Is there really as little danger in it as Joseph says?'

'Aye. There's more danger from the weather than from the Customs' men. They ha' so few boats you'd ha' to be awful unlucky to get caught. 'Tis the folk we deliver to who are in the most danger, for the English coast is patrolled by foot soldiers. But 'tis not really fear that makes me glad we won't be goin' out so much.'

'What is it then?'

'I've missed you. An' the others too. I've missed havin' a family life, 'cos 'tis hard bein' at sea, or loadin' an' unloadin' contraband all the time. But mostly 'tis you I miss.'

'Aye. I know what you mean.' Isabella gazed out to sea, watching the tiny dots that were boats, bobbing like toys in a busy bathtub. 'I miss you too. It seems I have hardly seen you these last months, wi' you only home for a short few hours sleep in the afternoons. The loft has seemed empty wi'out you at night-times.'

Isabella felt Daniel's grip on her hand tighten and when she turned her face up to him, he was studying her with a strange expression.

''Tis startin' to get cool,' he said gruffly. 'We'd better go afore you catch a chill.' He stood, then, offering her a hand to help her to her feet.

'Aye,' Isabella agreed, puzzled, not feeling the slightest bit chilly. She put her hand in his and found it trembling slightly.

'Why, Daniel, whatever is wrong?'

He coloured quickly, looking away from her, shuffling his feet uncomfortably. 'Nothin'!' he said abruptly.

Isabella stood, her hand still in Daniel's, and suddenly his arms were around her, crushing her. She returned the embrace for a moment, then tipped her head back to look up at him. Immediately his lips were on hers, kissing her deeply, longingly.

At first she returned his kisses, then grew frightened at their intensity and pushed him away from her.

'No, Daniel, you mustn't. It's wrong.'

'Why is it wrong?' He looked agonised.

'Because we are — well — like brother and sister. It's bad to feel this way about each other.'

'But we are *not* brother and sister. Not even cousins. I think I have loved you ever since I first found you that mornin' in Castletown. It wasn't until after Catharine died, though, that I knew how much, or that it was not as a brother loves a sister. You feel the same way, don't you?'

Isabella was thoughtful, shaken. 'I don't know, Daniel. I'm not sure how I feel. I know I have a different feeling for you than for the others. That I love you more than the others. But I don't know if it's the kind of love you're meanin'.'

'Please, Isabella. Please care for me. I won't ever love another as I do you.'

'Don't push me for an answer, Daniel,' she agonised. 'This thought is new to me. I'm not sure how I feel. Please give me time to think. To put my thoughts together.'

Daniel nodded miserably, embarrassed that he'd acted so impulsively, and that he'd blurted out his feelings as he had. The power of his emotions and the loss of control they had engendered frightened him also.

Without another word he turned and began to walk, head hanging ashamedly, down the Brow. Isabella's hand slipping into his brought him some comfort.

'You won't tell Joseph will you?' Daniel finally asked in a voice not much louder than a whisper.

'NO. Of course not.' She squeezed his hand encouragingly.

That night Daniel, who had slept close to Isabella for the six and a half years they had been together, moved his mattress to the other end of the loft, beside James and Thomas.

Chapter 20

It was on the last day of August in 1764 that Francis Clague came rushing in, without as much as a perfunctory knock on the door. Sitting at the table, he stretched his long legs out under it.

Daniel looked up from his carving, this time a dog for Elizabeth, then stood up and moved to sit by Francis.

'There's some funny goin's on wi' the new Duke o' Atholl, I hear,' Francis started.

'Oh, aye?' Joseph leaned forward, immediately attentive. 'What've you heard then?'

'Well, you know how desperate the English have been gettin' to stamp out smugglin' from the Island?'

'Aye. But they have been for many long years now. There's never been much they could do about it.'

'Well, they may have foun' a way now. It all depends on the Duke, an' whether he does what they want?'

'What's that, then?' Daniel chipped in.

'Well, it seems a few weeks ago he got a letter from the English Treasury, sayin' they wanted to buy the sovereign rights to the Island.'

'Who'd you hear this from?' Joseph was sitting bolt upright now, frowning.

'From that fellow who hangs aroun' the hotel. Calls hissel' the Duke's equerry. If there is such a thing.'

Joseph nodded. 'Aye. I know who you mean. He does work for the Duke. I've seen him wi' him.'

'Right. Well before the Duke had time to reply, they — the English I mean — sent him an order tellin' him they was goin' to station cutters an' cruisers in the harbours an' aroun' the coasts o' the Island too.'

'They can't do that!' Joseph roared, thumping his hand down the table. That'd be an illegal, aggressive act against the rights o' Lady Charlotte. This was her Daddy's Island until he died this year. The English has no rights here. That would be war!'

'Aye, well, this equerry fellow says the Duke said the same as you. He figured 'twas no more than a bluff. But it seems he's considerin' it. He told 'em that as he was only newly in possession o' the Island he was unsure o' the value o' his rights an' has invited the English to make him an offer.'

'He can't sell *our* island, can he?' Daniel's face was a mask of disbelief.

Joseph shrugged. 'I dunno anythin' about these things. I suppose if the rights are his, then he must ha' the right to sell them. The English Treasury mus' think so, or they wouldn't be tryin' to force him into it.'

Francis nodded his agreement.

Suddenly Joseph roared with laughter. Startled, everyone turned to stare at him. Cathy stirred, whimpered, then decided it wasn't worth waking and went back to sleep.

'God almighty,' Joseph roared. 'We must have them worried if they want to buy the whole island to stop us!'

'Would that mean you'd stop smugglin?' Isabella asked hopefully.

'No, lass,' Joseph replied solemnly. 'It jus' means we'd ha' to be a mite more careful.'

A few weeks later, having plied the equerry, yet again, with a few ales, Francis came forth with the news that the Duke had received yet another letter from the treasury, asking for full information concerning the value of every branch of his revenue on the Island. Without allowing him the time to reply, they had then communicated, yet again, informing him that the British Government now declined to go any further into a treaty, as their intentions could best be served by an Act of Parliament.

After that it all seemed to die down. The smugglers plied their trade as usual, and at times Joseph was tempted to think it had all been in Francis' mind.

Summer rolled into autumn, then the beginning of winter, with its short days and long, cold, crisp nights.

To Isabella's delight, Cathy continued to thrive, growing quite plump. In no time at all, it seemed, she was walking, into every kind of mischief and leading her adoptive mother a merry dance.

Daniel had never again spoken to Isabella of his feelings for her.

Part of her was sad and wished he would but her main feeling was of relief, for she felt she was not yet ready to deal with any more commitments or complications. She had not the slightest doubt she loved him very deeply, but was neither old enough nor experienced enough to be sure of just what form her feelings for him took.

'There is a rumour of a dreadful disease sweepin' Britain,' Agnes told Isabella, one day in early December.

'Which disease? Is it diphtheria?'

'I didn't hear the name o' it. Why do you ask o' that?'

'Daniel lost his family in an epidemic o' it. That would be twelve years or more ago though. But by all accounts it is a dreadful disease. He watched all his family die wi' it!'

'Aye. That's what took Catharine's young brother, Alexander, too.'

'Alexander? Aye. Of course — that's who I'm thinkin' o'. Wi' Daniel's family 'twas somethin' else. Some sort o' pox, I think.'

Isabella's brow furrowed as she tried to recall the name, but it eluded her.

As the weeks went by, more and stronger reports kept arriving from the mainland. A terrible illness, they heard, the victims suffering an awful, burning, consuming fever. Then they would be covered in pus-filled sores which left, if the victim was lucky enough to survive, the most hideous scars. Hundreds were dying all over the country.

Then the inevitable happened. At the well one morning in mid-December, Isabella heard one of the townswomen, in tears, telling another that her sister's daughter had taken ill with the awful sickness from "across". 'Smallpox, they call it!' the woman said.

Isabella recoiled from the well in horror, grabbing her bucket in one hand and Cathy in the other. The disease was unknown to her, but she had heard enough about it in the past few weeks to be terrified lest any of her loved ones should contract it.

Almost running, her heart stammering with fear, she rushed up the hill to home, with Cathy scampering alongside complaining all the way that her legs were hurting.

'Agnes. Agnes — it's come!' she gasped out, finding her friend standing in her doorway.

'What's come? What is it?' Her eyes were wide with fear, but of what, she knew not.

'The pox. The sickness they're all dyin' o' "across". 'Tis on the Island.'

Agnes blanched, her hand fluttering to her mouth. 'Are you sure?'

Isabella nodded. 'Aye. I heard a woman at the well say her sister's child had it.'

She took Cathy's hand then and went home, a part of her wanting someone to talk to, but another, stronger part not wanting others near. Others might be harbouring this terrible disease. Carrying it around. Spreading it. No one seemed sure of how it travelled — just that it did — and rapidly. Behind her, she heard Agnes' door close abruptly and realised that the other woman, usually so friendly, had not invited her in. Her fear had shown, like a reflection of Isabella's, in her eyes.

Isabella shut her own door firmly, as though that act would keep out whatever it was that caused the awful disease. Cathy played on the floor with the doll Daniel had made, while Isabella busied herself around the house. She went about her chores automatically as though in a dream; or more likely a nightmare; of terror.

When people had talked of the pox rampaging and killing so many "across", she had spared it little thought. It seemed so remote, happening to folk far away, not real at all. But now, suddenly it was here, on her island, threatening her and her loved ones. It was no longer someone else's fantasy. It was real. And unrelenting. And deadly! And *here* on the Island amongst them, like some dark, hateful, threatening stranger.

'Well, it won't get my family!' Isabella vowed through clenched teeth. 'It won't! I won't let it!'

James and Thomas exploded into the cottage after school that afternoon, chattering excitedly, each shouting as he tried to make his voice the one that delivered the news.

One of the girls at school had been taken with the pox, they yelled. They seemed almost pleased about it, Isabella thought in horror. Something noteworthy was happening and, in the callous way children have of enjoying others' suffering, they found it exciting.

'Tis nothin' to be pleased about,' she remonstrated. 'From all accounts 'tis the most awful disease. We must pray it doesn't get none o' us.'

Elizabeth was more subdued, appearing almost as frightened as Isabella herself

Joseph and Daniel had heard the awesome news on their way up

from the harbour. It was strange how quickly bad news travelled —
almost as fast as scandal — like a disease itself.

'We'd best keep the childher away from school until this menace
has gone. It seems to pass easily from one person to another, so you
all should stay indoors as much as possible. Keep away from other
folk all you can,' Joseph ordered.

Isabella nodded, the power of speech having deserted her
momentarily. 'But I must go to the market, an' the bakers, an' the
well,' she whispered through lips that had gone dry.

Joseph fell silent for a while, frowning, deep in thought. Finally,
he nodded, as though concluding a conversation with himself.
'We'll do that. Me an' Daniel. Then we'll sleep on the boat until
this thing has passed.'

'Oh but why? I'll ha' need o' you here. I'll be scared to be on my
own here wi' this thing aroun'!'

'This is the way it must be, Isabella,' Joseph said strongly. 'We
will have to stay away for fear we might bring the disease home to
you. You an' the childher must stay here, in the house an' keep away
from everyone. Open the door to no one, for anyone might bring
the pox in wi' them!'

'But what if we should take ill? There'll be no one to help us.'

'Daniel an me will come every day wi' food an' water for you, so
you'll be well watched over. Don't be worryin' girl, it'll be a'right.'
Joseph could see the panic in Isabella's eyes and sought to calm her.

'But what if you and Daniel should get the pox an' die? What
would become o' us?' Isabella was sobbing now, her lips trembling.

Joseph moved to put his arms around her, crushing her close to
his chest, and Isabella could feel his strength flowing into her. Then
he said quietly, 'We must pray, my love. We can only pray. Surely
God has taken enough from us already.'

Joseph and Daniel stayed at the cottage that night, feeling that
since they were already there it could do no harm. Daniel said little,

but that night he moved his mattress back beside Isabella's and they lay in each other's arms. She could feel the stirrings of deep passion in him, but he just held her very gently, protectively.

The days which followed were difficult for everyone. James and Thomas, always active, played well together at first, wrestling at times, as they had always been wont to do. But then they became like caged animals they who loved to roam free — and soon squabbled incessantly.

Sarah grumbled all the time, pestering Isabella to take her walking on the Brow, to see the robins, crows and seabirds.

Bored to distraction, Cathy just got into as much mischief as she could find, or wailed at the top of her powerful voice.

Elizabeth was the only one who made life bearable, for she would either lie in the loft, quietly reading a book, or try to keep the two little girls as well amused as possible.

Nerves became ragged. Tempers frayed and flared.

Daniel and Joseph came daily, laid the provisions on the doorstep knocked, then stood well back. The news they brought was not good, and grew worse each day.

The pox claimed more victims with every day that passed and doctors seemed able to do little. Reports started coming of people dying.

'I heard this mornin' that Agnes and Henry's elder daughter has it now.' Joseph's face was grey with worry as he gave Isabella this item of news.

Isabella gasped, her hand flying to her mouth as bile rose to burn her throat. 'Oh, no! Not Maria!'

Joseph nodded sadly

'I must go to her. I must help Agnes'

'No! Stay away!'

'But she's my friend,' Isabella agonised. 'She's helped me so many times. Given me a shoulder to lean on when I've needed strength. I can't just ignore her at a time like this!'

'You can't help, Isabella. There's nothing you can possibly do. 'Tis bad enough havin' the disease jus' two doors away. If you go aroun' there you'll surely bring it back wi' you. You must put yourself an' our family first this time. Only God hisself can help the Quirks now.'

Isabella knew he was right. To go there would be to risk bringing death to her own family. Sense made her stay home, but her heart yearned to offer help.

It struck Thomas quite suddenly, just two days later. One moment he was playing happily and in the next, it seemed, he was sobbing because his head hurt.

Looking at him, Isabella thought he appeared flushed, and when she laid a hand on his forehead it burned alarmingly.

'Perhaps you've jus' bin playin' a bit wild,' she said hopefully. 'Go an' lie down for a while an' maybe you'll feel better. Lie in your Daddy's bed. It'll be easier for us both than runnin' up an' down the steps.'

Isabella watched over Thomas, worriedly fussing, tending, bringing drinks of water when he asked. But as the day wore on he worsened. Afternoon turned to evening and when supper-time came he refused to eat, saying he felt sick.

At night, when all the others were asleep, Isabella, scared to move too far from Thomas, crept into bed beside him. Feeling him shivering beside her, she rose to find any warm covering she could, piling on top of him an odd assortment of clothing. Then she lay beside him, wrapping him tightly in her arms to afford him as much warmth as possible.

All night Isabella lay awake, frightened, repeatedly pleading, 'Please, God, let it be only a feverish chill. Please God, don't let it be the pox.'

And all night Thomas shivered ceaselessly, while at the same time his little body oozed perspiration. Isabella quickly found her petticoat saturated and uncomfortable.

It was a relief to her when the first pink haze of dawn started to find its way through the tiny window, casting soft, misty shadows in the room.

Quietly Isabella slipped out of bed, her teeth soon chattering in the bitter cold of the winter morning. Moving quickly to the fireplace, she soon had a good fire roaring in the grate.

That was something they must have, she thought, if there was illness in the house. They would need plenty of wood, and at the moment there was very little in the cottage. She must keep a good fire going. Even if it was just a chill Thomas had, he would need to be kept warm. Joseph and Daniel would have to bring fuel for the fire — a great deal of it. She must remember to tell them when they came today.

Isabella stood at the window staring out at the lightening sky. Soon it would be morning and Joseph would come. He would be able to tell her what she should do. Maybe he would know whether it was the pox Thomas had or just a chill.

Thomas groaned and tossed in his sleep, pushing the mountain of coverings away. Isabella took a bowl of water from the bucket and, carrying it to the bed, she replaced the covers, then wiped his face with the cool water.

'I'm too hot,' Thomas whimpered weakly. 'Take the blankets off.'

'No. Thomas, you must keep warm an' burn out this fever. I'll wipe your face an' it'll make you feel better.'

Cathy woke and came noisily demanding breakfast, disturbing Elizabeth as she did so.

The older girl came staggering down from the loft, bleary eyed and half asleep. 'Is Thomas any better?' she asked quietly.

Isabella shook her head miserably. 'No. He has sweated terribly all night.'

'Do you think he has the pox?'

Isabella shrugged helplessly. 'I can't tell. We must keep praying, as I have done all night, that it's only a feverish cold. Will you keep cooling his face an' neck while I make the porridge?'

'Aye.' Elizabeth took her place beside the bed.

Isabella prepared the porridge, hanging it over the fire with a lighter heart. Performing an everyday task brought an air of normality to the day, giving a sense that things, perhaps, might not be as bad as they seemed.

Thomas refused food, though he drank thirstily. The rest of the family, to Isabella's great relief, showed no loss of appetite.

Finally, the anxiously awaited knock came on the door.

'The provisions are all here.' Joseph said, indicating the bags he had laid on the doorstep. 'Enough to keep you goin' for another day, I should think. Is all well here?'

Isabella shook her head. 'No. Thomas is sick. Very sick.' She felt her lips trembling.

Joseph looked stricken. 'Is it the pox?'

'I .. I don't know. He has a terrible fever.'

'It starts wi' a fever. Has he any spots?'

Isabella shook her head, instantly hopefully. 'Does that mean it isn't the pox?'

'No. No, I don't think so. I think the spots come later. I'll come in an take a look at him.' He took a step towards the door.

'No!' Isabella cried, 'You mustn't come in! If it is the pox you'll catch it too.'

'But we must help you, Isabella. You can't be left to handle it alone!'

'What if you take ill?' Daniel looked heartsick, his face drawn with fear.

'If 'tis the pox Thomas has,' she said quietly, 'then I will likely already have caught it, if I'm goin' to, an' there's nothin' you can do now to stop it. An' all the other children too. It will help no one for you an' Joseph to come in here an' catch it. But we will need more water, much of it because Thomas has an awful thirst. An' we need to keep the fire burnin' high to keep him warm. So if you can bring a lot o' wood — .'

'We will,' Joseph cried. 'We'll get you as much this afternoon as you could ever use.'

'Don't get caught,' Isabella said frantically. 'You will be no help to us in gaol.'

'There's no danger o' that right now,' Joseph assured her. 'The soldiers ha' more to worry about than folk cuttin' trees. We'll go down right now an' get the doctor to call.'

Joseph and Daniel brought the first of the wood early in the afternoon, and several more lots throughout the day.

Each time, on learning the doctor had not yet called, they went in search of him, always being given the promise that he would be there soon. Finally, at supper time, Joseph went to the man's house in a rage. Had he not been such a powerfully large man, he would most likely have been thrown out on his ear. As it was, he was told politely, but firmly, that the doctor was not home, it being such a busy time for him. His household did not know when they might expect him back, but they were quite definite that he would not be able to reach Joseph's cottage before morning.

Thomas' condition continued to worsen and Isabella spent another sleepless night cooling the boy's brow, whilst trying to keep blankets over him. All night she kept the fire stoked high, praying continuously.

'Isabella!' Thomas screamed suddenly, curling in pain, clutching at his stomach. Then with a sudden spasm of muscles he emptied a tummy full of green bile on the floor.

In terror, Isabella wondered what to do. Nothing in life could ever have prepared her for this. She stared at Thomas through eyes like huge, blue saucers.

He seemed to doze, quite peacefully, for a while, then whispered, through cracked, dry lips that he was thirsty.

Automatically Isabella offered him water and he drank greedily. But his stomach threw it back quickly and violently.

To her relief, Joseph came at dawn. On learning of his son's condition, he stormed straight down to the doctor's house. 'When I come back, he'll be wi' me!' he vowed.

Daniel was left in the roadway, to speak words of encouragement to Isabella through the closed door.

How he wished she would open the door. He would gladly risk catching the pox to be able to put his arms around her and comfort her properly.

God — how he loved her! If anything were to happen to her! He shuddered at the thought. He felt sure he could not go on living.

True to his word, Joseph returned within the hour, with the doctor, red-faced, blustering, very angry and wearing only a night-shirt under his coat.

Having once propelled the man into the cottage, he told Daniel, 'The lazy bugger was still abed an' all the household asleep. So I pounded on the door till they opened it, then I walked in an' pulled him out o' bed!'

'Good God!' In spite of his worry, Daniel found himself laughing. No wonder he's angry.'

'Well, I weren't goin' to be fobbed off wi' a lot o' lies an' false promises that he'd come soon. We had enough o' that the day Catharine an' the boy died. I want my son seen to today.'

Inside, the doctor, calmer now, listened to Isabella's description of what had occurred so far, nodding his head all the time, as if it was a very familiar story.

Then be pulled back the covers to visually examine the boy's body. Shaking his head gravely, he straightened again.

'You see all the marks on his face and trunk?'

Isabella, sitting on the bed for a closer look, saw the strange red blotches. Looking fearfully up into the doctor's face, she nodded her head.

'Well they're going to be spots. I'm sorry, but there is no doubt the boy has smallpox!'

Chapter 21

Smallpox! A killer disease in her house! In her family! Isabella stood, stunned, staring in horror at Thomas. It was impossible to believe. But the doctor had said so. It must be true. Smallpox! She felt her stomach turning like a windmill and unshed tears pressed painfully behind her eyes.

Smallpox! Until now it had all been a bad dream. Now, suddenly, it was here, its evil all around, clutching at her little family. Thomas had smallpox! Moments after the doctor left, the door flew open and Joseph stood on the threshold.

'Don't come in!' Isabella said quickly, a flutter of panic at her heart.

'He *is* my son. I must be wi' him.'

'There's nothin' you can do. The doctor said so. Except pray!'

'Then I'll pray by his bedside.'

'No! 'Twouldn't do no good. He won't know you're here. He's too ill to recognise you, an' it will do him no good for you to catch the pox.'

Joseph hesitated where he stood, knowing the sense in what the girl said, but desperately wanting to give comfort to his child. Behind him, Isabella could see Daniel's pale, anxious face, clearly reflecting the agony he too was suffering.

Finally Joseph took a reluctant step backwards. 'I s'pose you're right.' be mumbled. if he gets any wuss I'm goin' to be wi' him. Or if it gets be too much for you to cope wi' you must tell me.'

Isabella nodded mutely. Closing the door behind Joseph, she leaned trembling, panting with fear. Panic rising in her breast, she tried frantically to remember the doctor's words. He hadn't said much really, except that there was nothing much he could do for Thomas. The disease had no cure. Just time. If nature would allow him it!

It was all up to her, it seemed. Most important was that she had to keep Thomas warm. Fine. Well she had been doing that. And she must make him drink, the doctor had said. Make him drink as much as possible, but not to let him take huge gulps, no matter how thirsty he claimed to be, nor how much he begged. Just let him have no more than a mouthful at a time, else his stomach would reject it and it would do more harm than good. The best advice he could offer, the doctor had finished, was to pray an' to keep on praying, for it was in God's hands now and He, alone, could save the poor unfortunates.

Thomas thrashed, asleep, but moaning in some private agony and Isabella moved to wipe his face with the cool rag of wet flannel.

In horror she saw the marks on his face and body were beginning to form into blisters. There could be no mistaking it now — the doctor had been correct!

Throughout the day she nursed Thomas, with help from Elizabeth, wrestling the cup away from him when he tried to drink too deeply.

The other children had become strangely subdued since the doctor's visit. James, in fact, had crept straight up to the loft and lay in the farthest corner, curled in a ball.

After a while Isabella became concerned about him and climbed the ladder, to look over the edge of the loft at him.

'Are you ill?' she asked anxiously.

He shook his head miserably, but said nothing.

'Well, what's wrong then? Why don't you come an' join the rest o' us. Come down by the fire where 'tis warm.'

James shook his head. 'I'm scared,' he whispered hoarsely.

'Of what?'

'Of the pox. I'm scared to go near Thomas in case I get the pox from him,' he admitted shamefacedly.

'I think 'tis probably too late to worry about that, don't you?' Isabella asked gently 'But you can come down here wi' out bein' too close to him if that's what you want.' James still looked hesitant, so she added, 'Hidin' away alone up here will just make you all the more miserable and frightened.' Then she left him.

Several minutes later Isabella heard him shuffling across the loft, then he came downstairs, giving Thomas a wide berth, to sit, embarrassed on the floor near the fire.

When Cathy refused her tea, Isabella felt her forehead, her heart sinking, like a lump of lead, to her boots. 'Elizabeth,' she said fearfully, 'I think Cathy has the pox too.'

Elizabeth looked up from Thomas's bedside with pained, water-logged eyes. 'Not Cathy,' she whispered. She's all we ha' left of our Mammy. God can't have her too! He can't!'

Isabella went to the door. As soon it opened. Joseph was there, as she knew he would be. All-day he had waited outside, determined to be there the moment he was needed, sending Daniel for whatever the family required.

'I think Cathy has it now,' Isabella told him tremulously.

Joseph caught his breath, closing his eyes, his face contorted by his mental agony. 'No!' He whispered dryly. 'No more. Not my baby.'

He refused to stay outside then. If any of them were to die it, was his right to be with them at the end.

Soon after, there came a knocking on the door. Joseph, with Cathy in his arms, crossed to it. 'Who's there?'

'Daniel,' came the reply.

'Well, lay the wood by the door an' step well back. In fact it might be best if you go back to the boat. We won't need you again tonight.'

'Why are you inside? What's happened?'

'We think Cathy has the pox.'

They heard Daniel's sharp intake of breath. 'Then I wish to come in.'

'No, boy. You must not. We need you outside — an' healthy. Stay clear.'

'I'll get the doctor!'

''Tis a waste o' time, lad. There's nothin' he can do!'

'Well what can I do to help? I must do somethin'!' Daniel's voice was pitched high with emotion. He felt so helpless — so frustrated.

'Jus' be there when we need your help. An' pray all you can. Go back to the boat now. Please, lad.'

'I'll be back early in the mornin' then.' They heard his footsteps dragging reluctantly away down the street. After he had gone, Joseph opened the door to bring in the wood and he heard the most awful commotion of weeping and wailing coming at them from along the road. Grabbing the bundle of sticks, he closed the door hurriedly and moved to stoke the fire. But he had not been quick enough.

'That sounded like Agnes,' Isabella said, looking anxiously towards the door.

'Aye,' Joseph agreed miserably.

'It must be Maria.'

'She must ha' died,' Elizabeth spoke the words that were in the minds of the others.

'I must go to her. Give some comfort if I can.'

Joseph offered no argument this time. It could do no harm, he knew, as the pox was already in his home. And he was sure it would ease Isabella's conscience to show Agnes she cared.

'Aye. You go! She may need a woman's shoulder to weep on

Elizabeth an' me'll manage here. Stay as long as you're needed.'

Isabella threw her cloak around her shoulders and ran to the cottage two doors away. With a quick rap on the door, she let herself in.

Agnes was on her knees on the floor, laid across a tiny body on the bed, weeping and constantly muttering, 'No! It can't be. I love you, Maria. Come back to me. Please, dear God, give her back! Don't do this to us,' she beseeched finally.

Henry looked around on Isabella's entry, his eyes sunken and tortured, hollowed in huge black shadows.

'You mustn't come in here, Isabella. Stay away.'

'I had to see if I could give you any comfort. Is there anything I can do to help?'

'"Tis kind o' you, love. But there's nothin' you can do. The pox has taken Maria. For your own sake you must not come near. Leave now.'

'Twill do me no harm, Henry, to stay. The pox is in our house too.'

Henry winced and Agnes raised her head, seeming to notice Isabella for the first time.

'Who has it?' she asked huskily.

'Thomas was first. He's covered wi' blisters now. An' it looks as though Cathy has it too.'

Then you must go home. They need you more than we. It helps us just to know you cared enough to come. Go now, an' our prayers will be wi' you.'

'An' ours wi' you,' Isabella said feelingly. Weeping, she staggered home.

In the days that followed, Thomas' blisters grew huge and painful-looking, then they burst and erupted into angry, red, weeping sores. Joseph was the one to bathe these, for the look of them made Elizabeth and Isabella sick.

Cathy's fever worsened, and when the first tell tale marks appeared on her body, they were left in no doubt she was another victim of the dreaded pox. Her spots seemed to itch more than Thomas's and she kept trying to scratch, so Isabella hurriedly made some mittens from a rag of flannel, to try to protect her face from scarring

Thomas lapsed into a state of delirium, sometimes sleeping fully and, at others, crying out, moaning or chattering incoherently After a while he started convulsing, twitching and making frightening sounds in his throat. He took a deep, shuddering breath and lay still

Isabella and Joseph stared in dread, first at Thomas, then at each other. Fearfully, Joseph knelt to put his ear to his son's chest For a moment he was still, his eyes tight closed.

Isabella, with Cathy clutched in her arms, watched wide-eyed, mouth moving in silent prayer, as did James and Elizabeth. Even Sarah, usually boisterous, seemed to realise the need for silence.

After a lifetime Joseph lifted his head, moving it slowly from side to side. His face was a mask of stunned disbelief. A tear broke from the well in his eyes, to scurry down his cheek and roll off his chin. Isabella thought he looked like a little lost child. Running to him, she put her arms round his neck as he knelt.

It was that same evening Isabella began to feel ill. At first she said nothing, hoping it was only the shock of Thomas' death. But then she started to sweat and her tummy felt bad.

'I think I am goin' to be ill,' she told Joseph, and saw the horror on his face.

He stumbled to the door, sobbing. 'Isabella has it now!' he blurted to Daniel.

'No!' the lad cried. 'Not my Isabella. Now I *must* come indoors to help.'

'No, Daniel. You'll still be more help to us out there. I'll take care o' your sisters myself.'

'Isabella is *not* my sister. She's more than a sister. I love her! With all my being I love her. I must help her!'

Joseph's expression, for a moment, was of shock, then he realised

Daniel was right. So long, had they been together, he had come to regard them as his own children; his own flesh and blood. Brother and sister to each other and his children. But of course, they were not. They were completely unrelated. As he thought of it, so protective had Daniel always been, his love for Isabella should have been obvious.

Gently he said, 'I understand, lad, but the best way you can help Isabella is by stayin' well yourself. There's little chance o' that in here. The best thing you can do for her now is to bring some more water an' as much wood as you can get. I'll get you the pail.'

Daniel nodded dejectedly, then went to the well.

* * *

All talk at the well was of the epidemic. Everyone spoke in muted tones, as if to talk aloud would rouse the pox and make it angrier.

Cathy's blisters worsened, until her face was a complete mask, seemingly fighting a valiant battle against the disease which ravaged her tiny body.

Isabella's condition deteriorated until, quite quickly she had little awareness of what was going on about her.

Joseph and Elizabeth, with a good deal of assistance from James, who seemed, finally, to shake off his terror, slaved day and night, to care for Sarah and the two victims of the disease,

Outside, Daniel did his share, keeping the family provided for and as comfortable as was possible, but frustratedly feeling he should be doing more. Joseph arranged for Thomas to be buried in his mother's grave. Then on the agreed day he and Henry dragged Maria and Thomas, their little boxes on the one sled, to Braddan Church for burial. It was a very short service, the minister being as busy as he was at that time. Then they hurried home to relieve Agnes, who was looking after both sick families in their absence.

Joseph started with a cry of horror, rushing to pick Cathy from her cot when the laboured rattling of her breathing quite suddenly went silent. Readying himself for the worst, he looked down, to find to his joy, two bright little grey eyes looking intently back at him, the face almost smiling. Pressing her face to his cheek, he found it to be cool.

As abruptly as it had started, her fever was gone. Broken in a moment, and she had won her battle for life.

'Glory be!' he yelled. Looking towards heaven, he fervently said, 'Thank you, dear God.' And he unashamedly let his tears flow.

Rushing to the door, he threw it open, almost shouting at Daniel, who was sitting on the step, 'Cathy's awake again. Her fever's gone. She's goin' to be well. Tell Agnes. 'Twill give her hope for her George.'

Daniel hurried to tell Agnes. There was a spring in his step now. If tiny Cathy could win against this thing, and there was hope for George, then there must certainly be hope for Isabella too.

Isabella was a fighter. He knew that of old. There wasn't much of her, but he knew her to be far tougher than she looked.

She fought on for days, and many times Joseph thought she had taken her last painful breath. Then she would draw on some inner strength and her battle would resume.

Suddenly one morning he had a feeling of being watched. looking at Isabella, he found her eyes, only half comprehending, following him as he moved around the room.

Rushing to her side, he knelt by her bed. 'Are you feelin' better?' he asked.

Isabella looked puzzled, as if she did not quite understand the question. then suddenly, comprehension came and she tried to sit up, trying desperately to look around.

Joseph placed a hand on her shoulder, gently pushing her back to the bed. 'Hush, now, girl. Just take it quietly. You've been terrible sick.'

'Cathy?' Isabella rasped through dry, cracked lips.

'Cathy's fine. Up an' runnin' aroun'. She's sleepin' jus' now, though,' he added as her eyes started roving in search of the toddler.

'The others?'

'All well. No one else caught it. I should think they won't now'

'Daniel?'

'Daniel's fine. But he's been frightful worried about you. Nearly out o' his mind. I must tell him right away.' He rose and went to the door.

Daniel, sitting in the snow outside, looked up fearfully when the door opened. but the look on Joseph's face told him all he wanted to know. Isabella heard his yell of joy, as did most of Douglas.

* * *

The disease ran its hideous course on the Island and by the end of March 1765, it finally petered out. In its wake it left twenty-eight dead of the Island's twenty-thousand inhabitants. For three and a half months it had raged, wreaking its destruction — a period the Islanders would not forget for many a long year.

To Isabella's relief, Cathy came through it with no significant scars on her face, while Isabella had only a small smattering of unsightly ones.

By the time the horror was well behind them, the children, imprisoned for so long, were relieved to return to school. Especially Elizabeth, the bookworm, who loved her studies so much.

Isabella, watching James and Elizabeth go off together that first day was filled with a dreadful sadness and emptiness. She would gladly have returned to the days when she had to fight to get the boys off to school. It would be worth it to be given Thomas back.

However the clock could not be turned back and he would be safe with his mother now. Catharine, she knew, would be pleased to have his company.

Chapter 22

Francis scarecely knocked before he entered, to stand just inside the door, clearly very agitated. 'Can you spare a few minutes, Joseph?' he asked, frowning worriedly.

'Aye. Sit down.' Joseph inclined his head towards the table, both men and Daniel moving towards it.

Isabella watched Francis, his knitted cap pulled tightly down over his ears (or at any rate, where his ears used to be) and felt sad for him. He was such an odd sight and seemed to become more self-conscious about his appearance with every day that passed. Nowadays he never seemed to take his cap off at all, not even when he was, as now, with old friends. She wondered whether he even removed it in bed.

How different his life might have been if he'd kept his ears, she reflected. Perhaps he might even have married. She knew Agnes often had admitted to terrible feelings of guilt that she had ruined his life.

'I just had a few ales wi' the Duke's man.' Francis started agitatedly. 'Real drunk he was. Seems that while the epidemic was ragin' on the Island, the British Government was not standin' still on its plans to quell the smugglin' from the Island.'

'What have you heard?' Joseph leaned forward attentively.

'Well, it seems that in January a fellow, the Right Honourable

George Grenville; First Lord o' the Treasury an' Chancellor of the Exchequer he is; introduced into the House o' Commons a Bill to stop what he called 'the illicit an' clandestine trade to an' from the Isle 0' Man', whatever that may mean. The 'Mischief Bill', he called it.'

'The what?' Joseph shook his head. 'Well they've got that wrong. There's no clandestine an' illegal trade *into* the Island. 'Tis all brought in legal enough, none o' it smuggled. 'Tis only whatever he said it was when we take it off the island an' over to Britain — or Ireland. Did your friend say how they was plannin' to stop the smugglin?'

'Aye. This Bill they was talkin' about, if it'd gone through, would ha' given the British Customs the right to search and seize vessels in Manx waters. An' they'd have had the power to make arrests both on the water an' on the Island itself, an' then taken their prisoners for trial in English Courts.'

'That would be intolerable! How could they possibly hope to do such a thing? Tynwald would not allow it. Our Government would never permit the English to violate our three miles o' water. Or come on the Island to take our people off, for that matter.'

'There was talk o' them usin' force, or by military occupation o' the Island!'

Joseph erupted in a fury. Thumping his huge fist down on the table, he half stood, his face only inches from Francis', glaring angrily into the other man's eyes.

A hen that had been scratching for crumbs near the table rose a foot in the air and raced off, flapping and squawking to the far end of the room.

'They can't do that!' Joseph bellowed.

Startled, Francis flinched and drew back hastily, almost tipping his chair over backward.

"Tis no fault o' mine, Joseph,' he protested.

Joseph re-seated himself, drawing a deep breath. 'Sorry, Francis.

But they cannot do such a thing. This island is not theirs. The English don't control it. How can any responsible government hope to enforce such a law in a territory it has no jurisdiction over?'

Francis shrugged. 'Well, they talked o' stationin' soldiers all over the Island. But then the Duke's man says his master sent a petition to the House o' Commons about the middle o' February, objectin' to it an they wrote back then sayin' possibly a treaty might be entered into for the purchase o' his rights. The Duke thinks the British Government were jus' usin' the threat o' the Mischief Bill to force him to give in to their wishes.'

'An' is he goin' to give in, do you know?'

'Aye. Well, at least his man says he is. The Duke an' Duchess propose to surrender the island and all their rights, jurisdictions an' interests herein. Only they're to keep their manorial rights, landed property an' one or two other things — like the patronage of the bishopric.'

'They can't do that, can they? Just give our Island away.'

'They haven't given it away. They've sold it — to the English — for seventy-thousand pounds. An' the Irish are to give them two-thousand pounds a year — Irish pounds, that is — for the rest o' their lives! That was what the English Treasury offered the Duke an' Duchess, an' they've accepted it. There's some Bill goin' through Parliament; the Revesting Act, I think he called it; to make the transfer o' rights.'

'Tynwald will stop all that. They won't let them get away wi' it!' Joseph said decisively.

'They already tried. When news came to Keys, o' the Revestment Bill, at their meeting at Castletown in March, they sent a deputation immediately to London, to argue for the rights o' the people o' the island. But the best they managed to get was a promise that goods that are manufactured an' produced on the island will be allowed duty-free entry into England.'

Joseph sat in silence for a while, shaking his head in disbelief. Then suddenly he laughed harshly. All eyes turned to him, startled.

'I fail to see any joke,' Francis said a trifle huffily. 'Our livelihood is at stake here.'

'I was jus' thinkin',' Joseph said, 'That the English mus' be terrible worried by us if they'll pay seventy' thousand pounds for a chance to control us.'

Francis nodded. 'Aye. But 'tis not funny really. If they get their own way, it'll make it hard for us. If the seas are full o' Customs' cutters and the Island alive wi' soldiers, how will we stand then?'

'Does that mean you'll give up smugglin'?' Isabella asked hopefully. Startled, the men all looked up, not realising she had been listening and had moved close to the table.

'Bless you, no, lass. We won't give up.' Joseph shook his head vehemently. 'No Englishman will get the better o' me.'

'But it'll be awful dangerous won't it?'

'Not so bad. We'll jus' ha' to be a bit more careful, that's all. There might even be more money to be made from it, for the goods will ha' to be smuggled *into*, as well as out o' the Island then.'

'Why do we need so much money? What would we do wi' it all. Are we not happy as we are? Money's not so important to be worth losin' your freedom for!' Isabella stamped her foot.

'We need it to give us all, especially you childher, a better life, good food to keep you healthy. Most of all we need it to buy the house I promised Catharine. We're not so far short, now, o' havin' enough money for a fine house.'

'Do you think Catharine would want you to take such risks just for a house. She feared for you, just as I do now. Every time you're away I'm tormented wi' fear till you come back. You an' Daniel, both! Just as Catharine used to be. What's so wrong wi' this house? 'Tis dry an' warm. What will become o' me — an' of Catharine's children — if anythin' happens to you? Will we have to end up on the streets, like Daniel an' me was when you found us? Do you want me there again? An' your own childher starvin' an' freezin' to death wi' me? Catharine wouldn't thank you to do that to us!'

Joseph took a deep breath, puffing his cheeks and letting It susurrate between his lips.

'Wow! This lass o' yours is turnin' into quite a little firebrand, Daniel. For such a little scrap o' flesh, she's got a lot to say!' Then to Isabella he said, 'Don't be worryin', girl. 'T'won't ever come to that. You won't ever be on the street again. Or have to go hungry, for that matter.'

Isabella had her teeth in, and was not about to let go.

'What use will a fine big house be if you are in gaol in England? Or sunk at sea an' killed? Aye — an' Daniel along wi' you! Have you thought o' him in all this? For wherever you are Daniel will be. What trouble you get yourself into, you'll get him into it wi' you! An' whatever happens to you will be his fate too!'

'Now calm down, girl!' Joseph jumped to his feet. 'Catharine wanted her children to grow up in a fine house, an' I always promised her they would. But you are one of her children — our children — so 'tis for you I want it as much as the others. This cottage is too small for us all. I promise you we will do nothin' that will put us in danger. We won't ever be caught.'

'How can you know that? How can you make such a promise?' Isabella shouted, her voice quivering with emotion. 'You can't know what the English will do. To what lengths they might go to capture, or even kill, smugglers. They must be desperate to stop you if they'd pay the Duke so much money. So how can you know you'll be safe if the island, and her waters, are bristlin' wi' English? If Catharine was alive she would no longer tolerate you smugglin' — an' takin' Daniel into danger wi' you. I suppose next you'll take James too!'

Whirling, she rushed away to sit, hunched miserably on a stool, staring into the empty fireplace.

Wide-eyed, the younger children had watched the drama. Now Elizabeth moved to kneel on the floor beside Isabella. Pressing her face against the older girl's, she took hold of her hand and found it trembling.

'Don't be upset,' she whispered. 'He won't ever stop until he's ready to. We'll just have to get used to it.'

'I don't think I ever will,' Isabella replied wearily.

Daniel watched for a few minutes, his heart going out to her. He found it unbearable to see Isabella so upset. Yet he owed so much to Joseph, his duty was to him. Rising, he went and laid a hand gently on Isabella's shoulder.

The cornflower blue eyes glistened with unshed tears as she looked up, giving him a watery smile.

'Would you like to come out for a walk wi' me?' he asked softly.

Isabella nodded. 'Aye. 'Tis a nice night. An' I need to get out o' here. I can't listen, any longer, to them talkin' about all this trouble.'

Picking up her cape, she followed Daniel out into the street.

'Let's go up beyond the Brow. 'Tis peaceful up there.'

It was a balmy evening, the sun starting to drop low in the sky, edging the occasional cotton-wool cloud with a glistening, silvery pink.

For a while they walked in silence, wending their way slowly up the hill, drinking in the last dregs of the day's sunshine.

'Try not to be too hard on Joseph,' Daniel said eventually.

'But he's so stubborn. He makes me angry. He could so easily go back to fishin'. The nets are there still, tied to the rafters. Oh, I know they will probably need a lot o' repair by now, but if we all did our share, they would soon be good.'

'Aye.' Daniel said thoughtfully. 'I think I'd enjoy fishin'. But Joseph seems set on the smugglin'. It pays much better than the fishin', he says.'

Isabella stamped her foot. 'Money! That's what it always comes back to, isn't it? Money that we don't need to make us happy. Didn't he learn from the pox that all we need to be happy is to be alive, an' well, an' together? It wasn't bein' poor that killed Thomas. All the money in the world wouldn't have saved him.'

'I know that. An' so does Joseph.'

'Then why is he so determined to risk his life — an' yours — just to get rich?'

'I don't think he has any thoughts o' bein' rich. 'Tis just this big house he wants. Some sort o' obsession he has. I think maybe because he always promised it to Catharine, an' he feels a bit guilty because she died without him ever givin' it to her.'

'Well, he'll ha' more to feel guilty about if he ends in gaol, an the rest o' us out on the streets!'

'Aye. Well, he's pretty careful, an' very clever. 'Tis unlikely that would happen.'

'But it could, couldn't it. And so very easily. Please will you talk to him, Daniel? See if you can persuade him to go back to the fishin'?' Isabella drew a long, tremulous breath.

*   *   *

They had reached the crest of the hill and stood, now, looking down past the gorse and young bracken ferns, to the shimmering pink sea. Above the harbour and the swirling, crying seagulls, they felt at the top of the world. Daniel was silent for a while, studying the scene. He dearly wished he could wipe Isabella's worries away.

'I'll have a word or two wi' him, but don't hope for too much. He's a stubborn man, an' he's set his heart on that house for Catharine's children.'

They sat on the grass, at the edge of the trees to watch and listen to the wildlife. Isabella was thoughtful, a trifle morose.

'Tell him you won't go with him any more. Tell him you're finished with the smugglin'.'

Startled, Daniel turned his head sharply to look at her, then shaking it emphatically, he said, 'No! I can't do that. I owe Joseph too much. I could never let him down that way!'

'Do you owe him your life? 'Cos that's what you might end up payin' if you go smugglin' wi' English Customs men an' soldiers everywhere. He's talkin' now o' smugglin' contraband past them *onto* the Island as well as out o' it. Didn't you hear him?'

'I heard,' Daniel replied tightly. 'An' in answer to your first question — aye, I do owe him my life, as you owe yours to him. If he had not found us when he did, an' had the kindness to give us a home an' put food in our bellies an' clothes on our backs, then we might well have perished quite soon. Do you not remember how it was for us? Have you forgotten how hungry we were? An' how cold?'

'I remember it well. Of course, I haven't forgotten,' Isabella replied quietly.

'Do you remember havin' to eat a rat to stay alive? An' the awful cold gnawin' at our bones. We were gettin' thinner every day!'

'That's why it scares me so much. That could happen again. Next time it could be us an' Joseph's childher.'

Daniel shook his head. 'But if Joseph hadn't given us a home we wouldn't have survived much longer. I can't let him down now. If it is important to him to keep up with the smugglin' till he gets his house, then I'll be at his side as long as he wants me to be!'

Isabella nodded slowly. 'I remember every bit o' our sufferin'. Better, I think, than you. That's why I don't want it to happen to our brothers an' sisters.'

Wretchedly, Daniel looked down on her, his overwhelming love for her conflicting with the love and duty he felt towards Joseph, his feelings tearing him in two directions at once. Knowing that if his hand was forced, his stubborn self-esteem would take him with Joseph. Yet seeing Isabella, so small, vulnerable and frightened, scraped an open sore in his heart.

Placing an' arm around her shoulders, he pulled the girl gently against him. Instinctively, Isabella wrapped her arms around him, pressing her face to his chest. The tears she had been fighting flowed now, streaming down her cheeks to soak into his shirt.

'I'm so frightened!' she sobbed, 'For both of you — an' for the childher. But mos' of all for you. If you were arrested an put in gaol or, worse still, shot an' hurt or killed, I don't know whether I could live on.' She broke off, shuddering, then continued a moment later. 'I love you too much. If you were to die I should want to go with you — as Catharine went with her baby boy.'

Daniel tightened his arms around her, feeling her body trembling. 'Don't talk like that,' he said huskily. ''Tis unlikely anything o' the sort will ever happen to me, but if it does, you must live on. Promise me.'

Isabella nodded, too choked to speak. Sniffing back a sob, she gazed up at him and his face was blurred by the tears in her eyes.

'I have to,' she whispered. 'I promised Catharine.'

Spellbound, Daniel lowered his head to kiss her, gently at first, then with increasing passion, tightening his arms around her, crushing her.

Isabella kissed him back, her emotions keeping pace with his, like a wave sweeping her along on its crest. Gently he pushed her back onto the grass and they clung together, neither wanting the embrace to end, their desire mounting. So strong was her love and need for him, she knew she could not, at that moment, deny him anything. Nor did she want to.

Then suddenly Daniel pulled away from her, rolling over to lie on his back. Isabella's arm lay lightly across his chest and she could feel him trembling quite violently. Raising herself on one elbow, she looked at him, puzzled, and saw a tear on his cheek.

'Why Daniel, whatever is the matter?'

He shook his head, turning his face away from her. 'I'm sorry. I shouldn't have …! I wanted to …! I almost lost control o' myself. Only because I love you so much. I find it very hard to live in the same house, an' to sleep only a few feet away from you. Almost like husband an' wife. But not husband an' wife. But I want us to be. An' my body wants you real bad.' He laid his arms across his eyes to hide from her the pain in them.

'I want it, too,' Isabella whispered, embarrassed. 'I love you an' desire you. If you want to we can do it.'

She took her weight from her elbow, lying herself half across his chest, tightening her arms around him again.

Daniel was still for a moment, save for his trembling, then he shook his head. Gripping her shoulder, he pushed her gently away and she could feel the agony in him.

'No. Not this way. It would be wrong for me to take you like this. I won't ever do you no harm. No one must ever be given the chance to call you a whore. I won't have you until we're married.'

'Married?' Isabella whispered the question.

Daniel sat up, looking down at her. She looked like a child, he thought, or a little doll. So sweet. So fragile!

Shaking himself from his trance, he nodded. 'Aye. That's what I said,' he surprised himself. 'Married. You will marry me, won't you?

Suddenly he was anxious.

Isabella sat, and pulling her legs against her chest, wrapped her arms around them, burying her face in her knees.

'Oh, Daniel, I don't know. 'Tis something I hadn't thought of.'

'There's surely nothin' to think about?' he said. If you love me, like I do you, then you must surely want to marry me.'

Isabella was quiet for many minutes, staring thoughtfully down to the harbour and the boats at sea, with the glory of the sunset reddening their sails.

Finally, she shook her head wretchedly. 'I — I'm sorry, Daniel, I must say no! I can't marry you.'

Daniel stared in stunned disbelief. 'Why not. I thought you loved me? Is it because we have grown up as brother and sister?'

'No. But I cannot be a smuggler's wife. I cannot live as Catharine did, worryin' always. If we married then there would be childher. An' I couldnt bear the waitin', not knowin' if their father was comin' home or not. I love you too much to live that way.'

'Yet a few moments ago you were willin' to make love wi' me?'

'Aye, but if you asked me now I'd say 'no'. I'm in control o' my mind again. An' as much as I love you I won't marry you while you're smugglin'.'

Daniel angrily punched his fist into the ground. 'I should ha' taken you when I had the chance,' he said harshly. 'You're no more than a tease!'

Seeing the tears spring to her eyes, he hated himself for the injustice of it. Gently taking her hand, he said softly, 'I'm sorry, love, I shouldn't ha' said that. I know it isn't true.'

Isabella looked at him solemnly. 'If you still want to marry me when you're ready to give up smugglin', then ask me again an' the answer will be different.'

Chapter 23

An uncomfortable formality developed between Isabella and Daniel during that summer of 1765.

Though Joseph noticed a tension in the atmosphere, he put it down mainly to them being at a difficult age. If he were to be honest, he thought Isabella was mostly at fault, because she so strongly disapproved of their means of livelihood.

In the course of time the islanders learned that the Revesting Bill had been rushed through the British legislative system, having taken only eighteen days from when it was first introduced into the House of Commons, until it received Royal Assent by Commission in the House of Lords.

'Damn the Duke!' Joseph growled, when he heard the news. 'Damn him to Hell. How many times did he give us assurance that he would not sell?

It did not augur well for the island, he was sure. Or for the Manx. He had an awful feeling of foreboding about this whole sorry business. It would not be only the smugglers who would suffer.

News was spread that there was to be a ceremony held at Castletown at 11 a.m. on the 11th Day of July 1765, to proclaim the change of rule on the island.

Hoping to learn, better, what the consequences of the revestment might be, Joseph and Daniel left home before dawn on that morning to sail to Castletown.

George Drinkwater and Francis Clague both, for different reasons, had expressed a wish to accompany Joseph and Daniel, and were waiting for them by the *Louisa*.

Douglas Harbour was crowded, but Castletown even more so, for it seemed folk were sailing in from every corner of the Island.

Joseph gazed around him, his face flushed — and not only from the heat of the summer sun. 'I've never seen so many soldiers in my life!' he said under his breath.

'Nor have I.' Francis' eyes were restless, searching the crowd, picking out the multitude of military uniforms.

There was a lot of pomp, but with an underlying, almost oppressive atmosphere, Daniel felt, of apprehension. A poignant tension in the air, like the breathless calm before a summer storm.

In Castletown's market square, gathered like vultures for the kill, were the Governor, the Deemsters and Members of Tynwald, while the Attorney General read the Royal Proclamation to the gathering.

Then accompanied by much heckling from the crowd, the colours of the Island were struck and the English ones hoisted in their place.

Following this, the Duke and Duchess formally surrendered the Island to the English Crown, by handing over the Sword of State, Public seal and other regalia, together with the castles at Castletown and Peel

'As simple as that!' Joseph said, dumbfounded.

'Is that it, then?' Daniel asked, still open-mouthed. 'That's our Island sold from under our feet!'

'It looks like it, boy,' Charles growled.

The growing murmur amongst the crowd died away as the Governor-in-Chief and Captain, John Wood, rose to deliver a speech which stated:

'Gentlemen: I need not engage your time with recounting the many incidents that have brought about this Revolution amongst you; let it suffice to say that you are now become the immediate care of a Prince as distinguished for his goodness, as renowned for his power; a Prince who is pleased to take you into his Royal protection, that you may participate with the rest of his subjects the advantages of his love, and that he may communicate to you the blessings of his mild and paternal government. To this end I have his Majesty's instructions to tell you, that every encouragement shall be given to the fair and open trader; he will hear your complaints, he will listen to your grievances and relieve your wants; ardently desirous to promote your happiness in common with all his subjects.

Permit me, gentlemen, to exhort you no longer to look back on a trade, confined, hazardous, uncertain as it has been, but direct your views to the pleasing prospect before you — the substantial advantages that flow from an honest and virtuous industry. You see, gentlemen, and you already feel the good effects of his Majesty's royal inclinations toward you. He has sent you troops, not to oppress, but to protect you in your properties, and to circulate their money amongst you; and it is his Majesty's earnest desire that most friendly intercourse may subsist and a constant harmony served between his soldiery and the inhabitants of this Isle Gentlemen, when you reflect seriously on the real benefits you will derive from his Majesty's constant attention to your welfare. When you see that all he does is calculated for your interest and good, will, I doubt not, by every dutiful and thankful return, express your gratitude and testify your obedience — and give me leave, gentlemen, to assure you that nothing shall be wanting on my part that may conduce to the great end of making you a happy, a flourishing and a prosperous people. And now gentlemen, I must address myself to you particularly that are in office under his Majesty and signify to you that it is his royal will that you

*demean yourselves in your several capacities civil, judicial, and
military in an uniform and steady exercise of your duties, with
a constant attention to the laws of Great Britain as they respect
this Island and its dependencies; and that regard most especially
the rights and prerogatives of the Crown, and preserve the same
in their due and legal extent; ever watchful to protect the people
and secure to them the peaceable enjoyment of all their just and
lawful privileges.'*

'What did all that lot mean?' Daniel asked, scratching his head
in puzzlement.

'Roughly speaking, and in simple language,' Charles said, 'They
would like to have us believe that all these troops are here for *our*
good, to look after our interests and safety and that we shall all be
a lot happier and better off under the protection of the Prince and
his Government'

'D'you think there's any truth to it?' Francis, frowned, biting his
lower lip.

'None at all, I shouldn't think!' Joseph shook his head decisively

'They promised six months for merchants to dispose of their
goods.' said Charles, thoughtfully. 'I hope to heaven they keep that
promise else I shall be left with a fortune in goods that they'll class
as contraband.'

'What difference will it make?' Daniel asked, puzzled. 'We'll
able to smuggle it "across" for you just the same.'

'No, lad, it won't be the same at all. It will be much, much more
difficult!'

'How so?' Daniel furrowed his brow.

'There will be a great number of problems. First of all, it will be
very difficult to load contraband cargoes in Douglas, because of
the troops.'

'Surely, if we had good lookouts posted, we should manage that
through the underground passages. On a signal, we could stop

loadin' an' stay out o' sight until the danger was past,' Charles suggested.

'Aye, but the King's men could come on board an' search any time they want. Then, if we did manage to get it all loaded, how would we get safely out of harbour, with all the customs vessels that will be around?'

'Do you think there will be so many?' Daniel asked.

Charles nodded. 'Without a doubt. The sea outside all the main harbours will be alive with excise cutters and cruisers.'

'Then we shall just have to sit back an' watch for a while. If they keep to their word o' a truce, then we can convey your goods openly an' wi'out a problem. But if they don't, then we will ha' to find another way o' doin' it.'

'Aye,' they all agreed, and it was a thoughtful crew who sailed the *Louisa* back to Douglas that evening.

When they had made the boat secure, they all stood on the harbour, surveying Douglas with a feeling of icy chill. Little was said, each man overwhelmed by the strange, strained atmosphere that had overtaken the town along with the swaggering, overly obvious militiamen.

'I don't like the look of it at all!' Charles observed. 'I have an awful foreboding that my days on the island are numbered.'

'Difficulties can be overcome.' Joseph assured him. 'We shall find a way of gettin' your goods off the island and safely away.'

'The difficulties, as you choose to call them, will be tremendous. I have the two large cellars full to the roof, and also three of the largest rooms in my house. There would be very many boatloads, and it is my opinion you would be lucky to get even one load past the harbour-mouth without detection. Even if we could manage it, there would be no more.'

'No more? Why not? I don't understand.' Joseph was growing more agitated by the minute.

'Well, it is simple, really. With the island now under English rule, we'll no longer be able to import goods legally without paying English taxes. So if we wished to continue, anything we wanted to smuggle to England would first have to be smuggled into the Island. We will no longer be able to use the harbours, and the seas will be bristling with customs vessels, so to continue in this business would put us all in more danger, I think, than I am prepared to risk.'

'What do you plan, then?' asked Francis.

'Well, I'm no young man, now. So if I can just get these goods "across", and sold, that I'm at present holding, I think I might be content to sell my house here and return to Whitehaven to live near my son and his family.'

'Well, I'd be sorry to see you go,' Joseph said — and meant it.

'Aye — an' many more on the Island,' said Daniel, feelingly.

'In the meantime, we must pray the English keep to their truce with you merchants, but if they don't — then we'll find a way, somehow, o' getting your stuff "across".'

The promised truce, as was expected, was not granted. In fact, none of the expectations expressed in the Governor's speech, concerning the welfare of the people, were realised. What did follow the revestment was a period of intimidation, brutality and broken assurances.

The merchants and manufacturers of the Island were the first to feel the hardships caused by the restrictions of the Act, for the promised six months armistice to allow merchants to dispose of their goods was never implemented. As Charles Drinkwater had predicted, those goods immediately became classified as contraband.

'We're not the only ones to suffer either,' Charles was divided between bewailing his own problems and sympathizing with others for theirs.

'What else have you heard, then?' Knowing his whole future was at stake, Joseph was more than just mildly interested.

'Well, before the act was passed, Manx manufacturers were promised a subvention on goods produced on the Island. But in fact, only herrin' and linen have been given bounty classification. The result is that the farmers; in fact, the whole agricultural industry; seems to be heading for a state of collapse.'

'Aye. I've heard as much,' Joseph agreed. ''Tis hittin' everyone though, for the prices o' everythin' have gone up so much just in this short time — an' still risin'.'

During the weeks since the revestment, he had been hearing all sorts of rumours. While the children had repaired his nets, to give him an air of authenticity when he sailed, he and Daniel had spent some hours every day strolling in the streets talking to the townspeople, but most of all watching and listening.

They had learned of the desperate plight the island was getting into. There were many stories of merchants who, unable to get their goods off the island, were being forced to find hiding places in which to secrete them. Many of these supposedly secret caches were being discovered and either looted, or their locations sold to the authorities.

''Tis gettin to be a dangerous game to have contraband concealed anywhere on the island,' Joseph continued. 'For I've heard there are armed bands now roamin' the countryside either stealin' from the looters or forcin' entry into houses in their search for any goods they can make use of.'

'Aye. I've heard of a lot of that. I'm beginning to worry about my merchandise. There are too many people who know about it for my comfort. It is only a matter of time before my stores are raided and stolen.' Charles was becoming increasingly nervous with every moment that passed.

'The boy an' me's been lookin' aroun' a bit these last weeks, haven't we?' Joseph looked at Daniel, who nodded his agreement. 'We've done a bit o' fishin' to make it look good. Thought if the excise men was watchin' us, they'd see we was genuine, an' it wouldn't hurt none if they searched the boat a couple o' times — which they have done.'

'I saw you going out — thought you must have turned honest and gone back to fishing.'

'Good! Well, I hope the excisemen have the same belief. Daniel an' me have checked the coast an' south o' here, about half a mile past Little Ness, is a bay. The road passes close by it there. If you can get your merchandise there we should, under cover o' darkness, be able to load it an' get it "across" before daylight.'

'Little Ness? Yes. Yes, there should be no problem with getting it there. I have enough trusted men to transport it for me. Just as long as we don't run into any of these gangs of armed bandits on the way.' Animation had returned to Charles' face and he was almost trembling with excitement.

'We'll have a go at it, if you're willin' to take the risk.'

'Oh — I'll chance it. No doubt about that. It will be less of a risk than keeping the wares here a day longer than I have to. I'm much obliged to you, Joseph.'

'We'll take the first load tomorrow night, if you can have it at Little Ness by dusk. Daniel, lad, we'll go out in the mornin', fishin' south o' the Island. Then toward nightfall we'll head back so it looks as if we're comin' in wi' our catch. As soon as it's dark enough, we'll go in an' pick up the cargo an' be off.'

'I'll find someone tonight to sail "across" with word to my son in Whitehaven, and he can meet you to pick up the cargo.'

When Joseph and Daniel told Isabella of their plans, they very quickly wished they had not.

'Have you two gone completely insane?' she raged. 'Do you really consider the customs men are so simple that they won't see through you? If they see you headin' towards Douglas, then catch sight o' you goin' "across", wi'out ever bringin' your catch in, don't you think they'll stop you an' search the boat?'

They've already searched us two or three times an' found nothin' but fish. 'Tisn't so likely they'll search again in a hurry.'

'Well, I think you're fools, the pair o' you. You'll end up rottin' in an English gaol for the rest o' your lives. Have you, for a single moment, thought what will become o' those four children then? An' me, for that matter!' With that, she glared hotly at Daniel.

'You worry too much, lass,' Joseph tried to pacify. 'There's no real danger.'

Isabella snorted and turned her back on them. Transferring her anger on the pot that bubbled over the fire, she stirred so vigorously that the broth splashed out over the edge.

Joseph glanced at Daniel, who raised an eyebrow and gritted his teeth. Truth be told — he agreed with Isabella, but he couldn't let Joseph down.

In the morning Isabella continued to make her disapproval felt when she served their porridge, slapping it into their bowls so sharply that they both got sprayed. The children, however, were treated with a little more decorum.

*   *   *

Joseph and Daniel left home when the new day had just taken the night's purple blackness from the sky and turned it misty pink. When they reached the harbour, the sun had just fought its way above the horizon, and shone the full length of the ocean's width like a slash of molten copper.

Charles was waiting for them with the news that he had managed to send word to his son. All being well, he should be there to take delivery of the goods, which were, even at that early hour, being loaded onto sleds for removal to Little Ness.

'Don't take more than a boatload,' Daniel reminded him, and he shook his head.

'We'll see you tonight, then.'

Daniel and Joseph set about readying the *Louisa* to sail. William and Phillip arrived soon after and, with Francis also there to lend a welcome hand, they had put to sea in no time, turning the bows southward as soon as they had cleared the harbour.

It was a perfect day for fishing, with many sunny periods and warm, gentle breezes. The herring, apparently incautious in the warmth, were easily caught and they made a good haul. It was almost with pleasure, therefore, that Joseph found himself intercepted, and subsequently searched, by a customs' cutter just off Castletown as they sailed north late in the evening.

The treasury men poked around well with sticks but found only fish. Grudgingly, Daniel supposed, they took their leave, empty-handed, their captain giving Joseph no more than a curt nod as they sailed away to seek more satisfactory prey.

*　　*　　*

Charles was waiting in the designated spot, having managed to bring his cargo safely to the meeting point.

Very swiftly, the transfer was made, by longboat, to the Louisa, where it was carefully buried under the mountain of herring.

'No change in the arrangements, Charles? Everythin' as usual at the other end?' Joseph made a final check.

'No change. The lighter will meet you. Same time. Same place. Just remember, though, if you run into any trouble, dump the cargo. It's worth a lot of money, but not enough to be worth going to gaol for.'

'Don't worry. We'll get it there for you.' Joseph waved cheerfully as the longboat carried his friend into the black velvet blanket that was night.

Chapter 24

'Well lass, this will be our last trip for Charles.' Joseph said cheerfully.

'Does that mean you'll give up smugglin' an' jus' fish for a livin'?' Isabella asked uncertainly.

'Oh now I didn't say that, did I?' He looked to Daniel for support, but the lad, uncomfortably studied his shoes and made no answer.

'Well what *do* you plan?' Isabella growled.

'Charles and most of the other merchants are goin' back where they came from — England and Ireland that is, mainly — so they'll be givin' us no more work. I know for certain Charles will be gone the moment he can sell his house.'

'How much chance does he have o' that, though,' Daniel asked. 'I heard that wi' the collapse o' the agricultural industry, an' the doublin' o' prices on everythin' 'cos o' the Prince's broken promises, people are leavin' the Island in their hundreds — most o' them Manx men, an' jus' walkin' out an' leavin' their cottages empty. So who will there be left to buy his house?'

'If we can get enough money together — we will!'

'Us?' Isabella's mouth hung open for a moment. Snapping it shut, she asked. 'That huge house? It has three floors! There must be at least nine rooms! Where could we ever get the money for a house like that?'

'Wi' what I've saved over the years, an' Charles will gi' me a good sum for these last six cargoes — seven wi' the one we're takin' tonight, we shouldn't be a long way short o' the price o' the house. I can likely get a loan for the rest.'

'Could we pay back a loan out o' the money you would make from the fishin'?'

Joseph shook his head. 'Herrin' won't pay for it. But there will be a lot more money to be made from smugglin' wi' the merchants gone!'

'There'll be no work for you then, will there?' Isabella asked hopefully.

'Aye. More'n ever, for we'll be able to smuggle goods into the Island as well as out o' it, an' make an awful lot more money.'

'No! you cannot! You must not! You've taken too many risks already. It is surely time for you to settle down to an honest life?' Isabella stood defiantly before Joseph, her hands clenched at her sides, lips trembling.

'I will go on until I have that house! When 'tis mine, an' paid for *then* I'll return to fishin'. An' not one moment before!' Joseph stood looking unflinchingly into the furious blue eyes.

'An' you? What will you do?' Isabella turned on Daniel, glaring angrily.

Daniel fidgeted unhappily. 'Whatever Joseph wants, is what I'll do,' he said quietly, his eyes unable to meet the fire in hers.

'Can you not be man enough to tell him you don't want to do it any more? Will you not just choose what you want to do with your own life an' have the courage to tell Joseph? You know fine an' well you don't want to go on with this way of life. This house is his obsession, not yours!'

'I owe Joseph a lot. An' so do you. An' if it's so important for him to keep his promise to Catharine, then what I *do* want to do is help him get it. You know how much Catharine wanted that house. You should want to help Joseph too!'

'I'm not quite seventeen years old yet an' mother to his four children — isn't that help enough. An' I'm left here to manage on my own most o' the time. If it hadn't been for Agnes I'm sure I would ha' lost my senses long ago. How much more is expected of me? Have either o' you ever thought Catharine would rather her children have a father than a three-floored house?'

Joseph listened to this exchange, a stricken look on his face. 'Don't do it for me, lad. If you want to give up an' go fishin' I'll understan'. I don't want you with me if you'd rather not. Probably Francis would crew for me.'

'No!' Daniel said stubbornly, 'Whatever you want to do — I'll be with you. *That* is what I want to do!'

*   *   *

When they had left, Isabella's anger dissolved into a flood of tears. Sitting at the table, she laid her face on her folded arms and let all her misery flow.

While the two younger girls gazed, wide-eyed and uncertain, Elizabeth rushed to give comfort.

'Don't be upset, Isabella. Daddy will surely see sense.'

*   *   *

Joseph watched Daniel from the corner of his eye as they walked down the hill. The lad had grown into quite a man and he had hardly noticed it happen. And Isabella! Well, she was certainly a child no longer. He wondered if perhaps he had put too much responsibility on her. Life had treated her harshly, he thought. As *he* was doing now, he realised with a sudden stab of remorse.

'How do you truly feel about smugglin', Daniel? Would you rather give it up?'

Daniel looked up at him thoughtfully. 'Whatever you want, Joseph. I know how much it means to you to get that house.'

'That's no answer, boy. I asked what *you* would like. And I want you to be honest wi' me.'

'I…I think,' Daniel started hesitantly. 'No. I know I would rather just fish, but I *will* not leave you. I asked Isabella to marry me, you know — a long time ago — but she said not while I was smugglin'. She won't consider it until I'm in a lawful occupation.' He raised his shoulders and flapped his hands in a gesture of hopelessness.

Joseph sighed and shook his head. 'You should ha' told me this sooner, lad.'

*   *   *

After yet another good day's fishing, Charles' final shipload of cargo was safely picked up from Little Ness and buried under the herring.

Charles stood on the deck, looking down into the hold with an expression of relieved satisfaction. In the three weeks since they had started moving his merchandise "across", he seemed to have shed years and now, in the misty moonlight, looked almost a young man again.

'Well, I just can't thank you enough for all you've done for me, Joseph. If I had lost all you've shipped for me in the last weeks, together with what I will lose if I can not sell my house, I would have been a very poor man indeed.'

'I'm pleased I've been able to help. We've been friends for many years now an' you've always been a fair master. We'll miss havin' you about, but I was wonderin' if I might talk to you about your house?'

Charles looked puzzled. 'My house?'

'Aye. I was thinkin' I might buy it if I can find the money to meet your price.'

Charles nodded thoughtfully. 'Come and see me when you get back to Douglas tomorrow. Maybe we can work something out.'

As soon as Charles had left the *Louisa* they set sail, northeast towards Whitehaven and soon a heavy mist started to sweep in.

Joseph stared into the haze, nodding in satisfaction. 'Let's hope this lasts until we're safely across. As long as it's not so thick at the other side that we can't see their signal. Just keep your voices down, lads, sound carries well in this weather.'

Half an hour out, Daniel heard, faintly, the sounds of barked commands through the mist. Looking around urgently, he signaled the rest of the crew, and they stood listening in apprehensive silence as the voices came nearer.

The creaking and groaning of the *Louisa's* hull, and the whistling song of the wind in the rigging, sounded painfully loud in Daniel's ears. His mouth moved in silent prayer that it would not be heard by the other ship.

It came so near they could hear the conversation of the other crew. The voices were English, bringing a fair certainty they were excisemen.

Almost scared to breathe, lest it be heard, the four on the *Louisa* peered towards the voices, Daniel, almost certain he could just discern the ghostly outline of the other boat.

Then they were past, their sounds fading into the distance towards the Island. Daniel unaware he had been as tense as a tightly wound spring, felt his body relax as he let his breathing return to normal.

The remainder of the journey to Whitehaven was uneventful, the fog clearing just enough for them to see the signal beacon at exactly the prearranged moment.

Joseph swung a ship's lamp briefly in reply and within minutes they had made contact with the party from shore. With the usual efficiency, the cargo was transferred and the crew of the *Louisa* waved goodbye, for the last time, to Charles' son.

As they turned the bows towards the Island, the atmosphere aboard the fishing vessel was somewhat heady.

'We can return in safety, now,' Joseph said with relief. 'Let the customs come an' search us if they wish.'

*   *   *

Which is just what they did. As the Louisa rounded Onchan Head, the Treasury cutter hove into view, bearing down on them with alarming speed.

An armed party came aboard, searching the boat from stem to stern, to leave, disconsolate and empty-handed half an hour later.

The captain of the cutter eyed Joseph suspiciously. 'I have doubts about you'. ' he growled. 'I sense you're up to no good, an' one day I'll catch you out.'

In joyful triumph they sailed into Douglas harbour with the cutter trailing at a distance, standing off watchfully as they docked.

'All go well?' Charles stood anxiously on the wharf.

Joseph looked up, smiling. 'Aye. Passed close to a cutter, we think, in the fog on the way over. Then got searched by that one on the way back.' He gestured towards the watching customs' vessel.

Charles glanced over, nodding.

'Best not let them see us talkin' together too long. We'll get the herrin' unloaded, then I'll meet you in the hotel.'

'Right.' Charles touched a finger to his forehead, then with a last quick glance at the cutter, strode briskly away.

'Daniel. don't you worry about helpin' us here. You get home an' let Isabella know we' re safe. We've cared too little for her worries in the past.'

'Aye.' Daniel, having had Isabella heavily on his mind since the previous day, was glad to take his leave. Almost leaping up the steps in his hurry, he threw the cottage door open, standing dramatically with his arms spread wide.

Instead of the excited, relieved welcome he had expected, Isabella spared him only the quickest glance, before returning her attention to the bread she was making. Elizabeth did not even look up from her book, and there was no one else there.

'I'm home,' he said lamely.

'I can see.' Isabella didn't look up again and Elizabeth continued to ignore him.

The next hour or so was an agony of tension, the girls talking and laughing between themselves, carrying on as though Daniel did not exist, whilst he huddled in a corner — sulking.

This was the scene Joseph arrived home to about an hour later.

Puzzled, he looked from one to the other of the trio in the room.

'What's goin' on here?'

Daniel shrugged.

Isabella said nothing.

'You two had a fight?'

'No!' Isabella glared haughtily.

'How can we fight when she won't even talk to me?'

Joseph sighed. 'Why won't you talk, Isabella?'

The girl shrugged. 'Jus' can't think o' anythin' I would want to speak to him about.'

Exasperated, Joseph shook his head. 'Well I *do* have somethin' I want to discuss, so will you all come an' sit at the table.'

Isabella gave the broth a last stir, then moved to join the others.

'As Daniel knows,' Joseph began, 'I've been havin' a word wi' Charles about his house by the harbour.

Isabella snorted derisively, winning her an icy glare from Joseph.

'To continue,' he said, looking pointedly at the girl. 'if you'll allow me?'

Isabella shrugged and studied her fingerails.

Joseph shook his head and sighed. 'Charles has had no luck sellin' his house, because all the merchants, along wi' many others, are quittin' the island. So we have come to an agreement, Charles an' me, an' the house is to be ours when he leaves, which is to be one week from today.'

The cries of excited jubilation he had expected did not come, and instead, he was met with a deathly silence.

Isabella and Elizabeth exchanged looks which he was at a loss to comprehend, whilst Daniel hardly seemed to have heard him.

'Well, has no one got anythin' to say?'

Isabella stood up and with quiet determination said, 'The rest o' you may do what you want an' live where you like, but I will not be comin' wi' you!'

There was a stunned, total silence for a few moments.

'I don't understand. Where will you go? What are your plans?'

'I will stay here. I will not live wi' you in that house until you both are rid o' this desire for smugglin'.'

'An' I shall stay wi' Isabella!' Elizabeth stuck her chin out defiantly.

Startled, Joseph eyed the two girls incredulously, then surprisingly he started to laugh.

'We have a fine pair o' vixens here, Daniel! Well, lasses, if you'd had the patience to hear me out, you'd have saved yourselves the trouble o' making those little speeches. For the agreement Charles an' I reached was that we should have the house for half o' what he had been askin' plus the payment he owed me for shippin' these last few cargoes for him!'

'Does that mean we can get the house wi'out a loan?' Isabella eyed him doubtfully.

'Aye, lass. An' better'n that — we'll even have money left over from what I've saved through the years. Quite a bit o' it. We should be able to live in reasonable comfort, even with only a fisherman's income!'

Isabella's blue eyes brimmed. 'You're givin' up smugglin' then?' Her question was a breathless whisper.

Joseph's smile was warm. 'Aye, lass. You'll ha' the house Catharine wanted for you all, an' us in honest work.'

Without warning Isabella launched herself at him, throwing her arms tight around his neck. Like a feather, he picked her up, swinging her in the air.

'But how can Charles afford to sell so cheaply?' Daniel asked, puzzled.

'Well, he's made a lot o' money through the years from the goods we've smuggled. An' as things were, there was no business here for him an' he was goin' to have to leave wi'out sellin' the house at all. So when he knew I was interested he decided that a little over half o' what he wanted was better'n nothin' at all. So we all gained by us buyin' it.'

Daniel caught at Isabella's hand. 'Will you walk wi' me?' He asked quietly.

The girl nodded and followed him outside. As soon as the door had closed behind them, Daniel turned to take her in his arms. 'Isabella' you said I should ask again, when I'd given up smugglin'….'

Isabella slipped her slender arms around his neck, gazing into the strangely different eyes. 'The answer, this time, is YES,' she mumbled as her lips closed with his.